PRAISE FOR E.M. POWELL

'The plot moves swiftly. As a stand-alone novel, this book more than holds its own. A great follow-up to the first two books in the series – and highly recommended.'
—*Historical Novels Review*

'E.M. Powell has created an immensely likeable pair in Stanton and Barling, in this exciting new medieval mystery series. Action-packed and laced with sly humour . . . I was completely riveted by *The King's Justice*.'
—Mary Lawrence, author of *The Alchemist's Daughter*

'E.M. Powell's medieval murder mysteries are like mead: sweet, potent, and seductively addictive. One sip and you won't be able to stop reading.'
—Jane Holland, bestselling author of *Girl Number One* and *Lock the Door*

The Monastery Murders

OTHER TITLES BY E.M. POWELL

Stanton and Barling Mysteries

The King's Justice

The Fifth Knight Series

The Fifth Knight
The Blood of the Fifth Knight
The Lord of Ireland

E.M. Powell
The Monastery Murders

A STANTON AND
BARLING MYSTERY

THOMAS & MERCER

Published by Thomas & Mercer, Seattle

www.apub.com

Amazon, the Amazon logo, and Thomas & Mercer are trademarks of Amazon.com, Inc., or its affiliates.

ISBN-13: 9781503903241
ISBN-10: 1503903249

Cover design by Ghost Design

Printed in the United States of America

For Paul Fogarty: indefatigable source of wisdom, wit and wine

Chapter One

Fairmore Abbey, North Yorkshire 24 December 1176

As a young man, Brother Maurice, novice master of Fairmore Abbey, had wondered why the old always seemed so ill-tempered.

He wondered no more. Had not wondered, in fact, for several years. Years which had taken his teeth, of which he had few now left. Which had taken his sight, completely in one eye, and with the same foul fog descending upon the other.

Years which had taken his mother and father, which, he supposed, was the way of things. Years which had taken many of his fellow monks too. Some had died after a long life, like his parents, while others had been called back to God after only a short time. The number of years mattered little. He could look into the dead face of a man he'd known for two decades and feel nothing. He could hold the hand of a man he had only known a few months as he slipped from this life and weep for days at his passing to heaven.

The prospect of his own death did not cause him any woe, though he hastened towards it daily.

For when it came he would sleep. Sleep properly.

Lack of rest, Maurice had long since concluded, was what made those advanced in years so quick to wrath. He would long for sleep throughout the day, have his head droop over and over as he prayed in the cloister, his slack mouth drooling on to the book that his useless eyes could no longer see. After the bell sounded for close of day, he would hasten to his sleeping mat in the monks' dormitory, the mat that currently lay under his wretched, sleepless bones. An hour, maybe two, would see him in blissful repose.

And then he would wake, not as he did as a young man, refreshed and restored, but in despair, for he knew he would not close an eye again that night.

At least on this night, this most holy of nights, others would have as little sleep as him. For the great feast of the birth of Christ was almost upon them. The night Office of Vigils would take place earlier than usual. He loved this feast above any other, even if it served to remind him of how few he may have left.

In the cold darkness of the dormitory around him, the other brothers slept on, in their familiar, maddening chorus of loud snores, sharp snorts, bubbling breaths and farted wind.

When the monastery bells sounded for Vigils, he would be up in an instant. For him, rising in the depths of the night was easy. He was already awake. For the others, the sleepers, especially the novices under his care, young men all, it was a sort of agony.

Maurice grinned to himself. At least he had that advantage over the young. He had little else any more.

He rubbed his face, listening out for the muffled sounds of the awakening of the sacrist, Brother Cuthbert, who slept in a separate chamber at the top of the dormitory.

The quiet sacrist was a diligent man, never late in his duties at the monastery bells. A boring fellow too, but dependable.

It should be any time now. Maurice waited a few more minutes.

Nothing. Only the continued sounds of slumber around him.

He frowned to himself and sat up, pushing his coverlet from him. This would not do. Not on the feast of Christmas. Not on any night.

He rose from his bed, pulling his woollen cowl straight and smoothing out its creases as he slipped his stockinged feet into his waiting soft leather shoes. Then he made his way along the clear path between the two rows of beds towards Cuthbert's little room. His poor sight deepened the room's shadows but he had no fear of falling. The floor would be tidy and without obstruction, as it always was. He reached Cuthbert's door and opened it without ceremony.

'Cuthbert.' His order was sharp, sharp enough to cause a few grumbles from those monks nearby. He peered closer.

Cuthbert's bed lay empty, the coverlet rumpled.

By the Virgin: had he, Maurice, missed the bell? *Have sense, man.* Of course he hadn't. Every other brother was still asleep. The deep peals to summon the monastery to prayer had not sounded.

Maurice made his way over to the tiny shuttered window and pushed it open. The icy wind that gusted in made him gasp. The heavy snow of the last two days had stopped, leaving the land a mass of formless white and a black clear sky above it. Maurice could no longer see stars but he could make out the blur that was the waning moon. He squinted hard. Barely. It hung where he feared it might. They were going to be late. Late for Vigils. On the feast of the Nativity, of all days.

Cuthbert: how could you?

Maurice slammed the window shutter and grabbed the wooden tabula and stick that sat beside Cuthbert's bed. 'Rise, brothers, rise!' He walked back out into the dormitory, struck the board loud and hard. 'The day of Our Lord's birth is here. Rejoice! Rise!' He made the most noise he could over his yawning, stretching novices – cajoling, herding them towards the night stairs that led down to the church. He knew the other monks would follow after. He fell in behind the last of the novices hurrying down the stairs. 'Let us go to praise—' He thudded into the novice in front. 'Move, boy. Move, all of you.'

A call came from below. 'We can't, brother.'

'Can't? Why not?'

'The church door is locked, brother.'

The other monks had gathered behind Maurice and drowsy, confused grumbles came from them.

'Brothers, why are you stopped?' asked one.

'Move down, move down,' said another.

Maurice's stomach tensed in his ire. They should not be stuck here like witless sheep in a pen. 'Here, use my key.' He handed it to the man before him, who passed it down the line.

He heard the church door open and another call came back up. 'The church is in darkness, brother.'

Shocked exclamations met the novice's words.

Maurice shared the shock. But he was angry now too. This was supposed to be a house of God.

'Well, don't just stand there!' he shouted. 'Go and light it. As many of you as possible.'

The novices did as instructed, Maurice hastening down the rest of the stairs and giving more orders as he entered the dark church.

'You and you, light the candles. You: fetch the books. You: go and wake the lay brothers.'

Lights were flickering in the church by the time the abbot walked in, his face like thunder at being told the news.

He marched up to Maurice. 'Why has Vigils been delayed, brother? What is going on?'

Maurice wondered if he had heard right. 'We are only in this church because of me, my lord abbot. Me. Cuthbert is nowhere to be found. Had I not been awake, we might all have slept until daybreak.'

'Then we commence the Office this very minute.' The abbot turned on his heel. No acknowledgement of Cuthbert's shortcomings. No acknowledgement of what he, Maurice, had done to save this precious day.

'His wicked slothfulness has brought sin on us all, my lord abbot!' Maurice was aware of every stunned face turned towards him, mouths open at his rudeness. 'You will need to punish the lazy cur.' He knew his temper was carrying him now. He couldn't have stopped it if he'd tried. 'Punish him. I'm going to find him, find him for you. Drag him back here to face his sinful, sinful shame.'

He stormed out of the church, past hands that reached out to try to placate him, stop him, and into the cloister.

'Cuthbert!' His furious yell echoed in the silent, freezing air as he marched along. He pulled in a deep breath to shout again.

Halted.

The night should smell of nothing except the fresh wind from the high moors.

But it smelled of . . . meat? Cooked meat?

No. Not meat. Not quite. It had a strange tang of metal to it. A horrible sweetness that went straight to the pit of his stomach.

Maurice was no longer angry. He was afraid. 'Cuthbert?' He set off again, at a run this time, uncaring of where he put his feet, running towards the stench, the stench that he now knew came from the monastery kitchen.

He flung open the door. And knew he'd found Cuthbert.

Afterward, in his prayers, he thanked God for his feeble, useless eyes.

They had spared him the worst of a sight that could only have come from the very depths of hell itself.

5

Chapter Two

Southwark, London 1 January 1177

While Hugo Stanton would never describe himself as a man of fervent faith, he did hold strong opinions about feast days. They were, without question, to be spent feasting. Feasting, drinking and, if his luck fell the right way, finishing the day in the arms and between the thighs of a willing woman. Yet on this, the great day of the Octave of Christmas, his usual plans had been ruined.

Instead, he sat in a damp wherry on the brown waters of the choppy Thames, waiting for a place at the busy landing at Southwark, being buffeted by an icy wind that drew no warmth from the colourless morning sun. He hauled his thick cloak tighter around him and tried not to think about spicy boiled beef, roasted capon, a number of sweetened cheese puddings, and cup after cup of good wine before a blazing fire.

'You see, young Stanton?' Aelred Barling, a senior clerk at the court of King Henry, sat opposite him, neat as ever in his dark robes and cloak and squinting in the brittle sunshine. The pale skin of Barling's thin face was blotched pink from the chill. 'The river is crammed with craft, as I knew it would be. I was correct in my estimation of the time it would take us to get here. It would not have done to be late. Lateness would mean we would see little of the bear.'

The bear. The one good thing about this trip with Barling. 'I hope we do get to see it,' replied Stanton. 'Looks like plenty of other folk have had the same idea.'

Above, the creaking wooden wharf teemed with happy, noisy people. Most headed away from the riverside and into the busy streets of Southwark, with few travelling in the opposite direction.

The clerk frowned. 'Fellow.' He addressed their oarsman. 'Make haste for us to land.'

'Yes, sir.' The man responded at once to his order, as people did. Barling was a small, slight man but carried with him the authority of the court and had the tone to match.

Although they now had a more amicable bond, Stanton had often faced a displeased Barling over the time they had been working together and he'd not enjoyed it. At all.

The wherry man forced their craft into a gap at the reeking, waste-clogged river's edge, drawing abuse and oaths from those in other boats.

'There you are, sir.'

'The blessings of the day be upon you.' Barling went to rise to his feet, almost overbalancing though the boat rocked little.

'Thanks, good fellow.' Stanton threw the man an extra coin. He grabbed hold of Barling and got him safely up the slippery wooden steps. The clerk might be twelve years older than Stanton's twenty-two and deeply learned, but his deftness in any physical task was woeful.

'You can let go of me now, Stanton.' Barling smoothed down his neat tonsure, which had blown about in the wind. 'We should hurry.' He matched his words with his actions.

No thanks for Stanton's help, just the usual determined stride through the crowd, ignoring the complaints of those he bumped into.

With a sigh and shake of his head, Stanton followed.

Stanton forced his elbows on to the chest-high wooden fence that surrounded the sawdust-floored bear pit. Its sturdy wall kept the gathering throng of loud, eager people out. It would also, he guessed, keep the animals in. Bear-baiting was a sport he'd always wanted to witness. He'd heard tell of the size and strength and ferocity of such animals but had never seen one for himself.

Not so Barling. 'I have seen the spectacle several times,' the clerk had said when Stanton had mentioned he'd be going. 'A sport favoured by his Grace himself, with very good reason.'

Another enjoyable pastime to add to his feast day. Or so Stanton had thought, until he realised that Barling had decided to come with him. There was no way that Stanton could turn him down.

Worse, Barling was going to use it as one of his lessons. Barling instructed as master and Stanton learned as pupil, the King's clerk liked to say. Frequently. Stanton knew he had nobody to blame except himself. When he'd first encountered Barling, he'd been a messenger with the King's travelling law court, a position he'd been desperate to leave. Seven months ago, when he and Barling solved the mystery behind a number of brutal murders, he'd had the opportunity to seek another position but he had failed to take it. Barling had persuaded him that he had an uncommon talent for finding the truth and so should work for the clerk, helping to bring wrongdoers to justice. Stanton had wondered throughout the time that had since passed whether he'd made the right choice.

He enjoyed much of it, especially the duties that meant riding a fast horse or seeking out a missing individual in the city's alehouses. Other aspects had far less appeal. Like the lessons. Barling's leaden presence could lower the highest spirits. The clerk would use events to question and debate Stanton's judgements, sometimes for hours at a time. Still, even that was better than when Barling droned on at him about the law. He suspected that nothing would make Barling happier than to have

Stanton in his own image: robed in black, hair in a tonsure and devoted to dry, dusty manuscripts and pipe rolls. Stanton would rather jump in the freezing, stinking river.

In the bear pit before them, a fool playing a whistle pranced around the enclosure, sending up puffs of fresh wood dust into the cold air. A small dancing dog dressed in the same yellow and red as its master followed him. The heavy wooden post in the centre of the pit stood empty, its dark, blood-stained surface giving promise of what was to come.

A fresh shiver went through Stanton, though this time not one of cold.

'Unfortunately,' said Barling, who stood to his right, 'there is nothing to be learned from this japery.'

The fool danced on, the dog ducking back and forth under its owner's high steps.

Stanton couldn't help a laugh. 'That little hound's very good, Barling.'

The clerk sniffed.

The performer finished his tune with a low, low bow. His animal leapt up on to his back to a chorus of merriment and clapping. Still bent double, the man whipped off his cap and circled the pit for coins.

'Perhaps there is one lesson,' said Barling. 'Which is that the man in there is less of a fool than those giving him their money.'

Stanton opened his purse to throw a coin as the man passed. 'Or perhaps it's that making folk smile is worthy of a reward.' He winked at the clerk.

The unamused set of Barling's thin lips told Stanton what the older man thought of his response.

As Stanton grinned to himself, a stir in the crowd came from one side of the pit.

'The nonsense has finished, which comes as a welcome relief,' said Barling. 'It would appear that Ursus is on his way.'

9

Finally. Barling or no Barling, this was what he wanted to see. Stanton leaned forward as far as he could, craning his neck for a better view.

The performer looked over at the source of the commotion and paled. He scooped his dog under one arm and was over the wall in a neat leap and gone. Gone too were the laughs of those watching, the smiling faces. Instead, mouths gaped in awe, as a low rumble of expectation loudened.

The gate to one side swung open and two men armed with long poles stepped through. The bearward walked into the ring, pulling a long, thick metal chain with one hand and holding a stout staff in the other.

And after him, at the end of the chain, lumbered the bear: the huge, black-furred bear.

Chapter Three

Stanton gasped aloud, as did many in the press of people around him. Others jostled to get a better look as excited shouts filled the air. Stanton stood firm to keep his place and he noted that Barling did the same.

'The bear!'

'God's eyes, he's a monster.'

'It's the bear!'

Stanton wondered if his eyes played tricks. 'Look at the size of that beast,' he said, turning to Barling. 'Just look at it.'

Even the clerk seemed impressed. 'I have witnessed a number of bear fights,' he replied. 'But never an animal as remarkable as this one.'

Stanton returned his gaze to the enclosure, hopeful now that Barling might forget the lesson and simply watch the action.

The chain the bearward held was attached to a stout leather-and-metal harness that encased the creature's massive skull and the top of its heavy snout. Nothing secured its four powerful limbs, limbs which ended in curved claws longer than Stanton's eating knife and which looked many times sharper.

Stanton's blood was up now, and he could sense the same in those watching – he could almost taste it on the wind. He wrenched one hand free from the crush of bodies and cloaks and blew sharp whistles to match those cutting the icy air.

The bearward locked the chain on to the post, watched at every moment by the men with the poles. The beast's small eyes in turn fixed on its master.

'You see the main combatant,' said Barling, his words for Stanton's ears only. 'What are your first thoughts?'

His first thought was that he would be very careful in future about telling Barling his plans. But he wasn't about to say that. He didn't dare. Instead he said, 'That the bear's a fearsome beast.'

Barling shrugged. 'That dancing fool could have told me that. As could any fool.'

Riled, Stanton added, 'And that it has no love for his master.' Where the little dog had looked at its owner with trust, the bear looked ready to feast on the man who controlled it.

'Better.'

Through the rising din came another chorus. Not one of human voices, but the clamour of dogs, their barks and howls telling of their readiness for the fight.

'And,' Barling added, 'here is the foe.'

The dogs entered the ring, three in total, smooth, mud-coloured coats rippling over solid muscle, straining against their leashes so hard that the men who held them could hardly keep their footing.

Stanton knew the breed well. 'Mastiffs. The finest dogs.'

'I would disagree,' said Barling. 'There are far finer breeds.'

'But they're the best suited for this. They have the strongest jaws. And they're going to need them.'

The bear no longer looked at its master, who had stepped back out of the way. Ursus's eyes were only for the heavy-set, snarling dogs. It opened its snout as much as it could in its tight head harness to send a snarl back.

Stanton gasped at its huge teeth.

The dogs answered the bear, showing vicious teeth of their own, powerful necks straining at their pointed metal collars as they bayed and tore at the ground with eager front paws.

'Ursus is off!' came a disgusted call from a man to Stanton's left.

Head down, the bear had turned and fled a few shambling short steps through the cloying sawdust. The chain snapped tight. Its head came up again. Now Stanton saw its fear.

'It knows it's trapped,' he said to Barling. 'Which will only make it more dangerous.'

Barling nodded. 'As is the case with all men. And all women.'

Stanton knew that only too well, had seen the devastating results for himself. And not only as he uncovered the horror of last summer's murders with Barling. He pushed the memory of his own loss away. Around him, folk shouted, drummed on the pit walls. His pulse banged faster in time with the sound.

'Let the dogs go!'

'The dogs! The dogs!'

The mastiff handlers slipped their animals' leads and the hounds charged their prey.

And Ursus stood. Stood tall on its hind legs.

'God's eyes!' yelled Stanton in delighted shock. 'It's like a man!'

The first dog jumped. With a wide sweep of one front paw, the bear sent the hound in a howling arc, its shoulder torn open in deep, red gashes that drew screams from the crowd. The second got a blow to the snout that sent it rolling away but unhurt. The third hung well back, silent, its ears flat against its skull.

'What make you of the foe, Stanton?'

'Those first two dogs are fighters. But it looks like the third one's taken fright. I don't blame it.'

Barling raised his thin eyebrows. 'If you say so.'

The bear's roar matched the crowd's as it dropped to all fours again, the better to slash at its attackers, spinning as deftly as its bulk would allow yet failing to land a blow. The first dog hadn't managed to get back on its paws. But the second dog went in again, throwing its whole weight behind its wide-open jaws as it clamped them shut on the bear's rear right leg. The bear howled in agony, thrashed its limb from side to side as the dog's teeth held firm.

Fur, then flesh, ripped in a spray of blood along with a bellow from the bear that echoed above the pulsing roar of those watching. But the bear hammered down on the dog in a clawed blow that rent the skin of his foe, and that hound went down too.

'Back, back. Now.' The bearward pulled hard on the chain of his animal and waved his staff in its face.

The bear lunged at him.

Stanton's warning sounded with a hundred echoes.

But the men with the poles moved in, lightning quick, jabbing the furious bear away to new cheers. Two of the dog handlers grabbed for their injured animals and pulled them out of reach as those watching broke into a flurry of exchanged coins, handshakes and oaths. The second dog bit its handler in its frenzy of pain and rage as it left the pit. The third handler stayed well back, merely whistled to his hound as it continued to slink behind the bear.

Heart hammering, Stanton turned to speak to Barling but the clerk cut across him.

'What of the third dog, Stanton?' The clerk pointed. 'The one that you declared not much of a fighter?'

'It isn't, it didn't even—' Then he saw. It didn't hang back because of fear. It was hanging back because it was watching. Waiting. Then running in a sudden burst of lethal, silent speed. It jumped on the bear's back. And fastened its powerful jaws on the neck of Ursus.

A new wave of shouts erupted.

The bear reared up in shock and pain, its front legs flailing in a futile effort to get free of the huge dog. It could not. The dog had locked its bloodied grip and was using its weight to try to pull the bear down. Ursus span, staggered.

Yet more shouts, more drumming on the sides of the pit.

Stanton joined in this time, hammering with a force that bruised his knuckles, willing his energy into the bear to fight back from the unseen attack. 'Come on!'

The bear went over. Hard. Hard in a thick cloud of flying sawdust as Stanton's shout met the crowd's.

So hard, the dog's grip loosened and it slipped from the bear's back to land on its own.

Ursus kicked out one back leg. Claws met flesh in a terrible strike. The injured hound tried to rise yet couldn't.

But Ursus could. And was up.

Up. Stanton could no longer form words, only think them as he yelled his lungs empty.

With a shake of its head and a roar of rage, the bear reared up and slammed its claws down on to the dog, over and over, crushing and tearing its foe.

Screams from the dying dog melted into the throng's in a piercing echo that made Stanton's head ring. But it was over. The bear had fought like the bravest warrior. And it had won. Stanton drew in a long, long breath.

'Now do you see what I mean by spectacle, Stanton?'

'I do. I'll remember this for the rest of my days.'

As the men with poles ran forward to push the bear off, a huge chant rose from the crowd: 'Ursus is the victor! Ursus is the victor!'

The scowling owner of the third dog hauled its corpse from the ring, leaving a smear of scarlet on the pale sawdust.

Stanton went on. 'That hound nearly won out by using its cunning. I was completely wrong about it. Thought I knew the breed better than that.'

Ursus sank to the ground as well, his own injuries showing as glimpses of red and wet, matted fur. The noise from the spectators lessened as the business of bets being paid out and argued over got underway, along with the first retellings of what had taken place.

'It was trained in a very clever approach,' said Barling. 'And one that came very close to succeeding. Remember too that a breed is still made up of a multitude of dogs. Though most will be alike, there will always be exceptions.'

'A shame that it ended up losing its life. But the bear deserved to win.' Stanton nodded at the exhausted-looking animal. It lay in an untidy heap on the ground, trying its best to lick its many wounds but prevented by its head harness. 'It was magnificent.'

'Was?' said Barling. 'The day is not over yet.'

As if hearing his words, a distant new chorus of hounds floated on the air. The bear's head shot up, injuries forgotten.

'They'll make it fight again today?' Stanton stared in surprise at Barling. 'After all it's done?'

'Of course.' Barling gave a tight nod. 'Otherwise people would riot. They need to have their fill.'

Stanton searched for the right words to argue back at Barling but stopped at a stir in the group of people next to him. A couple of the palace guards he recognised were making their way through, folk stepping back despite the crush.

'Sir,' said the guard to Barling. 'My lord de Glanville requests your presence at the palace, sir.'

'The King's justice summons me, on such a great feast day as this?' The clerk's reply told of his irritation at being disturbed. Stanton knew it well. Knew the look on his face too.

'Yes, sir. At once, sir,' came the respectful, if wary, reply.

Barling gave an impatient scowl but went to leave with the guards.

Stanton knew he would. Barling expected perfect obedience from those beneath him but followed every order from authority above him, no matter how unreasonable.

The clerk paused. 'I shall meet with you later, Stanton. We have much to discuss.' He was gone without waiting for a reply.

Fortune has smiled. As soon as Barling was out of sight, Stanton could go to eat and drink his fill, exactly as he'd intended.

He looked back at the enclosure.

The agonised, weary bear was climbing to its feet as the noise of the dogs came closer. The crowd roared into full voice once again.

Stanton didn't join in. But he didn't leave his place at the wall, either.

Forget feasting. He would stay to watch, though the sight no longer held any enjoyment for him. He knew what it was like to defeat a murderous enemy, only to have to face a new one. Knew the terror, the exhaustion it brought.

He only wished he had half the courage of Ursus.

Chapter Four

Aelred Barling watched the landing at Southwark recede at a rapid pace. The wherry in which he sat was a far finer one than that in which he had arrived. Both guards rowed hard in a matched rhythm that kept up speed despite having to travel upstream to Westminster.

Under usual circumstances, he would enjoy such a journey. On a clear day like this, the outline of London's many castles, monasteries and churches soared into the pale blue sky, a testament to his beloved city's greatness. The progress on the foundations of the magnificent stone bridge that was being built to replace the ancient, rotting wooden one was best viewed from a distance too. But he could take little pleasure from such grand sights. Again, he wondered about the urgent request, why King Henry's great justice Ranulf de Glanville would summon him today.

The King. Could something have happened to his Grace? That would be a grave matter – the most grave.

A ridiculous idea, Barling. If that were the case, de Glanville would not be wasting time in calling for him. But while he wondered what the request could be, Barling had no doubt that it was necessary. He had the deepest respect for de Glanville, a man whom the King had ordered to lead his travelling law court to the north last year. Henry had decreed that his law should be brought to every corner of his lands. Barling had been a member of that court. While he had not relished the prospect of having to leave his work in the King's scriptorium here, he was honoured to have been chosen. It had not turned out at all as he had expected. Barling had come face to face with terrible bloodshed and his path to resolving the matter had been a perilous one. Nevertheless, justice had prevailed.

'Not long now, sir,' said the guard in front of him, his work at the oar uninterrupted as he spoke.

Barling took a glance over his shoulder and nodded. 'We make satisfactory progress.'

Yes, justice had prevailed. But without the help of the young Hugo Stanton, a mere messenger with the travelling court at the time, it might not have. Now they were master and pupil. Of sorts. Much of what Stanton could do and do well was very satisfactory. He was a talented, fast rider with a seemingly endless knowledge of how to get from one place to another. He also had a far better way with the common man than Barling. Or common woman. Especially a woman. Barling frequently despaired at how his pupil used his blue eyes and hair the colour of newly mown hay to charm and more. Worse, Stanton was lazy. Barling had yet to succeed in changing that particular vice. Barling knew full well that Stanton had a lively intelligence but showed little or no interest or enthusiasm when Barling tried to instruct him on even the most basic matters of the law. There were times when this would irritate Barling beyond measure. A pupil should pay attention to his master, and Barling would be at the point of utter exasperation with his assistant. Then Stanton would track down a missing plaintiff or tease important information from a neighbour about land inheritance, and Barling would have to admit to himself that, yes, Hugo Stanton was indeed invaluable to him at

times. Not that he would ever utter those words. He had no time for
blandishments.

'Here we are, sir.' The guard's breath came cloudy on the cold air
from his exertion.

As the boat pulled into the stairs at Westminster, the higher bells
of the hour of Sext sounded from the towering abbey of Saint Peter.
Their peals told Barling that their progress here along the water had
indeed been swift.

He followed the guards as they led him from the landing place
towards the spacious house near the river that de Glanville occupied
when he was staying on the business of the court. Barling could discern
nothing that would suggest that an event of worrying importance had
occurred. The King was away with his travelling court, which meant
that the streets, squares and courtyards around the palace were quieter
than usual. On a feast day such as this, the great hall from which much
of the law was administered would be deserted.

The guards led him through the small gatehouse at the entrance to
de Glanville's house. The stout wooden doors were opened at once to
the guard's knock by one of the justice's servants. Barling pulled off his
outer cloak and gloves, which the servant took from him with a bow, as
one of the guards went into the hall to announce him.

'Aelred Barling, my lord de Glanville.'

'Enter, Barling,' came de Glanville's deep-voiced order.

The guard ushered Barling through and closed the doors behind
him.

'My lord.' As Barling gave his customary respectful bow, he saw
that the imposing de Glanville was not alone in the comfortable, high-
beamed room.

Sitting opposite the justice before the large lit fireplace was an
abbot.

Barling was a little surprised. Not because de Glanville hosted
such an important visitor – the abbot of the nearby Saint Peter's was

a familiar sight in these environs. But this man was not dressed in the black robes of that Benedictine house. Instead, he wore the white wool robes of the austere Cistercian order. Particularly fine white wool, Barling noted.

De Glanville waved Barling forward across the rush-covered floor. 'Come and join us.'

Barling did so, hands clasped, halting at a suitable distance from the two men. Even so, the heat from the huge burning logs reached him, welcome after the cold outside.

'Aelred Barling,' said de Glanville to the monk. 'One of my most experienced clerks.'

The monk simply nodded.

'Barling, this is Abbot Nicholas of the great Cistercian house of Linwood Abbey. We have a matter that we need to discuss with you.'

'My lord abbot.' Barling bowed again. The man had a noble bearing and exuded the confidence of one of the highest status. 'It is an honour to be in your presence. Linwood is an abbey of the highest renown. A place of great holiness.' The man's presence struck him as unusual. An abbot would not normally leave his monastery on a feast day and make the journey of some thirty miles to visit de Glanville.

'It is a holy house and a peaceful one,' replied the abbot. 'But I am not here on the business of Linwood. Am I, de Glanville?'

'No,' said de Glanville. 'Abbot Nicholas is here seeking my help because there has been a dreadful event at one of the other houses of the White Monks.' His voice deepened further. 'It appears that one of the brethren has been murdered.'

'And murdered in the most horrible way.' The abbot held up a letter. 'I received word of it two days ago. I set off for London as soon as I could.'

Barling inclined his head by way of response. His thirteen years' experience of serving the King's justices had taught him well about when it was best to keep one's counsel. To listen was far more valuable

21

than to speak, especially in a situation such as this where a clear picture had yet to emerge.

The abbot continued. 'The murder took place at Fairmore Abbey in the county of Yorkshire. Though our order favours locations that are secluded from the world, Fairmore is exceptionally remote. Yet its remoteness deep in the moors did not prevent evil from seeking it out. On the holy feast of Christmas, the sacrist of Fairmore, Brother Cuthbert, was found slain in utterly heinous circumstances.' Nicholas leaned forward. 'Strangled, and his body burned in the monastery kitchen.' He sat back. 'Well, half of it was.' He shuddered. 'His head and shoulders and the upper half of his body.'

Barling blessed himself, revolted at the idea of such a fate. 'May he be safe in God's care now.'

'A savage end.' De Glanville's expression was sombre but Barling knew him well enough to guess at the steely anger that flowed within him at the monk's fate. 'Yet the abbot of Fairmore, Philip, has no idea who committed this crime.'

'Philip says in this letter that he has questioned all of the monks at chapter,' said Nicholas. 'As he has the lay brothers. All have claimed that they have done no wrong, that they know nothing about it. Nothing.'

Barling kept his features expressionless. In his experience, such protestations meant little.

'The brethren of Fairmore live as every one of us in the Cistercian order does. Their regime is among the most challenging of all the orders, physically as well as spiritually. They devote their lives to God through prayer and fasting and hard work.' The emotion built in the abbot's voice as he spoke. 'They live in the cloister, not in a fortified castle. Just as a wolf savages the defenceless sheep, somebody has stolen in from outside and done this terrible deed. Whoever it is must be brought to justice. Must.'

'Of course, my lord abbot. Of course.' De Glanville raised a placatory hand. 'Which is why I will help, as requested.'

Still no clear picture. But de Glanville's next words formed one.

'Rest assured, Aelred Barling is definitely the right man for this enquiry.'

Chapter Five

Barling wondered if he had heard correctly. 'Me, my lord de Glanville?' To his dismay, he had.

'Yes, you, Barling,' said de Glanville. 'In his letter, Abbot Philip asks for you personally. He recognised you at the ordeal in York last June. He had travelled from Fairmore with a group of the brethren to witness the ordeal for themselves.'

'My lord de Glanville has given me an account of what you did for him and the other justices on that day,' said Nicholas, calmer-looking once more. 'Most impressive. A great lesson in the power of the truth for the crowds that were watching. An opinion which Philip shares.'

'Thank you, my lord abbot.' Barling would remember those sweltering weeks in June for the rest of his life. Not just the ordeal, where he had found proof of a man's guilt, but for what came after. 'Yet, if I might be so bold, my lord de Glanville, you say that Abbot Philip recognised me. I fear he must be mistaken. I have never lived in that part of the country. I was simply a member of the King's travelling court over which you presided.'

'Philip was a student at Paris at the same time as you,' said Nicholas. 'Philip de Franingeham.'

Paris. A sudden sweat broke out over every inch of Barling's body. *No.* He forced a polite smile to cover his deep shock at the unexpected mention of a part of his life that seemed now so distant. 'You will forgive me if I cannot recall him. I studied there over fifteen years ago. I was among two and a half thousand other scholars in that learned city.'

'A pale man, with dark hair and dark eyes,' said the abbot. 'Not very strongly built. Most talented in the study of rhetoric, as I understand you were.'

A memory stirred. A vague one, as were all Barling's memories of the faces and names from that time. Except one. One he could not, would not, think of. 'Then I believe I do recall him, my lord,' he said, marvelling that his voice came out so steadily. His training in matters of the court had served him well.

'Excellent.' Nicholas nodded in satisfaction.

'Yet, if you will permit me,' said Barling, 'I am still unclear as to why my help should be required. The Cistercian monks have many resources at their disposal.'

'I can see why you speak highly of this man, de Glanville,' said the abbot. 'He asks the correct questions.' He looked back at Barling. 'The situation at Fairmore, more specifically for Philip, requires sensitive handling. He has only been abbot for a few months. Naturally, he is the same age as you. Quite young for such great responsibility. His predecessor, Ernald, founded the abbey and was its father for thirty years. He died last summer, at a greatly advanced age. Philip, as new abbot, attended the General Chapter of our order last September, as did I. Though his grief at the loss of Ernald was apparent, he gave a good account of himself, considering how new he was to the appointment. I made a visitation to Fairmore in the weeks after that to make sure all was well. I found it to be mostly in good order.'

'Mostly, my lord?' asked Barling.

'I have explained to de Glanville that I came across some petty resentment at Philip's appointment. That was all.'

'But now the murder of Brother Cuthbert has taken place at Fairmore,' said de Glanville. 'The very opposite of good order.'

'Precisely,' said Nicholas, 'and it is Philip's responsibility to deal with it. Under normal circumstances, we could send another abbot to help him or I would arrange for a visitation, but coming so soon after the last, it would, Philip fears, imply that he is not capable of being in charge. That at the first sign of problems, he needs another senior monk's authority. I share his concerns. But your presence, Barling, would mean that Abbot Philip would have help in tracking this evildoer down, while leaving his spiritual authority intact.'

Barling met de Glanville's gaze and the justice gave a firm nod.

'Then I would, my lord abbot,' said Barling, summoning up every skill he had to sound as if he welcomed this, 'be humbled to provide the necessary assistance to Fairmore Abbey.'

'Then, may God be praised, the matter is settled.' Nicholas handed de Glanville the letter. 'I will leave this with you as it is a record of much of what we have discussed. Now, if you will excuse me, my lord de Glanville, I need to set off back to my own abbey. My place is with them during these holiest of days.' He stood up and de Glanville also rose to his feet.

'I wish you a swift and safe journey, my lord.' De Glanville walked him to the door as Barling gave him a respectful bow.

'Godspeed, my lord.'

The abbot paused on his way out. 'In the meantime, I will send a message to Philip, confirming Barling's imminent arrival. And thank you again, de Glanville. You will have a special place in our prayers.' The door closed behind him.

De Glanville looked at Barling. 'You will, I am sure, have questions. I have every confidence they will be the same as mine.'

'I do, my lord.' He wanted to ask why he had the misfortune to be thrust out from the safety and sanctuary of the King's writing office yet again, but he would never dream of revealing such insolent views to the justice. 'If I may be so bold, Abbot Nicholas was very certain that the murderer came from outside the abbey. Yet, could it be that . . .' He paused while he tried to find a tactful phrase.

'Barling, I know what you are thinking. It is perfectly possible that one of the brethren of Fairmore is responsible. All manner of men are capable of lying. Even monks. I did try to raise this with Nicholas, but he was highly insulted that I would even suggest it. In his defence, he has visited there, only three months ago. I questioned him at length about that visit, pressed him quite hard on his findings. But nothing appeared amiss. All the monks and brothers have lived there for many years. There are a few novices, but no new arrivals.'

'Nothing amiss, except of course for the resentment he mentioned at Philip's appointment.'

'Yes, I pursued that also. But it seems that such feelings are nothing out of the ordinary in the cloister. Nicholas has witnessed them himself in many houses, has had them in his own. He said they are easily addressed through prayer and reflection.'

'Then it is an outsider we seek.'

'It would certainly appear that way,' said de Glanville with a frown. 'Unless, by some unfortunate turn of events, you find otherwise.' He leaned forward, lowering his voice, although they could not possibly be overheard. 'Barling, I know I do not have to explain to you how delicate a matter that would be. You are a man who represents the King's law, while the White Monks are not only following the law of the Church but their own rules of discipline and punishment too.' He shook his head.

'I fully realise the implications, my lord.' The King. Saint Thomas Becket's murder. A terrible tragedy, born in arguments over the punishment of men of the Church.

'If such a situation were to arise, then you will need to seek my advice. As soon as you possibly can. Is that clear?'

'You have my word, my lord. I will always work to protect his Grace in any way I can.' Even if it meant setting off into the world outside the court again. An unpredictable, disordered, messy and unpleasant world.

'Delicate or not, it is vital that you get to the bottom of this, Barling.' De Glanville passed the letter from the abbot of Fairmore Abbey to him. 'Here, read it yourself. There is nothing in there other than what has been discussed. It is concise and well written, and the horror of what has happened is clear.' He crossed himself. 'No man deserves an end like that.'

'I will do my utmost, my lord.'

De Glanville leaned back in his seat again. 'I know you will. What you did last year at the village of Claresham was exceptional.'

'Thank you, my lord. You are most gracious. Yet I cannot claim to have succeeded alone. Which brings me to my next question.'

'Hugo Stanton?'

'Your reasoning is swift and sharp as ever, my lord. I would very much appreciate it if he could accompany me in this enquiry.'

'He has a lively mind and is braver than he knows,' said de Glanville. 'I knew that when I took him on as a messenger.'

'Indeed.' It was a tactful reply. Stanton's early days with the court had had Barling regularly doubting de Glanville's choice. Although Barling had tried to enquire why the young man had been chosen, his questions to both the justice and Stanton had been firmly deflected. He went on, sincere now in what he said. 'The outcome in Claresham would have been very different without him. Moreover, he is a fast, reliable messenger. If I did need to inform you of anything sensitive, we can trust him absolutely.'

'A most sensible suggestion. Take Stanton with you.' De Glanville gave a wry smile. 'Then it would seem you are returning to Yorkshire sooner than the King's justices, Barling.'

'It would, my lord.' He knew Stanton would be pleased at the opportunity of travelling, though Barling suspected that a monastery would not normally be the first place in which he would choose to stay.

As for Barling, his own displeasure was complete. He was being ordered once more from the security of the writing office. It was a world where he toiled with every diligence for the court: writing records and writs, recording appeals, copying judgements, keeping the pipe rolls in order. He performed every and any task that was needed to administer the King's justice. Now he faced an arduous journey and an enquiry that came under the authority of the Church and not of Henry. Worse, it seemed that he would have to reacquaint himself with a man who knew him from his old life, a life he wished to forget and had successfully put from his mind for many years.

'Then I wish you Godspeed on your journey, Barling.'

'Thank you, my lord de Glanville.' Barling found a smile from he knew not where, the better to mask his utter dismay.

Chapter Six

An icy rain spattered from the low clouds, whipped into Stanton's face by the strong, raw wind. He turned in his saddle to speak to Barling, who rode next to him. 'They said at that last village that we should be at Fairmore Abbey within three hours. It can't be much longer, I'm sure of it.'

'I do not need cajoling, Stanton,' came the clerk's testy response. 'Our progress will take the time it takes. Empty words will not hasten it.'

The mud-spattered Barling's bad temper came as no surprise. A poor rider with little skill, Barling had complained of being bone-tired and stiff-muscled within the first few hours of leaving London.

And they'd been riding for ten days.

Ten days since Stanton had returned from the bear-baiting and the clerk had given him an account of what had taken place between the visiting abbot and de Glanville. At first, he'd been puzzled. The murder of the poor monk in the Yorkshire house sounded horrific. Whoever did it should face punishment, no doubt about that. But it wasn't anything to do with them here in London.

Then he'd been puzzled no more.

Just like the bear, Stanton, we are being sent out to battle once more.

Barling's words had made Stanton's heart thud into his boots in disappointment. A monastery. They were being sent to a monastery. One that was hundreds of miles away. Winter journeys were always slow and hard. Stanton knew that well. Not only were roads muddier and slower under hooves, fords were more likely to be flooded and snow and ice would make the going treacherous. Riding in daylight was easier and safer. But midwinter days like these were over in a few short hours, shorter when the weather closed in. It would be no more feasts for him, then, not this Christmas. He'd miss the Epiphany, the best and richest of them all.

That wasn't the worst of it.

Had Stanton been on his own, he could've done what he always did when he was on the road and seek out the liveliest-looking inns. He could have slaked his thirst with plenty of ale and swapped songs and stories long into the night with folk he met, before a good fire. If his luck was in, he'd have had his bed warmed too. He'd happily travel another hundred days like that.

But he wasn't on his own, was he.

He had Barling in tow. Barling, who insisted on the quietest of lodgings and who looked at ale like it might poison him, demanding well water instead. Barling, who sniffed at food like it might contain a cow pat. Barling, who glared at the few people, the very few, who tried to talk to them and glared at Stanton if he smiled at a woman.

Yes, they were headed for a monastery, but, by God's eyes, Stanton was already having to live like a monk.

At least Barling had pressed on at a pace that surprised Stanton. Not the speed that Stanton could've ridden on his own. Very few riders could match him. But for a man who had all the skill of a sack of grain in the saddle, it wasn't bad.

No rider could go faster than their current pace, though. The land had risen steeply after the village of Gottburn, a small settlement that huddled in a narrow valley. The village was the last before the abbey and the track they rode on now led there and nowhere else. Thick snow lay on the high ground, slushy underfoot on the muddy roadway where streams ran across it or where the rain had started to half-melt it.

Stanton's horse laboured beneath him on the climb, as did Barling's. 'Better we weren't making this journey at all.'

'I have explained it all very clearly, Stanton.' Testy. Again. 'We have been tasked with this enquiry. It is our duty to undertake it without complaint.'

Without complaint? Stanton hid his wry smile.

'Who is that?' came Barling's abrupt, sharp question.

Stanton looked up from his careful watch of the rocky, unstable roadway underfoot to follow Barling's point.

A small band of people, four men and two women, were making their way towards them, walking down along the road from the top of the hill.

He took in their clothing, their appearance with a quick glance. 'They're not monks.'

'Outlaws?'

'Don't think so.' While not well dressed, the group wore cloaks and shawls to keep out the cold and all were shod.

'Yet they come from Fairmore.' Barling cast him a tight frown. 'And Abbot Philip's letter told of the suspicion of a murderous outsider.'

'It did.' Stanton shifted in his saddle, prepared for action. Though he fought hard when it was needed, he wasn't a natural fighter. His speed, on a horse and off, was a far better way of getting out of danger. 'If there's any sign of trouble, we kick these horses and get away. Those folk won't be able to catch us.' He hoped. Sudden pace on such steep ground was risky for both horse and rider. Especially one like Barling.

As they approached the group, Stanton saw to his relief that they clambered to the side of the road on the down slope to let Stanton and Barling's horses go past. Anyone planning an attack would head for the higher side. But they were still six, where he and the clerk were two. In a wild, inhospitable place with nobody else in sight.

'Nevertheless, I will speak to them,' said Barling in a low voice.

'No, don't, we should carry on and—'

'God keep you!' called Barling.

'And you, sirs.' A muttered, respectful chorus, eyes lowered, came in response as the horses drew level.

'You are a long way from home.' Barling halted his animal, forcing Stanton to do likewise.

He swallowed an oath at the clerk's dangerous pig-headedness.

'We're from the village of Gottburn, sir,' replied one man. No smile. The others let him speak for them all. 'We are returning there now.'

Stanton swept his gaze over every gaunt, sullen face, every hand, watching for any twitch that might be sign of an attack.

'Returning from where?'

'Fairmore Abbey, sir. Nowt else along this road, sir.'

'A long way to walk in such inclement weather,' said Barling.

Shut up, Barling. Move on. Quickly.

The man rummaged beneath his cloak.

Stanton drew in a breath, readied to pull Barling's animal out of there with his own.

And let the breath out again.

The man held a small loaf of bread. 'The monks give out alms, sir. We need them. This winter's been very hard, sir.'

Nods came from the others, with one woman showing Barling a basket with her equally meagre loaf.

'God be praised that you have the generous goodness of the monks' charity,' said Barling.

'Yes, sir,' was all the man said. The others said nothing.

Stanton didn't blame them. The small loaves weren't much more than three mouthfuls' worth. It was a long walk to get them. 'Then we wish you Godsp—' he began, in an attempt to shift Barling.

No good. Barling spoke over him.

'You will be keeping the monks in your prayers, I am sure. Especially after the murder of Brother Cuthbert.'

By all the saints, the clerk was trying to start his murder investigation. Here on a windswept open hillside. Outnumbered.

'A terrible tragedy, sir.' The man blessed himself while keeping his gaze directly on Barling, the others lowering theirs.

'And one which God will punish, no doubt.'

This time Stanton butted in. 'No doubt. With such a man on the loose, none of us wants to be caught out in the dark. Be on your way, good people.'

The group didn't need telling twice. They set off with a polite farewell as Stanton got both horses moving away.

The clerk, as expected, glared at him. 'How dare you conduct yourself in such an impertinent manner? I was speaking. I had not finished.'

Stanton glanced back over his shoulder. To his relief, all six people were steadily marching back towards their village. 'A bad time, Barling. And a worse place.'

'Do not attempt to tell me how to conduct an enquiry.'

'I'm not telling you how. But I am telling you where. This is not the place. It's far too risky. Had they been wrongdoers, we were far too open to attack.' His own sharp tone surprised him. He was as testy as Barling.

To his further surprise, Barling backed down. 'On reflection, you are probably right, Stanton.' He sighed. 'I fear I am letting my fatigue cloud my judgement. Our goal at this moment is to get safely to Fairmore, is it not?'

Stanton gave a firm nod. 'Fairmore.'

Two more for the abbey. That's good.

Crouched low in her hiding place behind a large, snow-covered rock above the roadway, Agatha Frane watched as the strangers rode past. No chance they'd see her, she was sure of that. Not only was her patched rough wool cloak the same colour as the windswept bare shrubs that had shed their covering of snow, she knew how to be completely still. Quiet.

They were a bit of an odd pair. Not from round here, no question about that. That was nothing new. People came from all over to visit Fairmore, people with hearts full of charity for a young beggar girl. She grinned to herself. And full purses.

But if the pair looked a bit odd, they sounded it too. Her ears were as good as her eyes, and her eyes could spot a hare in the snowy heather a hundred feet away. No, they were definitely not from here. The older man, the one in black robes, had started on at the Gottburn villagers about the murder, the one at Christmas. Agatha's jaw set. A Christmas that should've been very different for her.

Still, the older one looked like he'd have plenty of coins. Even from this distance, she could tell the dark cloth he wore was good, filthy though it was from travelling. He sounded like a man who had money too. But she reckoned he wouldn't part with it easily. She'd heard the way he spoke to the villagers, how they should be glad of the poor loaves of bread the monks had given them.

The villagers were trudging back to Gottburn now, not paying any mind to anything other than the long road home. There was a time when she would've been among them. Not any more. She didn't care. They were fools. She had a much fuller belly than them and didn't have to walk half so much.

She brought her gaze to the strangers again.

The other one, the younger one, looked a lot more promising. He'd have money as well, no doubt. He had a face that was far fairer than hers, which wasn't so good. Better was how he'd spoken to the villagers. He didn't seem over-lofty. Best of all was the way he sat on his horse, which told of a lean, muscled body. She knew her youth would get his notice, if nothing else.

The men were arguing between themselves now.

The older one was telling the younger one off. The younger one in turn sounded annoyed, talking about them being open to attack out here.

He was right.

She was up here, with them clearly in her sight. And they had no idea she was watching. None.

But outside wasn't the only place a person could get attacked. Brother Cuthbert had been attacked, hadn't he? And he'd been inside the abbey.

Now she heard the names of the strangers.

Barling, the young one called the older one. And the young one was Stanton.

Barling. Stanton. Two more. Two who didn't know her or anything about her.

What a nice, unexpected gift.

Chapter Seven

'There it is.' Stanton halted his horse, allowing the animal a short rest after the long, long climb up the snow-covered hill. 'Fairmore Abbey.' He might be looking forward to spending time in the monastery about as much as a man with a rotting tooth looked forward to a visit to the barber-surgeon. But at least their long journey was over. Even better, he'd managed to get Barling here in one piece.

'A very fine abbey.' Barling stopped his horse too. 'And in a remote location.'

'Remote? Desolate, more like.'

'The Cistercian brethren favour such places. Yet it is inaccessible even by their standards.'

If the hill they had climbed was steep, the one that fell away before them was even more so. The many buildings of the monastery far below nestled in a deep valley, with the yellowed stone of the buildings sheltered by the black branches of tall bare trees and large growths of evergreens. The outlines of several fields were visible around the abbey on the valley floor. Where the upward slope had been cut by a number of smaller streams, a much larger torrent carved its way down this one. A deep, dark slash in the snow, it gathered strength and size as it flowed down the rocky outcrops before disappearing into the small wood that grew beyond the abbey's walls.

'We'll have to take our time going down,' said Stanton. 'Let me know if you need to dismount.'

Barling merely nodded.

While they descended without mishap, it still took time and care.

Stanton was relieved once the land levelled out somewhat, could sense it in his animal as well. The low-lying valley meant that the snow lay less heavily on the ground, with patches of stony mud and coarse yellowed grass showing through in a few places.

'We've done it, Barling.' The clatter of their horses' hooves was loud on the deserted roadway. Though he couldn't see it, Stanton could hear the rumble and hiss of the strongly flowing river somewhere in the trees.

'We have.' Barling seemed lost in thought.

While this was nothing out of the ordinary for the clerk, Stanton wondered if he might be a bit worried about the task that lay ahead.

The gatehouse set into the sturdy walls loomed up ahead, its doors shut against the world: two large, which would allow horses and loaded carts to pass through, with a smaller one to the side.

Stanton slipped from his horse.

'You can ring the bell.' Barling dismounted with his usual clumsiness.

Stanton pulled hard on the knotted rope to the right of the smaller door. A loud jangle sounded from inside.

He noted that Barling pulled his cloak straight, squared his shoulders, the sign that he was ready to assert his authority.

Nothing.

A frown from Barling. 'Again, Stanton.'

He complied.

Still nothing. No sound. Only the nearby river and the snorting of their tired horses.

'This is intolerable. Again, Stanton.'

As Stanton yanked hard on the bell for a third time, a muffled oath came from behind the door, along with the clack of bolts.

The door flew open to the dying peals of the bell and a furious voice.

'I told you there'd be no more bread today. Be off with you, you lazy leeches.' An elderly monk stood there, clutching at the half-open door. Stanton guessed he'd be in his seventh decade. Hugely fat, his many-chinned scarlet face above his stained habit was screwed up in anger. 'Of—' He broke off. 'Oh. Sirs.'

A strong smell of ale came from him.

'Good day, brother. My name is Aelred Barling, clerk to King Henry. Your abbot will be expecting me.'

'Aelred Barling?' The chins arranged a smile. Of sorts. 'One moment.' He disappeared from view.

'Abbot Nicholas told me at Westminster that this house was in good order.' Barling's pale nostrils had pinched, always a sign he was annoyed. 'I can only assume he was received in a manner befitting his stature and not bellowed at like a common oaf.'

'Unless he came asking for bread, eh?'

Barling didn't smile at his companion's small jest.

More snaps of metal on metal came from within, along with huffs of breath. One of the large doors opened.

The monk stood there, mopping his brow. 'Please.' He waved them in, unable to say another word.

Stanton stepped back to let Barling lead the way. As he followed him in, the monk waddled past to close the doors once again.

Though they were within the walls, they were still only in the monastery's outer precinct. Stanton was familiar with the layout from his younger days as a monastic post rider. That was as far as he'd ever got in a holy house. The inner buildings were for the brethren only, which had suited him. He'd never had any need to go in and had no wish to, either.

Barling turned to him. 'I am most concerned,' he said in a low tone. 'I do not believe that this rude monk knows who I am.'

'Maybe not,' replied Stanton. 'But this one does.' He nodded to the right, where another monk came hurrying along a path that led from a number of buildings arranged around a small courtyard.

'God be praised, you have arrived, sir.' Tall and skinny, this monk was considerably younger than the first. Where the older monk's clothing was unkempt, this man's habit didn't have a mark on it. He came to a stop before Barling. 'The blessings of the Virgin be upon you on this day.' The monk bowed so deeply that his head almost touched his knees, then he unrolled himself again in one swift movement. 'I am Brother Silvanus, the guestmaster of Fairmore. It is my deepest honour to welcome the King's man. Deepest.'

'It is my honour that I am visiting this holy house,' said Barling.

Silvanus's gaze flew to Stanton, his beady eyes flicking to and fro and reminding Stanton of a weasel. 'And welcome to you also, sir.' The question was in his voice.

'Hugo Stanton is accompanying me on my visit.' Barling's tone didn't invite debate.

'A second visitor from the court of the King?' Silvanus did his remarkable bow again. 'I will be honoured to show you our hospitality also, sir.' He clasped his hands. 'Unfortunately, I have not yet had your room prepared as I was not informed that we were receiving you. Such a dreadful oversight. My deepest apologies, I will make sure it is done without delay. We have but the one guest here at the moment, so we have plenty of room. Now, please: if you would follow me. The stables are this way.' Silvanus led the way back along the path towards the courtyard. 'My lord abbot's heart will be full that you are here, as mine is too. He asked me to bring you to him the moment you arrived. The very moment.'

'We had a slight delay in arriving, Silvanus,' said Barling. 'It took us some time to rouse your gatekeeper.'

Stanton grinned inside. He knew how much the large monk's reception had annoyed Barling.

'Ah.' Silvanus gave a wide smile that was all sharp teeth and no warmth. 'My deepest apologies, sir. Brother Lambert is such a kind-hearted soul. But he gets a little' – he allowed a pointed pause – 'muddled in his ways sometimes. As I am sure we all do.' He clapped his hands and raised his voice as he left them to hurry over to what appeared to be the stable block. 'Daniel! Where are you?'

Stanton exchanged a look with Barling. 'Kind-hearted?' he muttered.

'Questionable, indeed,' replied Barling. 'And the reason for Brother Lambert being muddled will be found in an empty jug.'

A young man emerged from the stable block with Silvanus, carrying a pitchfork. He looked over as Silvanus, no longer smiling, hissed a rapid set of orders at him. Broad-shouldered and muscular, the scowling Daniel's appearance and dress marked him as a lay brother. As the dark hood that covered his shoulders wasn't raised, Stanton could see that, unlike the monks, his hair wasn't shaved in a tonsure but sat in a heavy fringe that reached his brows. Neither was he clean-shaven: he had a thick, short beard. Instead of a woollen cowl, he wore a long-sleeved belted tunic and braies of coarse cloth. At a last hiss from Silvanus, he leaned the pitchfork against the wall and came over with the monk to take the horses.

'Thank you.' Stanton handed him the reins, Barling too.

Daniel didn't meet their eye. 'Sirs,' came his surly reply. He led the horses off at once.

'No need for thanks: it is our honour. Our honour.' Though Silvanus spoke as if he hadn't noticed the lay brother's rude behaviour, his eyes darted a look after him that could have set him aflame in his muddy boots. 'Now come this way. This way.' He flapped a hand towards a gravel path that was screened by high evergreen hedges. 'My lord Ernald's lodging is this way.' The teeth again. 'Oh, my. Did I say

Ernald?' He crossed himself. 'I mean my lord Philip. So hard to get used to a new abbot. But I am sure we will.'

'I know of the loss of your esteemed Abbot Ernald,' said Barling. 'An event of tremendous sadness for this house.'

'The saddest.' Silvanus's sigh was louder than the crunch of their steps on the gravel underfoot. 'But he will now be in the arms of our Saviour in heaven. Eternal glory will be his.'

He slid his gaze back to Stanton, who made a point of not meeting his eye. He knew the man itched to ask about his presence here again. He didn't want to encourage him – he knew where Barling's conversation was headed.

'Indeed, the glory of heaven is that for which we all pray,' said Barling. 'But Abbot Ernald was not this house's most recent sad loss, was he?'

Silvanus's beady-eyed look was back on Barling. Displeased. 'You know much about us here, sir.' He crossed himself with wide gestures again even as he quickened his pace. 'No, it was not. We pray that poor Brother Cuthbert receives his eternal reward also.' He pointed ahead. 'You will see the abbot's fine lodging at the end of this path. A great welcome awaits you. Awaits you both.' Another hard smile for Stanton.

Stanton returned it with a nod and smile of his own. 'My thanks.'

Let this monk think he'd moved the discussion on from Cuthbert's murder.

It could easily be moved back. Knowing Barling, it would be.

Chapter Eight

'Please, come through, sirs.' Silvanus ushered Barling and Stanton into the hall in the abbot's lodging. 'I will seek out my lord Philip with all haste and let him know that his guests have arrived.' He scurried off, leaving them alone.

'He's not happy that I'm here, is he, Barling?' said Stanton as he made his way over to the lit fireplace.

'A moment.' Barling put his finger to his lips and opened the doors a crack. The vestibule outside was deserted and he closed them again. He walked into the spacious hall.

Unlike de Glanville's sumptuous room, this one was without any ornamentation, as he would have expected from the White Monks. The long table, the stools that lined it, the stone of the fireplace: all were well made and of the best quality but were without a single carving or decoration. Beeswax candles in single black iron candleholders lit the white-walled room. The only adornment on the walls was a large wooden cross.

'We are free to speak, at least for now.' He joined Stanton to stand before the fire. Although he ached from head to toe from his wretched days in the saddle, courtesy dictated that they should not sit until the abbot joined them. The abbot, Philip. Philip de Franingeham, as he'd known him. He'd thought of his fellow student many times on the journey here, thought of how one's past was always with one, no matter how carefully one tried to leave it behind. In a few minutes, it would catch up with him once again. He brought his attention back to Stanton. 'However, I did think it necessary to check that Brother Silvanus had left and was not still with an ear to the door. He appears not only disconcerted by your unexpected arrival but also immensely curious.'

'Disconcerted? Not as much as that gatekeeper.' Stanton flashed him a grin. 'Lambert.'

'His reception is not a laughing matter, Stanton.'

'Sorry,' he replied, looking anything but, adding irritation to Barling's tension.

'Yet I agree with your point. It was clear the man had no idea who I was.'

'I don't think he was confused only about you, Barling.' Stanton rubbed his hands before the flames. 'I think he's probably confused all the time. Looked very fond of his ale to me.'

'It is disgraceful conduct for a monk. He should—'

He stopped at the sound of the door opening, turning to see a man whom he had not seen or even thought of for many years before he was mentioned in Westminster. But as so often happened with the mind, the face of his fellow student of rhetoric became instantly familiar once it was before him again.

'Aelred Barling. You are here.' The voice too. 'May God be praised. I cannot tell you what your presence means to me, Barling.'

'My lord abbot.' Barling gave a respectful bow, relieved to note that Stanton did also. He could not always rely on his young pupil to behave in the correct manner.

As Abbot Philip made his way towards him, other memories from that time came back too and threatened to overwhelm him. He swallowed hard, banishing them.

'The years have treated you well, Barling. I thought that when I saw you at the ordeal in York last summer.'

'As time has been kind to you, my lord abbot.' A little above average height, Philip was not a powerfully built man, but his bearing had a confidence as befitted a man of his office. His dark brown tonsure, dark brown eyes and very pale skin were as Barling remembered, save for threads of grey in the hair and wrinkles around his eyes that Barling supposed would be equally apparent on his own face. As in his youth, Philip was almost the most handsome of men. Having a nose a little too long and a jaw a little too weak meant that he was not.

'Truly, words do not serve me in my gratitude.' He embraced Barling in a heartfelt kiss of peace, his gaze controlled yet clearly troubled.

'I am humbled by your gracious words, my lord,' said Barling. 'May I present my assistant, Hugo Stanton, to you.'

'Brother Silvanus has told me of your arrival, Stanton.' The abbot raised his hand in a swift blessing. 'May you also be welcome in our holy house.'

'Thank you, my lord.' Stanton responded with the necessary respect once more.

Philip indicated to a waiting trestle table against one wall upon which full washing basins waited. 'Please. Remove the dirt from your long journey. Silvanus is bringing food for us.'

Footsteps confirmed this.

Barling washed his face and hands, the freshening properties of the water helping him to fully regain his composure.

Three bearded lay brothers arrived bearing dishes, cups and jugs, with Silvanus close at their heels. They made quick work of setting their burden on the table and withdrew again to extravagant bows from the guestmaster.

Barling came to the table, Stanton with him, standing with heads bowed as Philip opened his hands and blessed the food.

With a chorus of 'Amen', Barling took his seat opposite Stanton, with Philip at the head of the table.

'Please, eat your fill,' said Philip. 'We do not impose our order's rules about food on our guests.'

'A most generous accommodation. Thank you, my lord.'

'You can address me as Philip, Barling. At least while we are in private.'

Stanton, he noted, was not included in Philip's invitation, which was to be expected. 'Your permission is most gracious.' Barling helped himself to modest portions of the dishes before him. Simple fare, as he expected from this order, which pleased him greatly: good bread, a plain vegetable pottage and a dish of the darkest green cabbage. He knew the addition of a small round cheese was for the benefit of him and Stanton as guests. A quick glance at Stanton showed the younger man's morose expression at both the type of food and the quantity.

'May I offer you some ale?' said Philip, pouring himself some water.

'I will also have water.' Barling filled his own cup and took a deep draught. 'Excellent.'

Stanton silently slid the ale jug over to himself.

'Our wells are fed by the river, which means they are very pure,' said Philip. 'My predecessor, Ernald, may have chosen a particularly remote place to found this abbey, but he chose wisely, as he did in all things. He was blessed with the deepest wisdom as well as holiness.'

'So I have heard,' said Barling. 'A great loss to this house, I am sure.'

'It was. And though we are sure he is safe in the arms of Our Lord in heaven, we grieve for him still. He was our beloved father.' The dark pools of Philip's eyes glistened for a moment and he blinked hard. 'A very great man. Sometimes I think he anticipated the evil act that was visited upon Brother Cuthbert.'

'How so?'

'It was Ernald's decision to go to the ordeal in York last summer,' said Philip. 'He wanted to see God's judgement of the water for himself, and he wanted many of his monks to see it as well. He was very sick and should not have gone but he was determined. I think it gave him the greatest comfort to see God's hand at work before his very eyes. The work of our lord King too, in the form of his justices. And of course, your work also, Barling. Though I had not expected to see a familiar face in the travelling court, I recognised you at once, to my great delight. While others expressed surprise at your cleverness on that day, I was not surprised in the least. I well remembered your outstanding intellect from our days in Paris.'

'I was but one among many sharp minds, yours included.'

'You are too kind.' Philip gave a dismissive wave. 'But only you could leave the masters struck dumb with their lack of response to your arguments.' He gave Barling a solemn nod, his gaze less troubled now. 'It is as if Ernald knew that something terrible would befall our monastery and his hand has guided you here to help me. I take great comfort from that.'

'The greatest comfort comes from justice,' said Barling. 'Is that not our experience, Stanton?'

To his irritation, Stanton was gulping down a long draught of ale.

'It is,' Stanton choked out in response.

Philip caught Barling's eye. 'Ale is always favoured by young men, is it not, Barling?'

It is very much favoured by your elderly gatekeeper as well. Barling did not put the thought into words. This was not the time. He merely smiled instead.

Philip returned the smile, though his was a sheepish one. 'Paris was not only hours of study and debate with the masters, was it? I seem to remember, to my deepest shame, drinking the taverns of Paris dry on more than a few occasions.'

Barling had no wish to revisit those events. But he had to be polite. 'To my shame too. I think every one of us had times when we acted foolishly when we were there.' He had seldom seen Stanton look more surprised: his pupil had even stopped drinking.

'Foolish does not even begin to describe it,' said Philip. 'The devil's monasteries, some called the taverns, did they not?'

Barling nodded, thankful he was unable to reply with a spoon of hot pottage in his mouth.

Philip went on. 'Though some were worse than others. The worst were dens of fornication, even sodomy, if the writings of Walter Map are to be believed.' He shook his head.

'A long time ago, indeed,' said Barling, hiding his discomfort at the topic of the taverns by concentrating on breaking up his bread. 'And I would hope that we have acquired wisdom since then.'

'I would hope so too,' replied Philip. 'Age and experience have brought us great rewards: me, an abbot. You, a royal clerk.' He gave a quiet sigh. 'Yet with great reward comes even greater responsibility.' Philip tapped the ale jug and looked at Stanton. 'But you see, my boy, how easy it could be to take a different path? To become ensnared in wickedness and sin?'

'Yes, my lord abbot.' Stanton gave a vigorous nod.

'Good.' Philip looked back at Barling, his gaze perturbed once again. 'And of course, Barling, the most terrible wickedness has descended on us here at Fairmore.'

'That it has,' said Barling, ashamed at his own relief that the abbot had moved the discussion to the appalling occurrence in the abbey.

'My fellow abbot, Nicholas,' said Philip, 'has let me know that he conveyed to you and Ranulf de Glanville what I wrote to him.'

'He did; hence I am here.' Barling reached for his satchel. 'In fact, I have your letter with me.' He took it out.

Philip's mouth set in a line, as if seeing his own neatly written words again brought him distress anew. 'That I should ever have had to write such a letter.' He glanced at Stanton, then back at Barling. 'We need to discuss it at the earliest opportunity.'

'We have no need to wait,' said Barling. 'You requested my help, which my lord de Glanville was happy to give, as am I. Stanton is here to assist me, which, again, de Glanville agreed as a course of action.'

Philip's brow cleared. A little. 'Then I have more help than I asked for. De Glanville will be forever in my prayers.'

'To help, we must have a full account.' Barling unrolled the letter. 'Shall we begin?'

Chapter Nine

'Philip, I realise it will be unpleasant to revisit the events of Brother Cuthbert's murder,' said Barling. 'But it is necessary.'

The abbot nodded. 'I understand.'

'Firstly, I need to establish that Cuthbert was your sacrist, was he not?'

'It is in my letter.'

'I like to confirm information.'

'Then, yes: Cuthbert is – was – my sacrist, and Abbot Ernald's before me. Had been so for many years. Cuthbert was responsible for maintaining our church. He took care of our liturgical vestments and the sacred corporal cloths, laundering them with care and devotion and ensuring their perfect cleanliness. His duties also included timekeeping, opening and closing the church doors as needed as well. Cuthbert was the one who had to ring the church bells to wake us or call us to the Divine Office or to Mass. That was what first alerted Brother Maurice to the fact that something was wrong.'

'Maurice?' Barling wished he had his tablet and pen to hand as well. But he did not wish to be so impolite as to take notes while he and the others were still eating. And he was pleased to see that Stanton was listening intently. For all his faults, his pupil had sharp recall. They could compose a complete record afterward.

'Brother Maurice, our novice master. Maurice told me he woke without any sound of the bell for the hour of Vigils, the night Office.'

'Which would have been around an hour and a half after midnight, would it not?'

'Normally. But this was the night before the birth of Our Lord, when Vigils are at two hours before midnight.'

'Then surely many of the brethren would still have been awake?'

'No,' said Philip. 'We go to sleep after the last Office at sundown. Which is already almost upon us today.'

'So early?' asked Barling in surprise.

'Early in winter, much less so in summer. I can tell you, it is welcome. We have a far stricter regime than the monks and brothers of other orders.' He drew himself up in his seat. 'They return to bed after Vigils to sleep the night away. We do not, but spend the dark hours in prayer and devotion. And work. All on the consumption of but one meal a day.'

A challenge indeed. 'Requiring the greatest fortitude of spirit, mind and body, I am sure. Yet Brother Maurice woke up?'

'He did. I think some of the older monks, of which he is one, have had so many years of answering the bell that they no longer need it rung.' He gave a rueful smile. 'I do not know if that time will ever come for me. I am very poor at rousing from sleep.'

'I doubt if you could be worse than Stanton here, Philip.' Barling nodded at Stanton, who was finishing the cheese and looking not in the least ashamed. 'As you were saying: Maurice was awake.'

'He was. He checked the chamber Cuthbert slept in, which is next to the monks' dormitory. There was no sign of Cuthbert. So Maurice set about waking the whole dormitory. He sent the novices down the night stairs, he and the other monks following. The night stairs lead from the monks' dormitory straight to the church. But the door from the stairs into the church was locked. No bell. Doors locked. No Cuthbert.' His voice dropped. 'Maurice used his key to open the church and I was sent for.'

'You sleep here, in your lodging?'

'I do. After so many years of sleeping in a crowded dormitory with all the other monks, I thought I would relish the peace and quiet. Truth be told, I find it a little lonely.' He took a sip of water. 'Anyway. There were some angry words said to me about Cuthbert—'

'By whom?' Barling did not hesitate with his interruption. Emotion was so frequently linked to a murdering hand.

'Maurice. He was very upset at Cuthbert's failure to wake everyone on one of the most important nights of the year. But at that point he was not to know the truth of the matter. I went to start Vigils and Maurice stormed out. He took it upon himself to track Cuthbert down. He was shouting about bringing him back to face his sins and shame. I think perhaps he was headed for the warming room, guessing that Cuthbert had sneaked in there and fallen asleep. It does happen from time to time.'

'But Brother Cuthbert was not in the warming room.'

'No. He was in the kitchen. Which is nearby. I was summoned immediately. I got the . . . the smell first.' Philip shook his head. 'It was a scene from hell itself. Cuthbert was almost unrecognisable. The murderer had stoked the kitchen fire beneath one of the iron grills. Cuthbert was face down on it over the red-hot embers. The upper half of his body was . . . cooked.' Philip dropped his head on to one raised hand, his elbow propped on the table, as if the memory of the sight weighed him down. 'Cuthbert had been strangled. My infirmary monk, William, found tiny pieces of thin rope buried in Cuthbert's neck when he was preparing the body for its eternal rest. The flesh was so damaged, he was not sure at first.'

Stanton reached for a deep mouthful of ale, pale as Philip now.

Barling knew his own visage would be the same. 'I wish I could say that I cannot imagine what it must have been like, Philip. Unfortunately, I can. Which is why we must discover who is responsible.' Barling patted the letter. 'And you conducted an immediate investigation?'

'I did. As I said in that letter, I questioned everybody at chapter. I have found nothing, except that all share the same distress. Cuthbert was a most decent man. Hard-working. Reliable. Quiet. Probably the quietest man here. He had no special friendships or closeness with any other. Unusual, given that he was a monk here for twenty years. But that did not mean he was not loved.'

'When you say you have questioned "all", Philip, to whom are you referring?'

'The seventy-five souls that are currently under my care. My seven remaining obedientiaries, the senior monks who help to run this house, of which Cuthbert was one. Twenty choir monks, six novices and forty-two lay brothers. I have spoken to them all.'

Barling nodded. It sounded as if Philip had been most thorough. But he pressed him further. 'Yet, surely,' said Barling, 'and I mean no disrespect, Philip, there may well be a wrongdoer amongst so many?'

'Are you suggesting any of them would lie, sir?' Outrage flushed into Philip's face, as de Glanville had said it had with Nicholas when he'd suggested the same thing. 'We live lives of peaceful order. These men have sworn before God, and they are men of God, that they have not done this foul, sinful deed. And I believe them.' His voice rose in tone. 'A murderer has come from outside. Slain our beloved brother. That is why I have asked for your help.'

Barling raised a hand. 'I am sorry, Philip.'

Philip gave a long sigh. 'It is I who should apologise, Barling. This has been a very heavy burden to carry. As well as my own grief for Cuthbert, I have had to carry the grief of the community. A community that was already grieving over the loss of our beloved abbot, Ernald.'

'Think no more of it,' said Barling. 'I completely understand. And I will be doing everything I possibly can to find the evildoer.'

'Then I can only pray you do,' said Philip. 'As does every soul here.'

'Thank you.' Barling rolled up the letter. 'As well as your prayers, I will need to have your assurances of the cooperation of the brethren. Stanton and I will need to view the place where Brother Cuthbert's body was found, along with other locations within the precinct. We may also wish to speak to some of the brethren.'

Philip pulled in a sharp breath. 'Barling, the cloister is not open to outsiders. The lay brothers won't like it but they will do as they are told. They always do. They have dull wits but at least are obedient. But the monks will not be happy. At all.'

Barling's irritation rose further, though he kept it from his voice. 'With respect, I am not interested in their happiness. My task here is to find out what happened to Cuthbert. To do so, we need a complete picture and that includes where he lived and died.'

'I see.' A deep frown dented Philip's brow. 'Then can I ask that we at least give the monks some warning? We meet every morning in the Chapter House, where I discuss matters of discipline, among other issues. I am not suggesting you should be present for those. But I can invite you in at the end, introduce you and explain the necessity and purpose of your presence.'

Barling wished he did not have to go through such an inconvenient performance. But if it would smooth the ruffled feathers of the monks, so be it. 'Very well.' Barling nodded to Stanton. 'We shall attend.'

From outside, a bell rang – not the jangle of the gatehouse, which in any case would have been too far away.

'If you have no more questions, I hope you will excuse me,' said Philip. 'The monks assemble in the north claustral walk at this time for a reading from me. I am trying to keep everything regular and in order at this time of upset.'

'I will not keep you further.' Barling went to rise to his feet.

'Please, stay and finish your meal,' said Philip. 'All I would ask is that, when you are finished, you make your way directly back to the guesthouse along the same path. I would not want your presence elsewhere to startle any of the brethren.'

'You have our word, Philip,' said Barling.

'Thank you. And thank you once again for your help in our hour of need. Good night to you.'

With that, he was gone.

Chapter Ten

As soon as the door closed behind Abbot Philip, Stanton downed his half-full cup of ale in one gulp.

'I see you are paying attention to Philip's wise and holy words.' Across the table from him, the clerk eyed him crossly.

'I'll keep a watch out for sin.' He refilled the cup. Hell's teeth, he hadn't ridden all these miles with a morose and complaining Barling to be lectured by him and the abbot again here. 'But I'm not letting good ale go to waste. And this is very good.' He drank again.

Barling took his writing materials from his satchel. 'Just make sure that you can recall everything for my record.' The clerk arranged the wax-covered wood tablet square in front of him and tested the tip of his stylus while delivering a fresh frown at Stanton. 'That is of far more importance than supping ale.'

Stanton shrugged. He could do both. 'Won't most of what Philip said already be in the letter he sent?' He picked up a spoon and scraped it round the empty pottage dish in a hunt for the last scraps. He could've eaten all the food himself and had space for more, let alone divide it three ways. The other two would have been fine. The abbot had said that the monks were used to eating little and Barling ate less than any other man he knew – most women as well. But, curse it all, he was still ravenous.

'Much of Philip's account is indeed in the letter. But he also told us a great deal in addition to it.' Barling unrolled the letter again. 'I shall keep this open to check.'

Stanton took one of the last pieces of bread while Barling looked over the document in front of him.

'Well,' said Barling, 'Philip's verbal account was as definite as his written one. He is adamant that Brother Cuthbert was killed by an outsider.'

'And we saw half a dozen of them on the road this afternoon. Unhappy-looking ones too. I don't blame them.' Stanton held up his piece of bread. 'This is bigger than the loaves given out as alms.'

'Alms are for those most in need, Stanton. They are not meant to be a feast, for if they were, people would slide into a dependency of laziness and sinful sloth.'

Stanton held in a groan. No wonder Barling had been friends with Philip. Neither man could resist the opportunity to preach. He avoided a reply by getting to his feet and putting another log on the fire.

The clerk didn't even seem to notice, with his head down over his work.

'I have made a note for us to speak to the gatekeeper.' Barling sniffed. 'Though only if we need to. I am not sure that Brother Lambert will give any reliable information.'

'True.' Stanton sat back down at the table. 'The old fellow wasn't really in his senses.'

'He was completely drunk, Stanton,' came the clipped reply. 'That is the accurate description of Brother Lambert.'

Stanton knew better than to say anything to that.

Together, they went back over what Philip had said, that it was Brother Maurice, the novice master, who found the body, and about the numbers of people at Fairmore, with Barling making notes as necessary.

Barling looked up at him from his writing. 'I don't suppose you recall the exact numbers?'

'Course I do.' Stanton could never understand why folk struggled to recall details like that. 'Seventy-seven: seven obed – obed—'

'Obedientiaries. The senior monks that help the abbot run the monastery.'

'Obedientiaries. Twenty choir monks, six novices and forty-two lay brothers, and the abbot.'

'You have made a mistake, Stanton: that is seventy-six.'

He was waiting for the question. 'And the guest. Seventy-seven.'

'The guest?'

'Yes. Silvanus said there is one guest here.' He raised his cup to Barling and drank again. 'An outsider.'

The clerk raised his eyebrows in return. 'We know that this guest was present on the night of the murder, do we?'

Stanton clicked his tongue at the clerk's instant, accurate response. 'No, we don't.' He thought he'd bested Barling with this one.

'Nevertheless, an excellent observation. I had missed that remark from Silvanus. We will find out more.' Barling made a note.

Excellent, eh? Stanton didn't get many comments like that from the clerk. 'But whether it's seventy-six or -seven,' said Stanton, 'it's still many people who were living alongside poor old Cuthbert. So many, yet you said the abbot who came to see de Glanville said it couldn't possibly be one of the brethren. Philip was adamant as well. But you're not convinced, are you, Barling?'

'I am certainly not discounting it as a possibility. My lord de Glanville was of the same opinion.'

Stanton frowned. 'Then you and de Glanville think that they might be lying? Both abbots?'

'No, not at all. The fact of the matter is that genuinely devout men like them, men who live every moment for their God, simply cannot conceive that there are others among them who might be otherwise.'

58

Stanton took another mouthful of ale. 'Then we are back at many, many hands that might have killed Cuthbert.'

'No,' said Barling.

'No? But you just said—'

'What I mean is that we can discount the vast majority.'

'How?'

'I have visited many monasteries on pilgrimage over the years. The choir monks, the novices and the lay brothers are rarely, if ever, alone. They live, work and worship amongst others all the time. They do not even sleep alone. That is largely the same for the obedientiaries.'

'The abbot sleeps alone,' said Stanton.

'Naturally, he does.' Barling made a wide gesture with one hand. 'This entire lodging is his. A privilege that every abbot has.'

'I hope you don't end up accusing him. He was angry enough with you when you said about it being somebody from inside. He'll likely have us thrown out into the snow.' Stanton shook his head. 'Was he like that when you knew him in Paris?'

He watched as Barling looked away from him and went back to his notes. 'He was a fiery speaker, good at rhetoric. Despite his modesty earlier, he did impress the masters.'

Stanton couldn't resist. 'But you both liked your taverns, eh?' He'd had to hold in a huge laugh when Philip had drawn that out of Barling. Never, ever would he have guessed at that one. 'In the devil's monasteries.' Stanton grinned. 'With wine and sodomy and whor—'

'Stanton.' Barling snapped his name, stopped writing to stare right at him. 'You forget your place, I think. Philip and I fell prey to the foolishness of youth. As young men do. As you have. I hardly need to remind you of your disgraceful behaviour in York last summer. Now bring your mind to the task in hand. At once.'

'I'm sorry, Barling.' Stanton noticed the angry quiver in the hand that held the stylus. Noticed too the haunted look that flickered across Barling's face. He'd seen it a couple of times before, when they had investigated the village murders last June, when Barling had spoken as if to himself rather than to Stanton. Just like then, it disappeared as quickly as it had arrived. 'I meant no disrespect.'

'Very well. But take note of what I say to you.' Barling pointed the stylus at him, hand steady as a rock again. 'I am at least in a position where I have some understanding of your unsuitable behaviours. I am doing my best to teach you the correct way in which you should conduct yourself, and may God grant me strength in that endeavour. But Abbot Philip knows nothing of you. You have been a witness to a private conversation between us. If you go around making unsavoury, disrespectful jests about it, it could have the most serious repercussions. He is the revered father of this house and I am a royal clerk. You must guard that loose tongue of yours, do you hear me?'

Stanton nodded. 'Again, I'm sorry, Barling.'

The clerk drew in a long breath and checked his notes. 'Now, where were we?'

Stanton didn't dare say anything.

'Ah, yes. The obedientiaries. Each one of these monks will have important duties that take them all over the monastery on their own. We have already seen that Lambert is alone at the gate. Silvanus runs the guesthouse.'

'And Daniel, at the stables.' He kept a cautious eye on Barling. All seemed well. 'Looked like he was working on his own. Yet he's a lay brother.'

'True, and a point well made.'

Stanton let out a silent sigh of relief.

Barling went on. 'There may be individuals whose duties mean they are apart from the others, but it should be easy to find out who they are from Abbot Philip. Should the need arise, of course.'

A bell rang from outside, much deeper than the others Stanton had heard here.

'We have come to the hour of Compline.' Barling started to gather up his possessions. 'We need to go to the guesthouse as all the monks will be retiring soon. As should we.'

Stanton took the last loaf from the table and shoved it in his own bag. 'I'm still hungry,' he said by way of explanation as Barling shot him a displeased look.

As they walked towards the door, the final notes of the bell died away, the bell which would once have been rung by Cuthbert, but no more.

Stanton pulled the door open for Barling, yet he received no thanks from the clerk. Instead, he got another glare.

'And make sure you shave before you present yourself tomorrow morning, Stanton: you could pass as a wild man as you are.'

***

Stanton had not been at all taken with the skinny monk, Silvanus.

But at least the man knew how to run a comfortable guesthouse, even if that guesthouse was in a monastery with only monks and brothers for company.

Stanton took the bread from his bag and flung himself down on his back on the bed with a tired sigh.

His room, identical to Barling's, was one of a number that were up a narrow flight of stairs above the guest hall. Though the hall was empty and a large fire burned in the hearth, Barling had ordered Stanton to bed. He did not want either of them encountering the abbot's unknown guest at this stage.

Stanton hadn't argued, tempted though he'd been by the warm fire. Barling's mood had seen to that. He took a bite of his bread, chewing slowly to try to make it last.

As clean as it was cold and of good size, the room didn't only hold the bed on which he lay, with its clean straw in a wooden pallet and covers of soft white wool. It also had a small table and a large wooden chair, with a chest against one wall. Washing bowls and basins sat in an alcove by the door. The walls were washed white and a large wooden crucifix hung from one of them.

He swallowed the mouthful of bread and took another, scrubbing at his scratchy face with one hand. Barling was right, he needed a shave, but he'd do that in the morning. The good bed was too comfortable under his bones. No doubt he'd sleep well in it, especially after the hours and days in the saddle. It was dead quiet here, with only the distant rumble of the river to break the silence. Grabbing the coverlet, he hauled it round him for a bit of warmth.

But he didn't normally go to bed at this hour. He doubted if many folk did. The darkness might have fallen outside. But a decent hearth and good tapers would allow for a couple of hours or more of chatting, singing, music. Like on the winter evenings of his childhood, when his mother and aunt used to sew or spin. His uncle would play a peg-board game with him. He took another bite of the bread.

The dark evenings as a man were even better. The hearths became those in inns or taverns, where the songs were bawdy and filthy jests flowed with the ale and women would draw him into shadowed corners.

Unless he was travelling with Barling. May the saints preserve him from ending up a dry old stick like the clerk. Philip wasn't much better, but at least the abbot had found a life with the monks. Barling had chosen to live and work completely alone, save for the time he spent with Stanton.

The clerk seemed content like that. Didn't appear to be lonely. If anything, spending time with his pupil seemed to annoy him a lot of the time. Most of the time.

His pupil.

Stanton rolled his eyes to himself at Barling's fondness for calling him that. Without 'his pupil', Barling would probably be face down in a ditch five miles outside London.

He swallowed the last mouthful and gave a deep yawn.

There was no way he could live like Barling. Not alone like that.

Wherever he lived, he made friends, got to know every face. He hated being alone. Nothing made him happier than a full, lively room of people who hung on his jokes and wanted to hear his stories.

Well, one thing did make him happier, had made him happier, something he knew he'd never have again. He brought a hand to his eyes to scrub away the sudden grief that stabbed at him.

His Rosamund, his love.

Last winter, for the happiest months of his life, the onset of darkness would often bring them together. Sometimes it had been hours in a wide bed, others it had been for the shortest while.

Every moment that his hands had been upon her, that his mouth had closed on hers, every heartbeat that his body had lain with hers, had been one he never, ever wanted to end.

But it had. In the cruellest way possible, with an evildoer taking her from him, taking her life.

And the man at whose door the blame could be laid, King Henry himself, still walked this earth.

Stanton knew he could never speak of it, any of it. His life, spared by the King, depended on it.

But still: another night without Rosamund.

God rot the King.

Chapter Eleven

Stanton waited with Barling in the small parlour outside Fairmore Abbey's Chapter House. Daniel, the lay brother, had escorted them here from the guesthouse, the early morning as wet and blustery and cold as the previous day. They had entered the inner precinct through a wide, tall gate and gone along under the arches of the north claustral walk to arrive where they now stood. Daniel had left with a curt 'Sirs.'

'See?' Stanton had said as he left. 'He's on his own again.'

'Quiet,' said Barling. 'We do not want to risk disturbing the chapter meeting.'

Stanton mouthed a silent apology.

He could hear voices from within. Well, first one voice only. Abbot Philip's. Then others would answer, one by one. It sounded measured, orderly. Then, in response to Philip, one raised, then another. No longer measured. Angry. Speaking over each other. Philip's, higher in tone in response.

Stanton exchanged a look with Barling, the clerk's brows raised as he listened to the exchange.

The voices cut off and the door opened.

A flushed-faced Philip stood there. 'Barling, please enter.' Stanton only got a nod.

He didn't care. He'd do as Barling had ordered him: 'Say nothing. Nothing, Stanton. Nothing unless directly asked by Abbot Philip. Keep utterly respectful at all times. I do not wish to see your face move beyond the blinking of your eyes. Your task is to watch every face in there. But not to let them know you are watching. Is that clear?'

The clerk had been more snappy than usual. Stanton supposed he was tired. He certainly didn't look well rested.

Stanton walked into the large square room behind Barling, moving to stand next to one of the large stone columns on either side of the doorway. Stone seats lined the walls, each separated by a rounded pier, also of stone.

Almost every seat contained an angry-looking monk, each man dressed in an identical white cowl.

Stanton drew in a long breath. Barling had told him to observe, and he, Stanton, would follow his orders. He had a bit of a talent for picking up on details and for noticing things, a talent that Barling had recognised in him. Part of the skill was in knowing what was right in certain places and situations. Easy to tell in a crowded market if a man was shifty and up to no good. Such a man would keep his back to a wall, a hand on his weapon. But here? Stanton had no idea what to look out for. He'd have to learn. And fast.

Philip led Barling across the grey flagstones of the wide floor to halt in front of his own seat opposite the door. Both men remained standing.

'Brothers,' said Philip, 'I present to you Aelred Barling. A servant of our lord King who is here to assist us in finding the killer of our dear brother, Cuthbert.'

Barling bowed, hands joined, ensuring he took in the whole room. 'I am humbled to be received here, good brothers.'

'With the greatest of respect to you, sir, I must say to my lord abbot: I am at a loss as to why it should be so.' The deep voice came from a monk of advanced years who sat next to Philip's empty seat. He had a snow-white thick tonsure and grey eyes as sharp as those of a bird of prey. He would have been a tall, powerful man once but now sat hunched over in his seat, one gnarled hand clutching a stick.

'I have explained why, Reginald,' said Philip.

'Yet, unfortunately, I am still at a loss, father.' There was no mistaking the contempt with which the monk used the word 'father'. That he seemed to be at least thirty years older than Philip added to its power.

The flush in Philip's face went a shade deeper.

Reginald went on. Slow, deliberate. 'You have already asked us all here in chapter about our brother's murder. Here.' The monk struck the stone floor hard with his stick, the sound echoing to the high ceiling. 'Chapter. The heart of discipline in our abbey. Where all and any misdemeanours are confessed or reported. Yet there has been neither confession nor reporting of the great sin visited upon our brother Cuthbert.'

'Brother Reginald speaks the truth.'

Stanton recognised the hiss. Silvanus. Over to the right.

Next to him, Lambert, the gatekeeper. Sitting with his huge thighs apart under his cowl, his scarlet chins wobbling as he nodded and nodded.

'And you also insisted that every one of us also speak to you in private, my lord abbot.' This from a wiry, grey-tonsured monk in the left corner, a man of equal age to Reginald. He had one milk-white eye and the other cloudy, glaring from under a drooping lid. Missing most of his teeth, his voice was clogged with spittle. 'Which we have done. With willing hearts.'

'For which I am very grateful, Maurice,' said Philip.

Maurice. Stanton locked gazes with Barling for a second. The clerk had recognised the name too. Brother Maurice, the novice master. The man who had woken without the need for Cuthbert's bell. The man who had found Cuthbert's body.

'We do not need your gratitude, father.' Reginald again. 'We need you to believe us.'

'And as I keep saying, I do believe you.' Philip spread his hands wide, seeking out every face in the room with his gaze. 'But it is still necessary that the King's man is allowed the full freedom of our house.'

'Necessary?' asked Maurice. 'To have the cloister open to a stranger? Two strangers, in fact. That's the other one by the door, isn't it?' He peered over, pointing a bony finger at Stanton.

To Stanton's horror, all heads swivelled towards him. He didn't dare say a word.

Abbot Philip saved him. 'Yes, Hugo Stanton is the assistant to the King's man. Again, as I have explained.'

'To invite the world in to poke and pry is a terrible mistake. Father.' Reginald, yet again. To a chorus of agreement.

Philip held a hand up. 'Loud words are not necessarily the best ones.' He looked over to Stanton's left. 'Osmund: you have said nothing.'

The deeply uncomfortable-looking Brother Osmund was less than a decade older than Stanton. The sleek black hair of his tonsure still had the shine of youth, as did his deep blue eyes. 'No. No, I have not.'

Stanton could have sworn at that moment that he heard a snigger being stifled, yet every face was still. The sudden set of Philip's jaw told Stanton that he'd heard it too. 'Then perhaps, Osmund, you would like to do so? This abbey's cellarer should have an opinion on important matters such as this.'

'Ah. Yes.' Osmund clasped his hands, unclasped them. 'Well, I would say, I think, whatever you think, my lord abbot. I . . . I will be guided by your wisdom.'

'Thank you, Osmund,' said Philip. He turned to address the whole room again. 'I understand how painful this is for all of you. But it would be nothing compared to the pain of never bringing Cuthbert's killer to justice.'

Reginald opened his mouth once more.

Shut it as Philip raised a hand. 'Enough, Reginald. My decision is that the King's men should be free to walk in our world and speak to those of you that they need to. To that end, I am giving permission for you to speak where you would ordinarily be keeping your vow of silence. I realise this will cause you unease. But, and I repeat, you not only have my permission, it is a direct order from me. I should not have to remind any of you of your vow of obedience to me as the superior of this house. To the Rule. To God.' His tone hardened as he imposed his authority. 'For, mark my words, if I hear of disobedience in this matter, you will hear of it here in chapter. And I shall punish those who transgress.' His voice rose. 'Do I make myself clear?'

A subdued murmur of agreement met his words.

'Good. Then we conclude chapter for today. And, brothers, we should take comfort in the fact that an Aelred walks amongst us on this, the feast of the late Abbot Aelred of Rievaulx Abbey. Now, let us pray.'

He began a familiar psalm and Stanton joined in once he saw Barling did too.

But judging by the looks on the faces of many of the monks, he and the clerk would need a lot more than the name of a dead holy man to get the monks to quell their ire.

Chapter Twelve

As the monks filed out of the Chapter House, Stanton went to join Barling and Philip.

He didn't want to get in the way, standing in his place right next to the door. As he moved over he caught a few glances: some curious, others hostile.

The stooped, white-haired Reginald had yet to leave. It had taken him a little time to rise. A fussing Silvanus had tried to help him get to his feet but he was shaken off by the old monk and waved out of the room.

Now Reginald made his way out past Stanton and his companions, bent over his stick, his steps slow and painful.

He didn't pause as he drew level. 'The blessings of the day be upon you all.' His unsmiling gaze moved over Barling, then Stanton.

'And to you, brother.' Stanton echoed Philip's and Barling's reply.

Reginald shuffled out, his steps quiet but the sound of his stick on stone firm and loud.

As the tap, tap, tap faded away, Barling asked, 'Reginald is your prior, is he not? I noticed he was sitting to your right.'

'He is,' replied Philip. 'My prior and my deputy. As he was Abbot Ernald's before me. He has been prior here for some twenty years. It is a great comfort to me to know that he presides here in my absence. I can travel as my post requires I do, knowing all the while that Fairmore is in safe hands.'

'Indeed,' said Barling. 'Quite forceful hands as well.'

Stanton saw a new flush rise in Philip's cheeks at Barling's pointed remark.

'My deepest apologies for Reginald's conduct – his and others',' said the abbot. 'But I can assure you that his words were not born out of any malice.'

'Worry not, I understand completely,' said Barling. 'This is not the first hostile reaction Stanton and I have had to our arrival in a strange place, is it?'

'Not at all,' replied Stanton. 'At least the monks weren't shouting and throwing things.'

'That has happened to you?' Philip's eyes widened. 'On the King's business?'

'Emotion,' said Barling. 'Always high at such times, which is totally understandable. My apologies, Philip. I did not mean to delay our task and further keep you from your duties. Shall we proceed?'

'My time is yours, Barling.' Philip pointed to an open arch set into one corner. 'The sacristy is through there. If you will follow me.' He set off across the wide floor of the Chapter House, Stanton falling in behind with Barling.

'Observe,' mouthed the clerk to him.

Stanton nodded. He was trying as hard as he could in this setting which was so strange to him.

He followed the clerk and the abbot into the sacristy as Barling put another question to Philip. 'Cuthbert was your librarian as well as your sacrist?'

The clerk stood in front of the open door of a large cupboard set into the wall. The wide wooden shelves were stacked with manuscripts.

'No, he was the sacrist only.' Philip pointed at a partition that divided the room, with a gap in it to allow passage from one half to the other. 'The library is through there. Fortunately for our abbey, it continues to grow. Less fortunately, it devours the sacristy as it does.' He gestured to the many chests that were piled up, one upon another. 'These all contain books as well.' He stepped over one to open another cupboard, full of clothing and a number of other neatly stacked linen items. The spotless white cloths almost glowed in the gloom and the fresh scent of rosemary came from them. 'This is where Cuthbert keeps – I mean, kept – all the vestments.'

'A diligent man,' said Barling. 'His care of the sacred cloths is still apparent.'

'He was.' Philip clicked his tongue in annoyance. 'I wish I could say the same of Brother Elias. This room should only be for the vesting of the priests.'

'Elias?' asked Barling.

'Our librarian. I know that Cuthbert despaired of Elias and his books. He does keep order, of a sort. But sometimes I think it is an order known only to him.'

A polite cough came from the arch that led into the sacristy.

Stanton turned to look.

A middle-aged monk stood there. Stanton remembered him from the chapter meeting. The man had distinctive red hair and green eyes and had been silent and still in the midst of the loud objections being raised by the other monks. He had not been like the others, Stanton had noticed that much.

'What is it, Elias?'

Philip's frown, Stanton guessed, was not so much for being interrupted as for potentially being eavesdropped on. In such a setting as this, Stanton would have to make extra efforts to ensure he and Barling didn't get overheard when they spoke in private. The monks moved quietly as ghosts.

'My apologies, my lord abbot.' Elias bowed. 'But I need to fetch a book for Brother Reginald. He requires a different devotional text today.'

Reginald again.

'Can he not fetch it himself?' asked Philip, even more irritated-looking now. 'You should be at your own devotion, Elias. Not doing Reginald's bidding.'

'He says his bones are especially stiff today,' said Elias. 'And I don't mind.'

'Very well,' said Philip. 'If you must.'

'I need to get past you to get into the library for it, my lord.'

Philip drew breath to reply, but Barling intervened. 'There is no need, brother. We are leaving.' He looked at Philip. 'I have seen all I need to. Shall we move on?'

'We shall.' Philip led the way out past Elias, who waited with his head bowed in respect.

Philip paused, his voice low. 'We are going into the church, which means we have to go along the claustral walk now. The monks will be at prayer, so I would ask that neither of you speaks until we are inside the church.'

When they stepped outside under the eastern arches of the cloister, they were not met with silence as Stanton had expected. Instead came the murmur and hum of many, many voices. Not speaking together, but each one with its own individual tone and rhythm.

As he followed Philip and Barling along the walkway, he saw why. Between each arch of the cloister was a small wood-panelled enclosure. He had noticed these on the way to chapter this morning. They'd been empty then but now he could see that each one held a monk, bent over a book or a manuscript. Whereas in the chapter meeting each monk's cowl had been lowered, now every hood was raised over every head. A stick leaning against one of the arches told Stanton where Reginald would be. Otherwise there was little to tell one holy man from another.

The noise of their reading was loud enough to drown out the sound of his and his companion's passing footsteps, though Philip's seemed to glide almost silently.

The closed entrance to the church was at the top of a short flight of stone steps that led up from the cloister.

Philip twisted the large iron ring that was the handle and ushered them through the door.

They stepped inside to a gasp of admiration from Barling.

'My goodness, Philip. This is magnificent.'

Chapter Thirteen

'I believe it is a wonder.' The pride in Philip's voice was evident. 'A wonder. Yet a wonder that so few see.'

'Magnificent,' repeated Barling.

Though he knew Stanton was not a man normally drawn to admiration of church architecture, he could tell that the younger man was impressed.

'It is.' Mouth open, Stanton stared around him.

Barling's gaze also roamed over the huge, quiet space.

He had not expected that the plainness of a Cistercian house could rival, indeed surpass, the gold, jewels, paintings and silk hangings of other orders. They had entered at the side of the stalls of the monks' choir, the floor beneath his feet patterned in a black-and-white check made up of hundreds of small tiles. To the right, flanked by a couple of smaller altars, was the high altar. Made of plain stone, it was covered with a simple linen cloth, as white as the snow on the mountaintop. A bare wooden cross stood upon it. The tall, arched windows had no coloured glass or images in them, only simple clear glass patterned with thin black whorls that might be clouds. The midday light that shone through them took on a greenish hue, as if bathing the church in water as well as light.

'I think it is here that I feel Cuthbert's loss the most,' said Philip quietly. 'He would open it. Light it. Prepare it for us.' His voice caught.

'I can understand.' Barling put a hand to Philip's arm for a moment to acknowledge his grief.

While he waited for Philip to regain his composure, Barling saw Stanton walk over to the rood screen that divided the church and take a look through the gap in the middle, then disappear through it in the direction of the nave. What on earth was he doing, wandering off like that? Barling itched to be able to order him back, but he could hardly start berating his assistant the length of the church with the abbot next to him, grief-stricken and struggling to compose himself.

Within a few brief minutes, Stanton reappeared. 'Is this where the bell ropes are, my lord?'

Ah. The bells. Rung by the late Cuthbert. There had been purpose, and a sound one, to Stanton's exploring.

Philip took in a shuddering breath, calm once more. 'Yes. In the west end of the nave. Beyond the lay brothers' choir.'

'Oh,' was all Stanton said.

Barling could not tell from his assistant's response if Stanton had found anything of note, but if he had, it was good judgement not to raise it at this point.

'Here are the night stairs.' Philip led them a short way to the right, where a smaller door than the main entrance they had come through was set between two pillars. He reached for his keys, which hung from his belt.

'This is always locked?' asked Barling.

'Yes,' said Philip. 'Until it is time to open up the church for the night Office, for Vigils, which Cuthbert always did.' He put the key in the lock. 'As I said to you yesterday, that was the first sign that something was wrong.' He pulled open the door. 'Come, follow me.' He led the way up the narrow stone staircase, which led to a passageway at the top. 'The night stairs and this passage connect the monks' dormitory directly to the church. The monks use this route at night so that they do not get wet or cold on their way to church. It is also quicker than opening up the whole cloister and lighting it. The dormitory is through here.' He came to another door, opened it without knocking and walked straight in.

Barling and Stanton followed him.

A long, long high-ceilinged room stretched before them. On the floor, laid out at exact, regular intervals, were the monks' beds. Each one was identical: a sleeping mat with a single pillow, neatly covered with a smooth woollen blanket. At the foot of each bed sat a square chest, presumably containing clothing and other personal items. *Interesting*, Barling thought. There was no privacy here. Of any sort.

'I presume the lay brothers' dormitory is the same?' he asked Philip.

'Like many of the rooms that the monks use, the lay brothers have their own. They live and work quite separately. A monastery within a monastery, if you will. But yes: the lay brothers' beds are all in one room together and the latrine block is at the very end. Do you wish to see that building?'

'Not at this time,' replied Barling. 'You mentioned that Cuthbert slept by himself?'

'Yes, this was his chamber.' Philip pointed to the left of the door, where one small section of the long room had been walled off with a wooden partition.

'May we look inside?'

'Of course.'

Philip opened the door and Barling looked in. Aside from the walls surrounding it, the bed and chest arrangement was the same as those outside. One other object was different: a candle clock sat on a table next to the bed, to help the sacrist judge the time for the bell.

Barling recalled what Stanton had said about the bells. 'Who has taken over Cuthbert's timekeeping duties now?'

'Brother Maurice,' replied Philip.

The half-blind novice master? 'Is that the same Maurice who discovered Cuthbert's body?' asked Barling.

'Yes, it is,' replied Philip.

'Is he not very advanced in years to have taken on such a responsibility?'

'It is only a temporary arrangement until I make my new appointment,' said Philip. 'And like I told you, Maurice is reliable. Probably more reliable than that candle there.'

'Indeed.' Barling looked at Philip. 'Lastly, may we please see the kitchen, where Cuthbert's body was found? And Philip, I completely understand if you do not wish to view it.'

'Thank you, Barling.' Philip gave a sad smile. 'But what kind of father to the brethren would I be if I could not do everything possible to help solve this? Come, both of you: follow me.'

They retraced their steps, the abbot locking the door to the night stairs once more and closing the church door behind them. They passed through the cloister, the air feeling so much colder after their time inside, but the sound of prayer and worship from so many male voices was undiminished.

'This is our kitchen,' said Philip.

If the cloister was busy with prayer, the enormous steam-filled kitchen bustled with the labour of the bearded lay brothers. Men hurried to and fro, some bearing large vats of vegetables, others trays of bread. Glances darted their way, but no brother said a word or stopped what he was doing in his haste to get the only meal of the day ready on time.

'May I help you, my lord abbot?'

Barling turned at the familiar voice.

Silvanus, the skinny guestmaster, stood there, teeth in a ready smile.

Where he had appeared from, Barling had no idea. He had not seen the monk when they came in.

'We do not require anything, brother,' replied Philip. 'Do not let us disturb your work.'

'Thank you, my lord.' Silvanus went over to one of the long tables, where loaves were being kneaded in a fog of flour.

'Silvanus is currently overseeing all the production of the abbey's food and drink,' said Philip. 'My refectorer has been laid up for many weeks in a Welsh house. He went there on pilgrimage but broke several bones in a riding accident.'

'An unfortunate occurrence,' said Barling. He noticed that Silvanus kept his beady eyes on the visitors to the kitchen, as if aware he was being discussed.

'Yet fortunate that I have such a competent brother to look after his duties.' Philip lowered his voice. 'Now, if you will step this way.' He led Barling and Stanton over to one of the huge brick fireplaces set into the wall. It was built up on either side to allow the positioning of an iron grill over it.

The fire burned brightly and the huge pot of water on top of the grill boiled in fierce bubbles and steam.

'This is where he was found?' Barling made sure his own voice was low too. Stanton kept his counsel, for which Barling was grateful. He berated himself for not asking to see the kitchen when it was quiet, for no reason other than that he could have handled this with far greater sensitivity. But what was done was done.

'Yes,' replied Philip. 'The fire had been damped down and covered for the night as always. But the murderer had brought it back to life even as he took Cuthbert's.' He lowered his voice still further. 'In case you're wondering, that is not the same grill. This one is a replacement. One of the lay brothers who works our forge melted down the one we found him on and fashioned a new candlestick for the church from it.'

'A touching gesture, as well as a practical one,' said Barling.

78

'It was. And unusually sensitive.' Philip took a quick glance over his shoulder. 'The lay brothers are hard workers, but not thinkers, if you see what I mean. Other than that, all is as I described.'

'Is the door we came in the only way into this kitchen?' asked Stanton.

'Yes, it is,' replied the abbot.

'But it leads from the cloister,' said Stanton. 'From inside the monastery.'

Barling tried to catch his assistant's eye. 'Stanton, stop. This is neither the time nor the place.'

'It is a fair question, Barling,' said Philip. 'And in answer to it, come with me.' He led them over to the tall windows. They contained no glass, only wooden shutters, which stood half-open to let the steam out. 'As you can see, this is all that covers the windows. They do have a locking mechanism, but that was rarely used. It is difficult to work and the shutters are opened and shut all the time. The shutters would have been closed, but not locked. It would not have been difficult to enter and depart by the same way, leaving them looking undisturbed.'

'I see your point,' said Barling. 'It is a shame they were not locked, then.'

'They have not been locked in thirty years before this terrible event,' said Philip firmly. 'But they are now.'

A bell pealed from outside. Maurice, no doubt.

'You may well have less of an appetite by now,' said Philip. 'But I would request that you join me in my hall. It is probably very presumptuous of me, but I did tell my guest that the King's men would be eating dinner with us today.'

'We would be most pleased to do so,' said Barling, with Stanton nodding his thanks as well.

And pleased indeed he would be.

For to eat with the guest would be to eat with the outsider.

That the outsider turned out to be a woman was most unexpected.

Chapter Fourteen

Lady Juliana Kersley pulled her fur-trimmed red-and-blue woollen robe more tightly around her as she and the guestmaster approached the abbot's hall along the gravelled path.

'Oh, Silvanus,' she said, aware that she was becoming short of breath. 'I must confess to being a little nervous.'

As ever, her dear Silvanus offered her his instant help.

'Nervous, my lady? Oh, I am sorry to hear you say such words. Is there anything I can do for you?'

'A moment, please.' Juliana paused, willing her fluttering heart to calm. 'I cannot quite believe that I am to meet the King's men. Here, of all places.' A place where there was not another woman for miles.

'Of course.' Silvanus stopped with her. 'You do look quite pale. Here, take my arm that you may steady yourself.'

She accepted his wool-clad arm, her own hands in her best soft leather gloves. 'Well, if my complexion is pale, then so much the better. At least I will not look like a weather-worn peasant.' She cast him a look from beneath her lashes, a look that had served her well for the majority of her forty years. And still did.

'A peasant? Oh, my lady.' Silvanus patted her gloved hand with his own bare one, which was red from the cold. 'That could never be so.

Even if you were to dress in the coarse wool of the penitent and daub your face with ash, your radiance would still shine through.'

Juliana met his broad smile with one of her own, as much as a response to the monk as it was to test that her white silk wimple sat securely around her face. She could curse this day's raw wind for threatening disarray to her appearance, but all was well. 'Shall we proceed, then?'

'Whatever my lady wishes.'

My lady wished she could run on ahead and confirm what Silvanus had already told her about the unexpected other visitors. Two men of the court. One of around her age, the other close to that of her daughter, a daughter who sat idling at home. Unmarried. If things went as she hoped they might, then after all the years of donating her late husband's wealth to the abbey, it looked as if she, Juliana, might be rewarded in ways of which she had never even dreamed.

But she needed to take measured steps alongside Silvanus. She'd laced her dress as tight as she could at the sides, the better to show off her still-narrow waist and her ample breasts.

Finally, they were at the door of the abbot's hall and Silvanus opened it with a flourish.

Juliana swallowed hard. 'Thank you, Silvanus. You have been most helpful.'

'I am sure they will receive you with every delight, my lady.' He lowered his voice and gave her a deep bow as he ushered her in. 'As I am equally sure your sweet presence will charm them utterly.'

She gave her most appealing little light laugh. 'Oh, Silvanus, you are too kind, as ever.'

'Lady Kersley.' Abbot Philip hurried to the door to greet her with a bow, as Silvanus left her with one of his own.

'My greetings to you, my lord abbot.' She kept her gaze on Philip's familiar thin face, lest she appear too forward.

Philip went on. 'My lady, may I present Aelred Barling, clerk to our lord King.'

Juliana looked to the fireplace, to where Philip indicated, her smile already bright.

It almost fell. Almost. Yet it did not. She was far too skilled at presenting a face to the world that suited the occasion and not what she was feeling inside.

The clerk was a short, slight man. With a thin, dun-coloured tonsure. Utterly unappealing.

'My lady.' The man gave a respectful bow.

At least he had good manners. *And he's from the King's court, Juliana. He's not some grasping local lord.* Her own fierce reminder kept her smile warm. Inviting. 'The honour is all mine, good sir.' She moved her gaze to the other man present. And briefly cursed fate twice. Once for making her old enough to be this handsome, blue-eyed young man's mother. Twice for having a daughter who was about as lively as a tree stump and not a great deal more appealing. 'And this is?' she asked.

'Hugo Stanton, assistant to Barling, my lady.' The abbot did not even bother looking at the young man. 'Barling, Lady Juliana Kersley is here as an esteemed guest of this abbey.'

'Why, Abbot, you make me sound like a bishop.' She hauled her gaze from the delicious Stanton and pursed her lips charmingly at Philip. 'I hope I cannot be confused with one?' She raised her brows at him.

'Never, my lady,' said Philip.

She turned to Barling again. 'Silvanus informed me of your arrival, sir. I was most keen to greet you in person.'

'And I you, my lady.'

Oh? This was better. Perhaps it was to her advantage that this man was so underwhelming. He would not be used to attention from a woman such as her. 'That is most kind of you, sir. I too desired to make your acquaintance but this has been the earliest opportunity. I have been secluded in Masses as part of my pilgrimage here. Private Masses, you understand.'

The clerk inclined his head to show that he did.

'Lady Kersley is one of Fairmore's greatest benefactors,' said Philip by way of explanation. 'May I ask that we take our place at table, my lady?'

'Certainly.' She did so, the others following, which pleased her. That would show her sumptuous robe at its best.

As the abbot blessed the food, she assessed the table's wares.

Good white bread. Pottage that contained large chunks of mutton. Three fish dishes. Roasted pigeon. A milk pudding. Wine. A feast, no question, and an especially fine one. The King's men could not fail to notice that she was a most important guest of the abbot.

Philip finished and took his usual place at the head of the table. Juliana sat in hers to his right, Barling to his left, which meant the clerk was directly opposite her. Excellent. As she removed her gloves, she glanced to where Stanton was sitting, further down the table. Definitely not a man held in much esteem by the abbot, despite being here with the clerk. That settled her decision. Despite the far more alluring prospect of flirting with Stanton, it was the clerk, Barling, whom she should and must charm.

'A feast worthy of this holy day, my lord abbot,' said Barling.

'And a feast worthy of a visit from a royal clerk,' said Juliana. 'It is indeed an honour, sir.'

'Thank you, my lady.'

Juliana waited for him to say more, as all men always did, her head prettily to one side to show she hung on his every word. Yet nothing was forthcoming. By the blood of the Virgin, this man really was as dull as he looked. Very well. She could make up for that. She said, 'Although, sir, the reason for your coming here is one of great tragedy. It was sad enough for me to arrive and not see Abbot Ernald, but to have Brother Cuthbert lose his life in such a dreadful way while I have been staying here . . .' She put her fingertips to her lips and shook her head in a fetching display of noble grief. 'This will be a visit that I will not remember as fondly as my others.' She gave a sad sigh. 'I have always held dear memories deep in my soul of my times of devotion with the monks and long rides alone in the hills, in order to aid my contemplation. Now my soul will be filled with distress at what has happened. I was tempted to leave but Abbot Philip persuaded me to stay, as did dear Brother Silvanus too.' She smiled at Barling again. 'I believe God guided Abbot Philip's hand,' she said. 'For, had I left, I would not have met such an esteemed man of the court.'

'Indeed.' Her reward was a small smile in return and a nod. 'Do you visit Fairmore often, my lady?'

She'd got his full attention. Such as it was. But she had it – that was the important thing. 'Regularly rather than often, good sir. I travel here every year during the week before Christmas, so I have time to rest and prepare for the feast of the Nativity. I have done so for the last ten years, since my dear husband, Hubert, died. Widowhood is among the hardest of crosses to bear.' She dabbed briefly at her eyes. 'I pray you have not had to endure such grief.'

'I have not, my lady,' came his swift response. 'For I have never been married.'

While his dullness made that understandable, it did not always follow. But he had confirmed what she'd hoped. Barling would be able to take a wife. Juliana thrilled inside, keeping her features suitably composed. 'It is the deepest joy, sir, to share in the holiness of a good marriage.' She had to be careful. While she had no doubt that Stanton would respond in a heartbeat to the promise of the lifted skirts of a woman, she knew with equal certainty that this dry little clerk would scare off easily. 'I make my pilgrimage here to pray for Hubert's soul alongside the brothers of this house. I remain until the day of prayer for all the benefactors has concluded.'

'Prayers that are heartfelt in their thanks too,' said Philip. 'Before his death, Lord Kersley gifted Fairmore a couple of buildings in York to help us in our wool trade. It has helped us no end.'

Juliana nodded politely, though Philip's interruption was most unwanted. At least it confirmed her great wealth. She spoke before Philip could do so again. 'And I have continued to support this house. This year, I have brought a donation of many books.' How pleased she was that she had. This was bound to impress the clerk. 'A collection without compare, Brother Elias said when he took receipt of them. And so many, he said too. He was quite overwhelmed, I think.' She gave another of her little sighs. 'To give is such a great joy.'

'Most generous of you, my lady.' Barling poured out some water, leaving his wine untouched.

A quick glance told her that Stanton did the opposite. She cursed the fates again, but it mattered not. At least the clerk would not be one to lose her carefully guarded fortune to drink.

'That is very kind of you to say so, good sir,' she said. 'But I am as my late husband was, and the abbey has returned that generosity many times over. For Hubert is buried here in the monastic cemetery. I will be granted the same. I could ask for no greater reward.'

She spotted an impressed twitch of the clerk's eyebrows. He would be well able to guess at the size of the donations to Fairmore that had obtained a resting place for the Lord and Lady Kersley.

'I am sure they pray that that will not be for many years, my lady,' said Barling.

'We do,' said Philip. 'Every day.'

Juliana ignored him and kept her gaze on Barling. 'As do I. Though I pray they will not be lonely years. I have grown so weary of those.' She cast the clerk a look that she knew would be sad. Brave. Moving. She waited for his response.

To her utter annoyance, it was Philip who answered again.

'I have no doubt that your parish priest will continue to try to change your mind until that day, my lady.' Philip sniffed in displeasure. 'We have the same problem here with the priest of Gottburn.'

'Forgive me if my question is impertinent,' said Barling, 'but what is the complaint of the priests?'

Juliana kept her features smooth, looked from one man to the other as if this interested her. In truth, she could strike the abbot for taking Barling's attention from her.

'The priest of the village of Gottburn spends much of his time railing at the fact that we have a graveyard here where some of his parishioners choose to be buried,' said Philip.

'Not the cemetery in which I will be buried,' said Juliana quickly, inwardly furious that the abbot could now be presenting a diminished view of her status to the clerk. 'I will be lying with my husband.' She tapped the tabletop with a fingernail. 'With the monks. Not some common villagers. Is that not so, my lord abbot?'

'Most certainly, my lady,' said Philip. 'Most certainly. You will be within our walls, the people of Gottburn will remain outside.'

Juliana nodded and took a modest sip of wine, searching for a sign that the clerk understood. Her fingers tightened on her goblet in delight. He was nodding.

'Priests can be unhappy when their flock look elsewhere for their souls to be guided, Barling,' said Philip. 'That is all. It is nothing new.'

'And I find that priests can be most irksome in their demands for tithes,' said Juliana, determined to bring Barling's attention back to her. 'That is also nothing new.'

Barling was taking a drink of water. But his reply, when he'd finished, was not what she was expecting.

'Now, if you will excuse me, my lord abbot, Stanton and I have much to see to this afternoon.'

She could see Stanton had not been expecting it, either. The young man still had a mound of food before him. He had a huge appetite. Of course.

'Do not let me keep you, Barling,' said Philip with a wave of his hand.

Her mind whipped through several suggestions. She had to find a way to meet the clerk again – and in circumstances where they would be alone.

Barling rose to his feet as Stanton did the same.

'My lady.' Barling bowed his leave of her. 'An honour to have met such a good friend of the abbey.'

She had to make her move before she lost her chance. 'As it has been mine, good sir,' she said. 'Perhaps you will join me for a ride some morning? It would be most enjoyable.'

But her suggestion was a poor choice: she could tell from his look.

'Thank you for your gracious invitation, my lady,' said Barling. 'Alas, I am presently occupied with the tragic event that has taken place here.'

One poor choice would not be the end of it. She would just have to think of something else. 'Of course.' She raised a hand, the better that he would see the heavy gold rings that encircled her fingers.

As he went to the door with Stanton, Barling paused. 'I am sorry to further interrupt your meal. But one question, if I may.'

Juliana's hopes leapt and then fell again as the clerk's question was directed at Philip.

'My lord abbot, what is the name of the priest of Gottburn?'

'It is Theobald,' replied Philip. 'May I ask why?'

'I like to have a complete record, my lord. That is all.' He left with Stanton before there could be any further enquiry from Philip.

Juliana took a deep drink of her wine. The clerk Barling was not at all what she had expected, but he would still be a great prize.

And so long as he was within Fairmore's walls, she would take every opportunity to win him.

Chapter Fifteen

Stanton hadn't expected the outsider to be a woman, but that wasn't the biggest surprise he'd had during their meal with the abbot. No. That would be the sight of the hard-eyed Lady Juliana Kersley, a lusty woman if ever he saw one, setting her sights on Aelred Barling.

'You left the abbot's dinner very suddenly, Barling.' Stanton kept his voice low as they followed the path from the abbot's house back to the guesthouse. The wind blew harder than ever and the rain on it had turned to stinging sleet and hail. 'I could've eaten plenty more.'

'As you always can, Stanton. Your belly is like a bottomless trough: open to whatever can be thrown into it and impossible to fill.' The clerk shook his head at him in distaste.

Stanton wasn't bothered: that sounded fair enough to him.

'Were you keen to get away from my lady? I know I would be.'

Barling frowned at him. 'What do you mean?'

'Well. She seemed to me a woman who was used to getting what she wanted. She's already bought her way into heaven from the monks. And she liked you a lot, I think. Maybe she was considering a bit of earthly paradise as well.'

'I beg your pardon, Stanton?' Barling stopped dead.

Stanton halted as well, his stomach dropping as he saw the look on Barling's face. Oh, damn it all. He should have known, but the clerk didn't seem to find any of this funny.

Barling went on. 'Am I hearing you right? Are you actually implying that I would be ensnared by lust? In a holy house, no less. With a respectable widow, a benefactor of the abbey?' Two spots of colour had appeared in Barling's pale cheeks. 'Have you gone quite mad, that you would address me so? That you would accuse me of such a sin?'

Stanton took a step back, such were the depths and suddenness of the clerk's anger. 'I'm sorry, Barling.' He held his hands up. 'Really sorry. I didn't think.'

'No. Yet again.' Barling's small fists were clenched now. 'You most certainly did not.'

God alive, he'd never seen the man in such a state. And so quickly. 'As I say, I'm sor—'

'I have had cause to warn you already here about that loose tongue of yours. If there is another such occasion, I will send you straight back to London, with a note for my lord de Glanville to deal with you. Do I make myself clear?'

'Yes, sir.' Stanton hadn't called Barling 'sir' in months: the clerk had told him not to. But Stanton felt he had to. He was genuinely sorry at whatever he had roused in Barling. He really hadn't meant to. 'I really am very sorry, sir.'

Barling's fists uncurled and his colour paled once again. He seemed calmer, swallowing hard before he replied. 'Very well. But remember my words.'

'I will.' Stanton meant it.

'Good.' Barling seemed almost completely back to his usual self. 'Now, we need to get on. In answer to your observation – that is, your sensible observation and not the disgraceful one – we left promptly because there is still some daylight left. I wanted to see the layout of the grounds and the land surrounding the monastery as well. I also wanted to use this opportunity to go through what we have gleaned today. This is our first chance to discuss it alone.'

Stanton nodded, relieved that his foolish words were no longer Barling's focus. He pointed over to the left, where a small path branched off. 'I don't know if you want to have a look, but down there are many of the buildings where the lay brothers work. The forge, the wood shed, the wool store, the grain barn.'

The clerk looked at him askance. 'How do you know that?'

'I got talking to that lay brother Daniel at the stables this morning. Before you and I set off for the Chapter House.'

'I did not ask you to do that.'

'No, you didn't. But I was checking the horses and he came in, so I took the opportunity. He doesn't say much. Doesn't like chatter, I don't think.'

'Despite going off without my permission, it is useful to have found out what you did.'

'I know.' Stanton winced as another blast of sleet and hail blew into his face. 'Ow.'

Barling ignored him, peering up at the sky. 'We need to press on. I am anxious to see if we can find ways into the abbey.'

'You mean other than the gatehouse?'

'Yes. Whoever murdered Brother Cuthbert was not likely to come and ring the bell and ask for admittance, were they?'

Stanton shrugged. 'If you put it like that, no. But do you really think it is somebody from outside? From what we saw this morning at chapter, there's enough strife here to bring the roof in. And they really don't want us here.'

The clerk nodded. 'There is certainly a great deal of tension. But it is understandable. What has happened here has had the most terrible effect on those who live within these walls. The brethren are distressed and, I am quite sure, afraid. Guilt-ridden too. As things currently stand, it could have been any of them who perished at this unknown hand. A hand, remember, that could have opened those kitchen shutters with ease.' Barling tutted to himself. 'If a simple lock had been turned, things might have been so different.'

'I thought the same,' said Stanton. 'And that must make them feel even worse.'

They went past the stables and the guesthouse, heading towards the gatehouse now.

Stanton went on. 'It still makes no sense, though, does it?'

Barling shook his head. 'No. Which is why I am keen to move outside. That may well give us our answer.'

They arrived at the gatehouse. A low snoring sound came from inside the small building where Lambert supposedly watched over the monastery.

Barling frowned even as Stanton gave a rueful grin.

'Brother Lambert,' said Stanton. 'I'd lay a wager on it.' He knocked hard on the door. 'Hello.'

The buzzing stopped abruptly. 'What? Who is there?' Clattering noises came from the door. It opened a little way and the scarlet-faced monk appeared in the crack.

'We wish to go out, brother,' said Barling.

'Out? Now?'

'Yes.'

With many huffs of breath, Lambert opened up the gate. 'You can't be long, mind. I'll be going back to the cloister soon.'

Stanton braced himself for the clerk's harsh words to fall on the monk, as they always did when anybody dared to put the slightest problem in his way. Barling had only just calmed down. It wouldn't take much to get him angry again.

But no. Lambert got a terse 'Very well' from Barling and no more.

'Maybe we should have asked him to wait for us,' said Stanton as they walked away to a slam from the gate.

'I suspect it would be wasted breath,' said Barling. 'Even if I did tell him to wait on a little later, he may well have completely forgotten. I would not relish being locked out of here overnight.' He stepped off the roadway on to a muddy path to the right that led towards the trees and the deep rumble of the river.

'Where are we going now?' said Stanton, following him. 'If we have so little time left?'

'I have thought of one place where somebody might have gained entrance,' said Barling. 'The walls are high and secure, but the river flows into the grounds of the monastery and is used by the monks for all their requirements for water. Where it flows in may be a weakness.'

Stanton nodded his approval. 'That makes sense.'

They soon found it.

A sturdy arched tunnel was built into the brick of the wall, into which the river flowed fast and strong.

'Well, you were right about the water going in through the walls.' Stanton could see the clerk's disappointment.

'But not right about the iron covering it.'

'Let me check it.' Stanton made his way over to the entrance of the tunnel at the river's edge, his boots squelching in the deep, soaking mud.

'Be careful,' called Barling.

Stanton squatted down to take a closer look. The iron bars had been welded into a sturdy lattice, letting water in and keeping large debris out. Judging by what was caught in it, it hadn't been moved for some time. He leaned forward, pulling at it to test it. Nothing. It was solid. He made his way back to Barling, shaking his head. 'It was worth a try.' Stanton looked up at the darkening sky. 'We should probably go back in.'

'We have a little longer.' Barling pointed back upriver. 'The land rises steeply from here. If we go up, we should get a good view of the walls over to the east. It would be a good way of checking without having to walk all the way round another time.'

Stanton nodded. 'But we can't take long.'

It was even darker here amongst the trees and not being able to see what was coming was starting to make him uneasy. He also had a feeling that eyes were on him. But every time he turned his head, quickly, to catch those eyes, he saw nothing but shadows and branches.

They began the climb, the riverbank turning rapidly from mud to solid rock, the channel narrowing even as the slope became steeper, the roar of the river becoming louder and louder.

'I can see why the old abbot chose this location,' said Barling. 'Fairmore will never, ever run out of fresh water.'

'If the river doesn't wash it away,' said Stanton. 'Look.'

A gap had opened up amongst the trees, for little could grow on the huge slabs of rock that made up this part of the hillside. Though not carved by man, they might be the moss-covered building stones of giants. Up here, the channel of the powerful river was compressed into just a few feet across in a roiling, rumbling torrent. Spray hissed into the air above it.

'How remarkable.' Barling went over to have a closer look, Stanton with him.

'Stop.' Stanton had to raise his voice above the noise of the water to be heard. He halted the clerk with a hand on his arm. 'Those rocks near the edge are all wet and mossy. One wrong step and you'll be in. Looks very deep as well.'

'You are correct.' Barling leaned forward. 'The water has not been able to carve space on either side. It must have worn away the rock underneath instead.'

'We really need to go back, Barling. It's got too dark to try to find any viewing point for the walls.'

The clerk nodded and turned from the torrent.

As they hurried back down to the gatehouse, Barling took a quick look round to make sure they were alone. 'My plan for tomorrow morning is that we will ride out to Gottburn village. We will find the priest of whom Philip spoke, this Theobald. He will know everyone and should be able to identify those in his village who might be capable of such a crime. We may find the outsider that we seek through him.'

Stanton thought about jesting with Barling that the clerk could invite Lady Kersley along, as she'd seemed so keen to ride with him. But he didn't dare, as Barling would surely have his tongue. 'A good plan, Barling,' was all he said instead.

Chapter Sixteen

'Are you ready, Stanton?'

The question came from Barling, already waiting on his own horse.

Stanton checked the girth on his saddle one last time. 'I am now.' He mounted his horse and glanced up at the sky. 'Nice day for travelling.'

The leaden clouds this morning looked full of yet more sleet and hail.

'The sooner we get to Gottburn, the sooner we can come back,' said Barling.

'True.' Stanton clicked to his animal and led the way out of the stable yard. 'At least Lambert's awake this morning.'

The main gates to the monastery stood open. A horse and cart which held two lay brothers and was stacked with raw cut branches trundled in. The brother driving it turned back in his seat to give a coarse shout. 'Have you no eyes? Watch where you're going!'

Stanton rode past them towards the gate.

'Keep your speed down, sirs,' said the cart driver. 'There are many folk in and around the gateway and you don't want to trample them.'

'Who could be foolish or idle enough to stand in the gateway?' asked Barling.

'Beggars, sir,' said the brother. 'Here from first light to last. Almost every day.'

Stanton waved his thanks as Barling drew alongside.

'Well, there were not any yesterday evening,' said the clerk.

'Who knows?' Stanton slowed his horse right down, keeping close to Barling's animal as well. He didn't trust the clerk's skill in controlling a horse in such a tight, crowded spot. 'We'll be through them in a few minutes.'

As they rode slowly up to the gates, where several ragged figures waited under their shelter, Stanton saw Lambert waddle out of the house, carrying a large basket.

The figures converged on him but were met with a roar from the monk.

'Back, you ignorant peasants! Back! Wait your turn to be called or you'll get nothing. You curs, the lot of you.'

'I can only see one cur,' muttered Stanton over his shoulder to Barling as they rode out.

A sharp tug came at his right boot.

He looked down to see a young peasant woman striding along on the road beside his horse, keeping apace, though she was small in height.

'A coin, sir?' Her bold look met his, dark grey eyes in a round, grubby face, and thick chestnut hair, which she wore loose under her patched hooded cloak.

'Be off with you, girl,' came Barling's testy order.

Stanton could swear he caught the flash of a pink tongue from a pert mouth, directed at Barling. Though the clerk wouldn't be able to see her, her cheek made him smile. He pulled out his purse and threw her down a coin.

She made a deft catch but still walked beside him. 'Thank you, sir.'

'Are you going to walk next to us all day?' he asked.

'Depends. Are you going to be riding all day?'

'Stanton.' Barling's tone held a warning.

'We need to head off,' said Stanton. 'Stand back, I don't want you to get hurt.'

The girl did so with a pout, her steps slowing even as his horse gathered pace. 'Will you be coming back, Stanton?' she said.

'I should hope so,' he said, to a disgusted noise from Barling.

'Then maybe I'll see you then,' she said with a sharp wink.

Stanton raised a hand in farewell and the girl did likewise.

'I'm Agatha,' she called. 'Just so you know.'

Agatha stopped walking and stood watching as Stanton rode off.

He gave a final glance back, a last smile, as she knew he would. She gave him another little wave.

The man he rode with, the one called Barling, turned around too, almost toppling from his saddle as he did so.

She caught back a laugh and waved at him as well, as she knew it'd really annoy him.

It did. She could tell from the set of his back as he faced forward once more.

Pulling her own small purse from its safe place under her dirty shift, she grinned to herself. She'd guessed at the kind of man Stanton was when she'd spied on him as he'd arrived here, and she'd guessed right. He had a head that could be turned by a pretty smile and a purse that would open willingly. If she could get near enough to him, away from everybody else, she could do a lot more than smile, and she'd get a lot more out of that purse. She'd met the likes of him before. Well, maybe not quite like him. For all his good looks, he had a kindness about him too.

'Get out of my way, you filthy beggar.'

Agatha heard the scornful female voice at the same time as she heard the clatter of heavy hooves.

She jumped back with an oath. She'd let herself be distracted by a man.

Just in time. A tall, glossy horse went past at a fast trot, urged on by the fur-cloaked noblewoman astride it.

'A coin, my lady?' Agatha knew it was useless. She'd tried asking this one before, every morning as the lady rode out, and every morning came the same response.

Eyes brown as hazelnuts and twice as hard glared at her in disgust without even seeing her. 'You'll get no coin from me. Now be off with you.'

Agatha watched the horse's backside disappear from view, the woman bolt upright in the saddle, as sure of her place in the world as she was of her own virtue. Then Agatha sucked up a full mouthful of foaming spittle. Let it fly. Course it wouldn't go anywhere near, but it made her feel better.

Nasty old bitch, that one.

Agatha hoped the sour-faced cow would break her neck, and that she'd be there to see it.

She turned back for the abbey gate.

Yes, Stanton was gone. But he'd be back. No doubt of that.

There was plenty for her to enjoy within the abbey in the meantime.

Like the cats that roamed the cloister, she could get to where she needed to be by stealth.

Find her usual warm spot.

And lie low until darkness fell, when it would be time for her to hunt again.

'I'd heard the monks have had trouble.' Standing in the doorway of the small house next to the equally small parish church, Theobald, priest of the village of Gottburn, glowered at Barling's brief introduction of himself and Stanton. 'But I didn't expect to be asked anything about it. And certainly not by a King's man.' The priest opened the door wider. 'You'd better come in.'

'Will the horses be safe where I've tethered them, sir priest?' asked Stanton, a half-step behind Barling.

'What are you saying?' The square-bodied Theobald lowered brows that were bushy as brush bristles. 'That the folk of this village are thieves?'

'No, sir priest—'

'My assistant was only concerned that we were not inconveniencing you, sir priest.' Barling stepped into Theobald's cramped home, making sure Stanton followed. He had not ridden over two hours in the hail and sleet on this foul-weathered morning to be simply turned away.

Theobald grunted in response and indicated that they should sit on the wooden settle placed against one wall.

A smoking central hearth over which an iron tripod and pot full of water hung made the room tolerably warm.

The priest sat on a stool next to it, the only furniture other than a couple of chests and shelves on the opposite wall that held a few possessions. 'The King's men, eh?' he said.

'We are,' said Barling. 'And we would, as I have said, like to speak to you about the murder of Cuthbert, sacrist of Fairmore Abbey. You said at the door that you had heard of trouble in the abbey. Is that what you meant?'

'What else would I mean?'

Barling went to reply but Theobald carried on.

'Not that they've told me or aught.'

'Then how did you find out?'

'From the folk that go over there regular, seeking out the monks' charity. They hear all sorts at the gatehouse.'

'Such as?'

'Who's visiting. Who's left. Who's fallen sick. Who's died.' Theobald shrugged. 'Long way to go for a morsel of bread and some gossip. And they don't have horses like what you have, young sir.' This last to Stanton. 'But there we are.' He returned his unhappy gaze to Barling.

'Do you visit there regularly, sir priest?'

'Me? No. Not asked. Been here over five years and never invited. Only seen them on the road. The lay brothers mostly, with the monk that's in charge of them. The abbot from time to time when he's off on his travels. Not that the beggars are asked either, mind. But it's one of the monks' rules that they provide charity. So they do it. Do it because they have to. And like as always with folk, when there's something going for nothing, they'll take it. I should know. I am a charitable man but I get bled dry. Sometimes I think I'm the one who should be getting the monks' alms.'

'You collect the tithe?' asked Barling.

'I do.' Theobald picked up the poker and prodded at the fire. 'But a tenth of what? This is a small parish. You see the land round here. Poor, like the people. Like me. But not the monks. The monks have plenty in their coffers. Stuffed full to the brim, they'll be.'

The man's voice dripped with an envy that lay dangerously close to covetousness. 'Yet the monks of Fairmore live the most modest lives,' said Barling.

'Do they?' Theobald grunted in disgust. 'Pretend to, more like. Lying on thin beds. Eating neither bit nor sup. And all the while they add to their piles of coin. They bring in dowries with every new arrival. Get huge grants of land and money from the richest knights and barons. Trade in their wool better than any merchant.' He laid the poker down. 'All the time seeking ways to get their hands on more. They've even started taking my dead parishioners from me.'

As Barling sought a suitable response, Stanton gave one instead.

'Are you talking about their graveyard?' he asked.

'I am, young sir.' Theobald nodded. 'I get paid for burying my flock. But only if I bury them outside my church, in my graveyard. The monks put ideas into folks' heads, tell them the closer they're buried to the abbey, the closer they'll get to heaven. And it works. The monks bury my dead and reap the reward. And all the time, my parish gets poorer than ever.'

'Have you tried appealing to your bishop?' asked Barling.

'What's the point? He's powerless over the monks. They only answer to each other. They have their world arranged for themselves. Themselves, and no one else.'

'Yet that world has now been disrupted in the most terrible way,' said Barling, 'with the murder of Brother Cuthbert.'

'I'm sorry the man's dead,' said Theobald, 'but I never knew him. Like I say, I've never been there. Looks like you've wasted your time coming all the way out here.'

'It has not been a waste at all, sir priest,' said Barling. 'Thank you for explaining what you know about the murder. But the brethren of the abbey are very definite that the murderer must be an outsider. Perhaps you could give some thought to your parishioners, about who amongst them may have a violent past or some other suspicious behaviours.' He waited for another diatribe.

But Theobald just laughed.

His reaction utterly confused Barling and a quick look at Stanton confirmed that his companion felt the same.

Theobald went on. 'I'm sure they're saying it'll have been an outsider. I wouldn't expect anything else from them. But I can promise you that there are no murderers in my parish. They may like free bread, but they're a godly people.'

'You cannot know all their secrets.'

'No, I don't. But I don't have to. Because I know where they all were, and that wasn't in Fairmore Abbey murdering Brother Cuthbert.

It took place on the eve of Christmas. Every one of them would have been home with their families.'

'Again, sir priest, I would ask how you know that.'

'The snow that day was some of the worst we've ever seen. It came down like a blanket. And I saw every one of my parishioners in my church on Christmas morning. No one could have made their way to Fairmore and back.'

Barling frowned. This latest revelation had serious implications for this enquiry.

'With respect, sir priest,' said Stanton, 'I would question that.'

'Are you calling me a liar, young man?'

'Stanton,' began Barling, 'I think you—'

His assistant cut him off. 'I only question your view, sir priest, because of my own experience. Because I travel often, I think there are still many hours unaccounted for in what you say. Somebody could have slipped from their home while others slept, made their way to the abbey and come back. Travelling in the snow is very difficult, granted. But it is possible.'

'It is possible,' replied the priest with a grudging nod of agreement.

Barling let out a quiet, relieved breath. He'd thought Stanton had blundered with the priest. Instead, it was a point well made, which Theobald acknowledged.

But the priest went on. 'Usually possible. But the old abbot, Ernald, who founded the abbey, chose his site to be as secluded as it could be. An old man in the parish remembers when the monks first came – he told me about it. Ernald was warned about that valley, but he'd have none of it. Monks always know best, you see. The depth of the valley and the steepness and height of the hills around it means that Fairmore Abbey can get completely cut off in the snow. If one of my villagers had got there, they would not have made it back.' He gave a sombre look at Barling from beneath his heavy brows. 'You mark my words: it will be somebody from inside. No question.'

Chapter Seventeen

The heavy clouds were bringing yet more sleet and robbing the day's light early. Stanton and Barling were on the descent back into the valley, with, Stanton was relieved to see, the abbey not far off. He wouldn't have wanted to guide Barling back in the dark on such treacherous slopes.

For most of the journey the clerk had ridden in silence, telling Stanton that he needed to think undisturbed. That suited Stanton fine. It meant he could enjoy being out of the monastery, enjoy the ride, even if it was slow and the going heavy under his horse's hooves.

'I believe we have an answer, Stanton.'

'Do we?' Stanton looked over at him. 'Are you saying you know who killed Cuthbert?' Hope rose in him, not only for justice for the dead monk but also that he could leave the confines of the monastery and return to the world outside. The real world. A world that had noise and chatter and song. Where he could sleep at whatever hour. His mind went back to Agatha at the gate. And women.

'No, I said *an* answer. Not *the* answer.'

'Oh.' Curse it. He'd hoped too soon. 'But Theobald said he didn't know anything. Didn't even know Cuthbert.' Stanton shook his head. 'That priest is so bitter. You could almost taste it in the air in that house.'

'Bitter, but very useful,' said Barling. 'And no, as I say, we do not have the answer, the answer to the question of who killed the sacrist of Fairmore. Not a complete one. But a definite one nevertheless. One which helps us to form part of the picture. It would seem that the murderer is likely to have come from within the monastery, which is most concerning.'

Stanton thought back to the disgruntled priest. 'Do you think that maybe Theobald was lying? He sounded like he'd be happy to see the abbey razed to the ground, and all the monks in it.'

'He was certainly speaking from the heart, albeit a sour one. But the most important detail that he mentioned can be easily checked.'

'When he said about this valley being cut off?'

The clerk nodded. 'Precisely. That is not something that he can invent. Given the lie of the land, I see no reason to disbelieve him. But, to go back to an earlier point, I said that the murderer was likely to have come from within the monastery. We still cannot totally exclude the possibility of an outsider. Yes, this valley may get cut off. But there are woods and other hiding places where the murderer could have sought shelter, including during the worst of the weather.'

'But Gottburn is the only settlement for miles and sir priest was able to account for all his parishioners.'

'The murderer may be an individual who is not known to anybody, either in the village or the abbey,' said Barling.

They had reached the road that approached the abbey.

'A complete stranger. An outlaw.' Stanton's neck prickled as he looked ahead to the high walls. An outlaw had been involved in the murders last summer.

'Indeed. In which case they may be long gone and we will never know who took the life of Cuthbert in such a violent way.'

'Or why.'

'Excellent point, Stanton.' The clerk actually had the hint of a smile on his face. 'And an important one. If Cuthbert had been found dead by the roadside, his purse gone, then we could more easily rest with the conclusion that it was a violent robber who killed him. But both the location and the manner of his death would seem to suggest that it was not the result of a chance encounter with evil. That it was very much planned. And that, in my long experience in the law, is the worst kind of evil.'

'And far harder to see. I know that well.' Knew it in a way that had shattered his heart.

Barling looked at him with curiosity. 'To what are you referring, Stanton?'

'Nothing.' Stanton shook his head, embarrassed that a past secret would almost slip from his lips like that.

'It did not look like nothing.'

Stanton's jaw tightened. 'I said it was nothing. Do you hear me?'

Barling raised his eyebrows in surprise but backed off. 'Very well. I have a plan of my own, which is as follows. We need to speak to everyone who could have been involved in Cuthbert's death. When I say everyone, I mean those individuals who move around the abbey unsupervised. There are several of them we need to see. In order to do that as quickly as possible, we shall divide the work between us.'

'Divide?' Stanton didn't like the sound of this. 'Does that mean I'll have to question monks on my own?'

'Yes, that is what "divide" means. It is not difficult to comprehend.'

Stanton ignored the jab. 'Barling, truth be told, I'm not sure I can do it properly.'

The clerk made an impatient noise. 'Ridiculous. You speak to people all the time as part of your work for me.'

'I know I do. But I speak to people who live out in the world that I know. That makes it much, much easier to tell the truth from a lie. But in the monastery?' He shrugged. 'I don't even know if they'll speak to me on my own. They know you're a royal clerk and a friend of their abbot. Me?' He shrugged again.

Barling gave him a long look. 'Good.'

'What do you mean, "good"?'

'I thought it would take me a lot longer to get you to start questioning your own skills, to start to look at the whole picture. I am glad to see its beginnings, though you have a long way to go.'

Stanton held a hand up. 'Not a lesson. Not now.'

'I can assure you,' said Barling, 'that I am far too cold and weary to even think about such a thing. But I would add, and I was about to before you interrupted me, that you are being too hard on yourself. I agree that you might not know the reality of life as a monk, but you are still a shrewd judge of men. And monks are, after all, men.'

Stanton could've fallen off his horse in shock at the unexpected praise. 'Thank you, Barling.'

The clerk ignored his response but carried on. 'Therefore, as I had planned, we shall divide our work as the monastery is run: I shall take the senior monks who work inside. I shall start with Philip.'

Stanton gave a low whistle. 'He won't like that.'

'He will not have any choice. I shall speak to him about it before he retires to bed and we shall lay out the plan at the chapter meeting in the morning. Also, he may be more honest with me. He has been saying that all is well within the house, which it clearly is not. I can understand why he would take that approach as he does have a position to maintain and it would be most unsuitable were he to go around airing every quarrel that happens within the cloister. Perhaps if he sees me alone then I can persuade him to be more honest in his appraisal. I will then speak to his deputy, Reginald the prior. Followed by Maurice, the novice master, and Elias the librarian. There is an infirmary monk by the name of William too. The abbot said it was William who discovered that Cuthbert had been strangled. I do not recall having encountered him, but I will track him down.'

Stanton ran through those whom Barling was due to speak to. 'Faith, I'm glad I don't have your list.'

'I suspect they will indeed be quite difficult. You will speak to those who have dealings with the outside. Lambert, the porter, Silvanus, our guestmaster. Osmund, the cellarer. Osmund also oversees all the lay brothers. He will tell you if any brothers work alone. It would appear Daniel does, so include any others with him.'

Stanton nodded. 'I definitely prefer my list. Even Lambert.'

'There is one more,' said Barling. 'The lady Juliana. Yes, strictly speaking, she is an outsider, but still within the walls. I believe it would be most productive if you and I were to speak to her together.' He looked right at Stanton, as if daring him to make a remark.

Stanton didn't want to say anything about Lady Kersley that might get Barling riled again. 'That sounds like the best—'

'Sirs!' The shout came from the gate ahead, interrupting him. 'Oh, sirs!'

'What on earth is going on?' said Barling.

Out of the gate, the huge Brother Lambert came running towards them. Badly. Clumsily. Fighting for breath. But running. And still shouting. 'Oh, sirs!'

Stanton feared the scarlet-faced man would collapse as he staggered to a halt in front of them, his breath puffing in uncontrolled gasps.

'Oh, sirs! Thank God you are back. Come quick, sirs. Come.'

'Brother Lambert,' said Barling, 'pull yourself together. What is the matter?'

More agonised, ragged breaths. 'There's been another murder.'

Chapter Eighteen

As Barling rounded the corner at the back of the stables, with Stanton and a breathless, gasping Lambert following, the sight that met him made his stomach rebel.

'Hell's teeth.' This from Stanton. Shocked.

The body of Silvanus, guestmaster of the abbey, lay on the muddy ground. The dead monk was on his back, arms flung out to either side. A pitchfork was buried in his chest, so deep that it remained upright, steady as if it had been plunged into a thick pile of hay. Yet hay did not seep blood like that which stained the front of Silvanus's white habit.

Despite his repugnance, Barling did not pause but strode up to the body. This was no moment to show any kind of indecisiveness.

Standing over Silvanus was a sobbing Maurice, the novice master's shoulders heaving in his grief. Another monk, younger than Maurice and about Barling's own age, stood with the sobbing man, a comforting arm around him. Barling recognised the other monk from the chapter meeting, though the man had not been as vocal as many others. He'd stood out because he was bald as a hen's egg.

'He was my boy once,' Barling heard Maurice say as he reached them.

'We have only just been informed of this terrible news,' said Barling. 'I do not need to confirm that it is true.'

'No.' Maurice turned his clouded eyes to him, venom in his voice. 'Even I can see what has happened here.'

Barling let the response pass. As always with a crime: emotion. Always emotion. 'I would ask that you move back a little, please, brothers.' He directed his request at the bald monk, in the hope of better cooperation.

'Come now, Brother Maurice,' said the monk. 'We need to allow space for the King's men.'

'Stanton. With me.'

They squatted down to look more closely at the corpse of Silvanus.

'Damn it all, Barling,' came Stanton's whisper. 'It's even worse than it looks from afar.'

Barling nodded. 'It is.'

Not only had Silvanus been impaled by the pitchfork, but a metal skewer had been shoved into the front of his neck. A dark, thick substance oozed from his lips.

'And what is that in his mouth? Is it blood?'

Barling leaned down closer to see, then sniffed hard. He gingerly put his fingers into the black substance, anxious not to touch the gaping lips. This felt like enough of a violation of the man as it was. His touch met a stickiness and he withdrew his hand, the tips of his fingers smeared with black. He sniffed at it again. 'It is wood tar.'

'Wood tar?' said Stanton. 'Why would—'

Barling gave a warning shake of his head. 'Not now,' he mouthed. He got to his feet and Stanton rose with him.

'Who found the body?' Barling asked Maurice and the bald monk.

'I did.' The voice came from behind them. 'Sirs.'

Barling turned.

Daniel, the bearded lay brother. The broad young man stood next to the back of the stable block. 'I ran for Brother William. Straight away.' He nodded at the bald monk.

'He did,' replied William. 'I was in the cloister, at my devotions.'

William. The infirmary monk. Philip had mentioned him, the monk who had found the charred string in Brother Cuthbert's neck.

'As was I,' said Maurice. 'I overheard the commotion and wondered if I'd fallen asleep and dreamed. But no.'

William went on. 'I came here as quick as I could. Tried to see if there was anything I could do.' The front of his white habit was mud-stained where he must have been kneeling on the wet ground. He gave a despairing shrug. 'I do not think he had been dead that long. His body had yet to become stiff. But once death has arrived, the time matters no more. It was hopeless.'

'Hopeless, yes. But evil too,' said Maurice, anger breaking through his grief. 'Evil. First Cuthbert. Now Silvanus. May whoever did this rot in hell for all eternity. Rot!'

'Have you informed your lord abbot?' asked Barling.

'What do you think we did, man?' Rage had completely stopped Maurice's tears. 'He also came at once. But now, instead of praying for the soul of Silvanus, he is in the guesthouse, comforting the lady Juliana, who is in hysterics.' He spat hard to a gasp from William.

'Calm yourself, brother,' said William. 'Please . . .'

'I don't care,' said Maurice. 'Women have no place anywhere near a holy house.'

Barling turned to Stanton. 'Go and fetch Abbot Philip. At once.'

As Stanton nodded and hurried off, Barling saw a group of lay brothers approach, carrying a bier between them.

'I sent for them,' said William to Barling by way of explanation. 'We need to take our brother Silvanus to the infirmary.'

'We need to take him to the church, William,' said Maurice. 'The church!'

'We will, Maurice, we will.' William patted him on the hand. 'But I need to give him back some dignity first.'

'Barling!' came Philip's call. 'Thank God you have returned.' The abbot hurried up, Stanton with him.

Maurice started to say something, but William hushed him, this time successfully.

'That we had not returned to such terrible news, my lord abbot,' said Barling.

'Terrible beyond words.' Philip crossed himself. 'Yet you have summoned me. Have you found something?' A spark of hope lit the distress in his dark eyes.

'No, my lord. But I need to speak to you in your hall. Alone,' said Barling firmly. 'As Stanton will be talking to Daniel. Alone.'

Stanton nodded his understanding of what Barling was requesting. Barling knew his pupil completely recognised the new urgency, given this appalling discovery.

Philip looked confused. Uncertain. 'I . . . I need to take collation and Compline. My brethren need me.'

'Reginald can do it in your stead,' said Maurice, hushed no more. 'As he has done so many times.'

'Then you need not worry, my lord abbot,' said Barling. 'We should make haste to your hall.'

Chapter Nineteen

'In the name of God, what is happening to us here, Barling?'

The words burst from the abbot the moment he closed the door to his hall. Though no one sat at the table, a half-eaten meal lay abandoned upon it.

Barling noted the man shook from head to foot. Understandable, given the dreadful events of the day. 'I think we should sit down, Philip. You look like you need to.'

Philip nodded and sank into his usual chair at the head of the table, his head in his hands.

Barling moved the food from in front of him, suspecting that the man would have no appetite. He picked up a jug of water and a cup and placed them before Philip, and then sat too.

'Thank you.' Philip poured himself a cupful and drank deep.

Barling waited for him to finish. As he had discussed with Stanton, he had intended to speak to Philip alone and glean information from him about the true nature of relationships within the abbey. He also needed to advise Philip that certain monks would have to be interviewed as well as Juliana. All of that had been in Barling's enquiry as it related to the murder of Cuthbert. But now, shockingly, they had the murder of Silvanus as well. Barling would have to adjust his questions accordingly. He was confident Stanton would do the same with Daniel. Stanton was very quick to adapt to new circumstances. Barling wished he shared more of that talent.

Philip emptied the cup and pulled in a steadying breath.

'Do you feel more restored?' said Barling.

'I do,' said Philip.

'One cannot underestimate what such events can do to our composure,' said Barling.

'I know,' said Philip. 'It was so the night we found Cuthbert. I thought I had lost my reason at times. But for another of my monks to be slain, for Silvanus to be . . .' He trailed off.

'When were you made aware of what had taken place?'

'I was here, eating dinner, with the lady Juliana. Daniel came to summon me. I was shocked enough. You can only imagine her reaction.'

'I believe I can.'

'Not only the shock at another murder. But the fact that it was Silvanus. She was very fond of him. He extended the proper kindness and care to all of our guests as required by the Rule and ran the guesthouse impeccably. But I think he had a special bond with her.'

'I see. So you made your way to where Silvanus's body was lying.'

'I did, and my lady insisted on coming with me. I should have forbidden her from doing so. She took one look—'

'And had hysterics. Yes, Brother Maurice mentioned it.' Barling paused to pour his own cup of water. 'It was indeed the most horrific sight.'

'Had you seen Cuthbert, you might not think it the most.' Philip swallowed hard.

'No, perhaps not. I am very thankful I did not and you have my deepest sympathies.' Barling took a drink. 'Up to that point, had there been anything unusual about the morning?'

'No, nothing out of the ordinary. Everyone was at their usual place in our world.'

'Where was yours?'

'As every morning. Cloister, church, chapter, work. It sounds odd to say, and I mean this with no disrespect, but after the disruption of you and Stanton yesterday morning, it felt so calming to be back in the usual rhythm of the day. I apologise if that sounds rude.'

'Not at all,' said Barling. 'I know precisely what you mean. I myself love the order of the court, the discipline of the law. Speaking of yesterday, I wanted to ask you about the chapter meeting.'

'How do you mean?'

'Not only was there anger at my and Stanton's presence, but there was quite a lot directed at you as well.'

Philip gave a sad smile. 'You noticed.'

'Impossible not to.'

'Things are very difficult here at present. And not just because of the terrible loss of Cuthbert.'

'No?'

'Because of Ernald. My predecessor.'

'But Abbot Ernald is dead, is he not?'

'Yes, he is.' Philip's voice dropped. 'That is precisely the problem.'

'I am sorry, Philip, but I do not understand.'

'Let me explain, or at least try to. Life in a monastery is like that of a family. The abbot is the father. Ernald was the father here for thirty years. It was even his house. He built it. A few of the monks were here from the start, having joined from other houses. But there are not many of them left. For the rest, including myself, all they, and I, have known was Ernald. And he was a great man. A great, holy man. A strict disciplinarian. But we worshipped him. When he died last year, it shook the place to its foundations. We were all broken-hearted. And still are.'

'I am sure.' Barling recalled the abbot Nicholas's words in Westminster: *Philip, as new abbot, attended the General Chapter of our order last September, as did I. His grief at the loss of Ernald was apparent.*

'It would all have been hard enough, except that when it came to electing a new abbot, the monks elected me. Me. At my age. I was stunned.'

'They must have recognised something very special in you. For you to follow the great Ernald.'

'Maybe they did. But I do not recognise it in myself. Being the father of this house is a burdensome and often lonely life. And it has never been more lonely than now, with not one but two of my monks slain.'

'I can imagine, and I am glad the burden is not mine. May I ask what position you held while Ernald was alive?'

'I was the cellarer. For ten years, from the age of just twenty-four.' The pride that came into Philip's voice was obvious. 'The cellarer is responsible for the financial well-being of the monastery, and all its estates and granges. I had to do all that, as well as oversee all the lay brothers. My father Ernald saw that I had a quick mind and that I was good with money.'

'Perhaps your election should not have been such a surprise to you. It is a logical step from cellarer to abbot.'

'Logical, perhaps. But maybe too high for me.'

Barling thought back to chapter and remembered the young black-haired monk. 'Am I correct in recalling that Brother Osmund has taken your place as cellarer?'

'You are. I have great hopes for him.'

'Excellent. He is currently a little lacking in confidence, perhaps?'

'Regretfully he is, and much more than I realised. I fear I rushed into appointing him and have made a mistake. But having appointed him so recently, I do not want to change my mind. So I have not made any other changes. I do not want to add to my errors. The house continues as it was under Ernald.' His voice dropped again. 'Or rather, it did. For now we have lost Cuthbert and Silvanus.'

'You have appointed Maurice temporarily as sacrist?' asked Barling.

'I have. And now I shall have to think about Silvanus's duties.' He rubbed a hand across his face. 'You see why it is so hard, Barling? I would like nothing more than to be able to mourn them, all of them. But everyone looks to me for a solution, all the time. I am their father now.' He let out a long, long breath, exhaustion etched on his face.

'Philip, I understand the weight of your worry. I have no wish to add to it.'

'Barling, you are helping me with the burden. Your presence here means more to me than you will ever know.'

'I am pleased that I am being of help. I have been compiling information into my enquiry, as I said I would. The next step, which I had already planned even before I found out about Silvanus, was that Stanton and I would speak to various individuals alone. I had wanted to come to chapter in the morning and speak to them about it first. But now that Silvanus is dead, there is even more urgency.'

'You think it is the same evil hand?'

Barling was not going to share his conversation with the priest Theobald, certainly not at this point. 'I do not know what to think. Not yet. We shall be making every urgent effort to find out. Stanton and I will get started as early as possible.'

'Very well,' said Philip. 'There will be objections, I have no doubt. Despite what has been going on. Please make me aware of any and I will deal with the individuals concerned. I would make one plea: that you avoid the hours of the Divine Office. Please. The monks need their prayer more than ever, as do I.'

'Rest assured, I will.' Barling went to rise. 'Now, if you will excuse me, I need to find Stanton.'

'Before you go, may I make one further request of you?'

Barling sat back down. 'Of course.'

'You are aware of the General Chapter? That oversees Cistercian houses?'

'Yes, Abbot Nicholas mentioned it to me.'

'I had to write to them after Cuthbert's murder to inform them of what had happened. Not only that, but I also had to let them know what steps I was taking to resolve the matter. Well, I did so, and they are aware that you are assisting me. But now I have to write another letter, telling them of the appalling news that there has been another death. May God help me, I do not even know where to start.' He passed a hand across his face. 'You are such a skilled man of letters. Do you think you could help me with the wording? Or perhaps write one to accompany mine?'

'It would please me greatly to be able to assist you in that task,' said Barling.

As tasks went, it would not be difficult. Writing an account of a murder was not problematic.

But solving it would be.

Chapter Twenty

Stanton ushered Daniel into his room in the guesthouse and closed the door behind them.

He'd spoken the truth to Barling earlier when he'd said how unsure he was about getting the truth from the monks. The clerk's response had been as surprising as it was welcome. Stanton would do his best. Yet he was still glad that he was speaking to the lay brother Daniel first. Not only had he, Stanton, already spoken to the man alone in the stables about the horses, but he also understood the world of the lay brothers a bit better than that of the monks. Theirs was a life more devoted to work than prayer, it seemed.

'Do you want to sit down, Daniel?'

The tall, broad lay brother shook his head. 'Not allowed, sir.'

The man hadn't shed a tear, not like Brother Maurice. 'I'm allowing you.'

Another definite shake of Daniel's head.

Stanton let his offer go. No point in pushing it. 'I'm sorry about the death of Brother Silvanus. It must've been horrible to find him like that.'

Nothing.

'It was you that found him?'

'Yes, sir.'

'Can you tell me what happened?'

'I was working in the stables, sir. The guesthouse. Like always. Went for my dinner with the other lay brothers. Went back to work. Like always. I needed to have a piss. I went round the back of the stables. And there he was. I ran for Brother William. In case he could do owt. That's all. Sir.'

'You work mostly in the stables, don't you?' With a pitchfork, no doubt.

'Yes, sir. And I do the heavy work for Brother Silvanus. Did.' Still dry-eyed.

'I'm sorry to be asking questions so soon afterward.'

Daniel said nothing.

Damn it all. If Barling were here, he'd order the man to speak up and Daniel would have done so. Barling had that effect on people.

Then Abbot Philip's words from the day he and Barling had arrived here came back to Stanton: *The lay brothers won't like it but they will do as they are told. They always do. They have dull wits but at least are obedient.* Stanton realised that he would only get an answer from Daniel if he actually asked a question.

'Did you enjoy working for Brother Silvanus?'

'No, sir.'

'No?'

'No, sir.'

'Why not?'

'He was always on at me for not doing enough work. Not doing the work the right way.'

'Did that make you dislike him?'

'Yes, sir.'

Stanton paused to collect his thoughts, choosing his next words with care. Daniel's short, direct answers actually made questioning harder. Longer answers not only gave more information: they gave time to get the next question ready. 'Did it make you want to hurt him?'

'I didn't hurt him, sir.'

Maybe his question had been too indirect. 'Did you kill him?'

119

'No, sir.'

'Did you see anybody kill him?'

'No, sir.'

'Did you see anybody with Silvanus today?'

'You, sir. And the other King's man, sir.'

God's eyes. At this rate, they'd be here until tomorrow morning. He tried a different approach. 'Daniel, I know that you're used to obeying the monks and doing everything you're told without question. I have to do the same a lot of the time for Aelred Barling. He's my master and I'm his pupil. I listen to him. But part of my work for him means that we talk together and he listens to me.' *Some of the time, anyway.* Stanton ploughed on. 'I'm not demanding your obedience. I want to hear what you have to say. Do you understand?'

'Yes, sir. I think so.'

'So, did you see Silvanus with anybody else?'

'Lady Kersley, sir. When Lady Kersley was setting off for her ride. I got her horse ready and was waiting for her with it.'

Better. A bit.

'Were they arguing? Angry?'

'No, sir. They were talking and laughing, sir. They did that a lot.'

'When was this?'

'This morning, sir. She went off and Brother Silvanus carried on with his work in the guesthouse. I carried on with mine. Emptying the pots from the guesthouse. Changing the water.'

Stanton gave an encouraging nod, not wanting to break his flow.

'Back to the stables. Cleaning out the horses. Fetching the hay. All my work. Same as I do every day. Nights too, if the horses need looking after.'

'And when did you last see Silvanus?'

'At the guesthouse, sir. After that, I was with the horses.'

'Good, thank you.' Now that he'd got the man talking, Stanton tried a different tack. 'Daniel, you said that you didn't like Silvanus. Did you like Brother Cuthbert?'

Daniel shrugged and rubbed his beard. Wary.

'You can tell me, Daniel.'

'No, sir. But I didn't hurt him either, sir. Didn't kill him.'

Now, this was interesting. Daniel, the man who on the face of it had slow wits and few words, was following Stanton's exact line of questioning about Silvanus. 'Do you like any of the monks?'

'Not really, sir.'

'Can you tell me why?'

'It's that they don't like us, sir. The lay brothers. We're here for our muscles and our strong backs. Nothing more. We do different work to them. The real work. The monks might serve God. But we serve the monks. And if we don't serve them right, we get punished. Brother Osmund, he's in charge of us. He does all that. He can make us sit on the floor to eat our meals. For days. Has the stick, the scourge. Same as Abbot Philip used to when he was in charge of us.'

'That can't be an easy life,' said Stanton. He meant it.

'It's not, sir. And some of us didn't choose it, either.'

'How do you mean?'

'When the monks get given land, men can come with it. The monks become the lord.'

'Those with the most power don't care much for regular folk, do they?'

'No, sir. Well, one monk here does. He's not bad.'

'Who would that be?'

'Brother Elias. The library monk. He brings books to read to us when we have a rest hour.'

Stanton nodded, recognising the name of the red-haired Elias. 'You like that?'

'Yes, sir. They have good stories in them.' His mouth twitched in a ghost of a smile. 'Like the one called the *Aviary* – it's a book of birds, all sorts of birds. Stories in there about how they do good deeds and that. I like it a lot and so do the others. Brother Elias shows us the pictures and explains them. The words too—' He stopped dead, smile gone.

'Go on,' said Stanton.

'The lay brothers are forbidden from reading, sir. It's in the Rule.'

'I didn't ask you that, Daniel. Have you been reading?'

'Please, sir, don't say anything.' Wary again. 'I'll get in the worst trouble, be punished.'

'I won't get you into trouble,' said Stanton. 'I promise. But I need you to answer me.'

'Yes, I can read. A bit. Brother Elias has been teaching me. He showed us the letters by the pictures so often, I began to recognise a few. I told him as I helped him carry his things back to the library. He asked me if I'd like to learn some more letters. I said it was forbidden. But he said it could be our secret.'

'Has he been teaching any other of your fellow lay brothers?'

'I don't think so, sir.' Another shrug. 'I think they're happy with the pictures.'

The deep bell of the church sounded from outside.

'That's Compline, sir. May I go, please? I'll be punished if I'm late. But I'll stay if you tell me.'

'No, you go.'

'Thank you, sir.' Daniel went to go.

'One last question, Daniel.'

'Yes, sir?'

'Did any of the horses need looking after on the night of Christmas Eve?'

Daniel thought for a moment. 'Yes, sir. One of them had a bad leg with a poultice on. I slept in the stables that night.' His gaze locked with Stanton's. Hardened. 'In case that brings another question, sir: yes, I was in the stables all night. And no, I didn't kill Brother Cuthbert.'

'Stanton!' Barling's call came from outside.

Daniel left without another word.

Chapter Twenty-One

The door to Stanton's room opened and Daniel walked out.

'Excuse me, sir.' The broad lay brother turned sideways to stamp past Barling in the narrow corridor.

Barling went into Stanton's room and closed the door once more. 'What have you been talking about with Daniel?' he asked. 'He looked most perturbed.'

'That's one way of putting it,' replied his assistant. 'I found out that he's not anything like as slow-minded as the abbot says of the lay brothers.'

'I see.' Barling took a seat on the single chair while Stanton sat down on the bed.

'But I'd still choose to talk to him over the abbot any day, Barling. How did you get on with Philip?'

'He has agreed that we can start the questioning without waiting to discuss it at chapter. I would have proceeded without his agreement as the murder of Silvanus has brought a new imperative. But I am pleased to have his agreement nevertheless.'

'Silvanus.' Stanton blew out his cheeks. 'I didn't like the man. But what a way to meet your end. It was savage.'

Barling nodded. 'And utterly inexplicable. Either the pitchfork in his chest or the skewer in his neck would have ended his life. Why would the murderer have used both?'

'Unless it was more than one person.'

'That would be one explanation,' said Barling. 'Yet we also have the wood tar in his mouth.'

'A third way to kill him.'

'I do not think so.'

'Why so?'

'Had someone poured such a foul substance into his mouth when he was still alive,' said Barling, 'he would have tried to cough or spit it back out in his struggle for his life's breath. There was no sign of that. I would surmise that it was poured in once he was already dead.'

'I hope you're right,' said Stanton. 'It doesn't bear thinking about otherwise but either way, it's a very strange thing to do to someone.'

'It was, as you say, savage. And, although we never witnessed the body of Cuthbert, it would appear that there is more than simply savagery and bizarreness of method linking both murders.'

'Such as?' said Stanton.

'Both murders took place where lay brothers work: the kitchen and the stables. Now, Cuthbert—'

'Behind the stables.'

Barling paused, distracted by Stanton's interruption.

'We must have accuracy, as you're always telling me, Barling.'

'Very well, then: behind the stables. But a few feet in this instance makes little odds. As I was saying: Cuthbert. Cuthbert was strangled, which could have been done by anybody. But the infirmary monk said that string or cord was used. The lay brothers use that in their work all the time. Silvanus? Again, tools used by the lay brothers: a pitchfork and a skewer. Wood tar will be kept in the wood shed. Or the forge. Daniel works in the stables. And now you are telling me that Daniel is not as slow-witted as he pretends. Did he tell you anything else of relevance?'

'That he didn't like Cuthbert or Silvanus,' said Stanton. 'That he slept in the stables and not in the lay dormitory on the night of Cuthbert's murder.'

'Relevant indeed.'

'But he was very open about his dislike. Admitted it straight away.' Stanton related the tensions between the monks and the lay brothers that Daniel had described. 'And he says he didn't kill either monk.'

'Well, of course he would say that, Stanton.'

'Yes, but I believed him.'

'Unless he's a very good liar. We met such individuals last year, did we not?'

'We did.' Stanton gave a sharp sigh. 'But while he spoke of his dislike for the monks, he did speak well of one.'

'Who?'

'Elias, the library monk.'

Barling listened with close interest as Stanton gave him his account of the lay brother's secret fondness for books. 'I think your account has settled for me who we should speak to first in the morning. We are still following my plan, but in a slightly different order. I will speak to Elias. You talk to Osmund, the cellarer.'

'A monk.' Stanton cast him a wry look. 'But I'll do my best.'

'Of course you will. And yes, he is a monk but he is close to your age. What is more, he is not the most confident of men. I sincerely doubt that he will present you with much difficulty. He is in charge of the lay brothers, as Abbot Philip was before him as cellarer.'

'Well, we know what Philip thinks of the lay brothers,' said Stanton.

'Stanton, take care that you do not allow emotion to cloud your judgement.'

'What do you mean?'

'I think you quite liked Daniel. First, you bond over horses. Like you, he is a young man, and like you, he bridles against authority.'

'That's hardly fair.' Stanton scowled.

'It may not be fair, but it is the truth,' said Barling. 'I am simply reminding you of the pitfalls.'

Stanton held up a hand. 'I take your point.'

'Good. Once we have spoken to Osmund and Elias, we can meet up briefly here at the guesthouse to discuss our findings in case there is anything of importance to be shared.'

'Speaking of findings,' said Stanton, 'did you get anything else from Abbot Philip beside his permission for us to go ahead with questioning folk?'

'I did.' Barling sighed. 'I learned from him that there is much discord here, as we have observed. A far less harmonious picture than I was given before I came here.' He went through his exchange with the abbot, his assistant listening intently.

'I would only say one thing,' said Stanton when he'd finished.

'What is that?'

'Take care you don't allow emotion to cloud your judgement.'

'What?' Barling glared at him.

Stanton grinned. 'First, you bond over Paris. Like you, he's a man of middling age. Like you, he loves his authority and order.'

Barling drew in a breath to admonish his brazen speech but Stanton held up a hand again.

'Please don't think you need to give me one of your speeches, Barling. I was only trying to make you see what you can sound like sometimes.'

'I see.' Barling sniffed and got to his feet. 'Then I shall leave you to get your rest.'

'It's not long gone dark, Barling.'

'We shall be rising at the bell for Vigils, Stanton, only a couple of hours after midnight.' He walked to the door. 'Sleep well.'

Barling closed the door on Stanton's loud groan of disgust. 'Midnight?'

And allowed himself a little smile.

Chapter Twenty-Two

'By all that's holy, Barling, I don't know how the monks do this every night.' Stanton stood next to him, breath foggy, shuddering with cold, as they waited outside the locked main entrance to the cloister in the pitch dark.

The only light visible was that in the high windows of the church, the rest of the buildings shadows against the darker shadows of the night. Vigils were drawing to a close, the distant sound of the brethren's voices raised in song echoing from within into the quiet.

'The priest Theobald was of the opinion that they have an easy life,' replied Barling. 'I think it perhaps a lot harder than he imagines.' A life that Barling had once believed was calling him, though he had not been able to answer.

The singing finished and the light in the church began to dim. The monks and brothers would be leaving the church to make their way to prayer and work.

After a few minutes, sounds of unlocking came from the door and it was pulled open to reveal dim lamplight.

'Jesu Christus!' the lay brother who had opened it shouted out in fright, alarmed voices answering it as others rushed to his aid.

'It's only us!' Stanton's call was immediate.

'Brothers, brothers,' said Barling. 'Do not take fright, it is the King's men.'

He glimpsed Osmund, the cellarer, amongst them.

'Stanton,' murmured Barling, 'I shall leave you to speak with the monk as discussed. I shall seek Elias.'

'Good luck,' came Stanton's low-voiced reply. He patted Barling on the back then stepped forward. 'Brother Osmund, a word, please.'

Stanton tried to bring order, started to explain what was going on.

Barling left him to it and set off for the claustral walk, where the monks would have gone to prayer, just as the lay brothers had been assembling for work.

Though lamps lit the way, they did not pierce the wider darkness but seemed only to make it deeper.

The chorus of voices in individual prayer and worship met him. Many of the monks were already settled in their wooden carrels in the cloister.

Barling made his way along, peering into each one as he sought Elias. He'd thought it would be straightforward to discreetly approach the red-haired monk but now he berated himself for his stupidity. Even though the carrels were lit by individual candles, every monk had his cowl raised, so it was impossible to tell one from another. He stopped outside one where the figure looked of the same build as Elias.

'Brother, if I may.' He put a hand to the monk's arm.

The figure turned and a startled-looking choir monk cried out in fright and shrank back.

The murmur of prayer stopped dead. Fearful gasps and calls replaced it.

'My apologies, brother—'

'What is happening?' A familiar deep voice. A furious one. Reginald, the prior.

Barling glanced to his left.

Reginald was looking out from his carrel. 'You,' he said in disgust. The white-haired monk emerged, leaning heavily on his stick.

All along the cloister, frightened faces of monks peeped out from their wooden shelters, some whispering to each other.

'How dare you, sir?' Reginald made no effort to keep his voice down. 'How dare you disrupt us from our devotion? Leave. Now.'

'Reginald.' Philip, stepping from his own carrel. 'Desist. The King's man sought my permission to seek out individuals. I gave it to him.'

'I am seeking out Brother Elias,' said Barling. 'As Stanton is speaking to Brother Osmund. We will not take long and will try not to disturb you unduly.'

But Reginald would not be placated. 'What are we now, my lord abbot? Peasants to be summoned on a whim?' His voice rose. 'Pigs to be driven with a stick?' Rose further. 'This is intolerable, intolerable. I . . . I . . .' He began to sway on his stick.

Philip moved quickly to his side, grabbed his arm to steady him. 'Reginald? What ails you?'

Barling went to help too, unnerved by the monk's near collapse, but the monk shook him off.

'Unhand me.' Reginald's knees buckled.

'Brother, brother. Take deep breaths.' William, the bald infirmary monk, bustled up. He slipped his arm under Reginald's free one. He looked from the abbot to Barling. 'I could not hear all that was being said. Whatever it is, I must insist that Reginald comes with me for bloodletting in the warming room. Then he will be in the infirmary for a day afterward recovering. Whatever you require him for, I am afraid you will have to wait. His health is of the utmost importance.'

'Of course,' said Philip. 'Let us get you there at once, Reginald.'

Reginald mumbled something but did not resist as they helped him away.

'You asked for me, sir?' A quiet voice at Barling's shoulder. Elias.

'Yes, I did,' said Barling, struggling to regain his composure. He disliked fuss intensely and his attempt to approach Elias discreetly had gone horribly awry. 'Shall we go to the library? I would like to speak to you in private.'

'This way, sir. Follow me.' The red-haired monk led the way along the cloister.

As they approached the library, Barling saw Philip and William disappear into the warming room with Reginald. The white-haired monk thankfully seemed a lot more revived and was talking freely.

Barling had no doubt that the monk was talking about him.

And he could take a very accurate guess at what he was saying.

Philip entered the light and heat of the warming room with Reginald, his arm still giving support to the older monk.

If Reginald was a little unsteady on his feet, there was nothing wrong with his tongue. Angry words continued to pour from him, directed at Philip. 'An utter disgrace. To be disturbed like that, in our own cloister, in the midst of our devotions. What was that man, Barling, thinking?'

No 'my lord abbot', of which Philip was only too aware. He felt his own ire rise at the open rudeness but he pushed it down, at least for the time being. It would not help matters.

On Reginald's other side, William offered the prior a calming response as he steered him in the direction of one of the wide stone seats built into the wall beside the huge brick fireplace. 'Don't excite yourself any more, brother.'

'William is right,' said Philip. 'It is not good for your health.'

The heat seemed to revive Reginald even further. 'I am not excited.' He shook off Philip's and William's hands, using his stick to get himself the last couple of steps. He dropped into his seat with a grimace of pain, glaring up at Philip from under his thick white brows. 'I am wondering what is happening to our abbey.'

'While you wonder, my good brother,' said William, 'I will need your arm.' The infirmary monk set about rolling Reginald's sleeve up as he spoke, brisk as ever in seeing to a patient.

Philip remained standing too, the better to assert his authority. 'You have no need to wonder, Reginald,' he said. 'I explained everything at chapter the day before yesterday, as I did just now.'

'Keep still, please, brother.' William had his small bleeding knife in one hand and Reginald's bare arm in the other, the bowl to catch his blood positioned beneath.

'Of course I can wonder.' Reginald pointed a gnarled finger at Philip. 'As I wonder about who leads this holy house.'

While concerns about the King's man were one thing, such an unacceptable personal challenge was quite another. Philip could hold back his own temper no longer. 'Reginald, I know you are not feeling well. However, I need to remind you that you speak to your abbot.' His voice came out higher than he intended, made him sound like the young novice he'd been when he first came to Fairmore and the imposing Reginald had already been the abbey's prior of many years.

'Then, father' – Reginald's sneer changed to a wince as William slipped the knife into his vein – 'I continue to ask myself how Abbot Ernald would have guided us through this time.'

Philip swallowed hard to ensure his next words came with full authority. 'And how, might I ask, do you answer yourself, brother?' He clasped his own hands together to hide their angry tremor.

'That Ernald would not have sought the help of those from outside our order. Ever.'

A rattle came from the door before Philip could respond.

He turned to see Maurice enter and his annoyance deepened. Now he would have not one but two dissatisfied voices railing at him. It was so frequently thus now that he was the father of Fairmore: monks, visiting abbots, benefactors, the General Chapter and many more besides. Every one of them with their own particular demands and every one insisting that theirs was the most important.

'Reginald, I heard you collapsed,' said Maurice, squinting hard at the prior as he walked over. 'What ails you?'

'A few moments of dizziness, Maurice,' said Reginald. 'Nothing more.'

'Is this true, my lord abbot?' Maurice turned his poor-sighted gaze to Philip.

'Reginald seems much recovered,' said Philip. 'Is that not so, William?'

'Yes, father.' William kept his voice low and his attention on the blood that fell drip by drip from Reginald's arm into the bowl, obviously not wanting to be drawn into the uncomfortable debate.

'The other thing I heard,' said Maurice, 'is that the King's man has been disturbing the cloister.'

'Then you heard correctly, Maurice,' said Reginald.

Maurice frowned. 'This is not acceptable. Not in the least.'

The two old monks glared at Philip, united in the confident power that their years gave them.

Philip squared his shoulders. Years, however many a monk had lived, could not match the power of his office. 'I need you both to listen to me, and listen carefully. The King's man, Aelred Barling, is doing what I have asked him here to do, which is to help find the devil who has murdered two of our brethren.'

'But—' began Reginald.

'Enough, both of you.' Philip raised a hand. 'As father of this house, I am responsible for ensuring the safety and well-being of every soul here. To that end, I must carry the burden of the deaths of Cuthbert and Silvanus. Not you.' His voice rose: he couldn't help it. 'So whatever I decide, those decisions must stand. Do I make myself perfectly clear?'

He still had to wait a moment for their replies but at least they had the sense to make the correct ones.

'Yes, my lord,' said Reginald.

'Of course, my lord abbot,' said Maurice.

Correct, yet their expressions did not match their humble words.

They looked at their abbot, their lord, their father, with a barely concealed seething hostility.

Chapter Twenty-Three

Of all the monks that Barling could have ordered Stanton to speak to at this ungodly hour, Osmund was by no means the worst.

Stanton had guessed from the chapter meeting that Osmund, the young black-haired monk who seemed so unsure of himself, wouldn't be one to become angry or difficult.

Judging by the raised voices that echoed over from the cloister where Barling had gone, somebody else was.

As they stood in the wide passageway inside the gate, Osmund spoke calming words to his bearded lay brothers after their initial scare at finding Stanton and Barling standing in the darkness. It was clear that the monk had had more of fright than they had. Most ignored him, standing solemnly as cattle until he finished. A few exchanged furtive glances. Daniel looked at him with barely concealed scorn.

'Brothers, here are the duties that need to be done today.' Osmund folded his hands, obviously trying to look commanding. All his action did was draw attention to the fact that they trembled. Badly. 'The . . . the forge will need to be fired up. We will need more firewood. The cows need milking. And there is a table in the monks' refectory that needs mending. Also . . .' He paused, clearly lost on whatever list he had made in his mind.

'You told us everything last night, brother.' This from an older lay brother. 'We'll be right. We know our work.'

'Yes, yes. Thank you.' Osmund raised his hand in a blessing. 'May God grant you strength and purpose as you labour in praise of His divine mercy.'

'Amen.' The brothers dispersed at once without a backward glance at Osmund.

'Well, sir.' Osmund looked at Stanton, his voice still unsteady. 'I am here and ready to answer your questions.' He swallowed hard. 'As you have ordered.'

Hell's teeth, the man was nervous as a field mouse. 'It's more of a request, brother. We're standing in a very open place, though. Is there somewhere we can speak more privately?' It was a genuine request for privacy. Stanton also knew that if they didn't get out of this passageway through which the wind blew unceasing frigid air, his backside would freeze clean off.

'We could go into the store room.' Osmund pointed to a door a few feet away.

'A good choice.'

Once inside with the door shut, Osmund set about lighting a covered lamp.

The store room was vast, crammed and piled high with caskets, barrels, sacks and bags and more. A large trestle table sat off to one side, holding a number of balances for weighing and untidy mounds of papers and documents.

'This is where you do your work – your work as a cellarer?' asked Stanton. He didn't want to start with a question about murder. He needed to get this fellow to calm a bit first.

'Part of it. This is where many of the provisions are stored and we have a cellar underneath. I keep all the accounts and records as well, for here and for the granges, the lands we hold elsewhere. Make sure we have money coming in from things like our wool sales.' The monk looked more and more defeated as he listed off everything he had to do.

'Quite a responsibility, then.'

'It is. So much. And on top of that, there's what you saw just now. I have to give the lay brothers their work and oversee it as well. Hold their chapter meetings. Make sure they are disciplined for any transgressions.'

Discipline lay brothers like Daniel, who deeply resented Osmund for it. The looks on the faces of the other brothers who had waited for Osmund to give them their work hadn't been the most content, either.

'How long have you been cellarer?' Stanton knew full well: Barling had passed on what the abbot had said. He just wanted to try to put the man at ease.

'Since last summer, sir. Since Abbot Ernald died. It was Abbot Philip before that.' He chewed his lip in anxiety. 'Philip was much better at this than I am. I try my best. But it's a lot to remember. I get a lot of things wrong.' He waved a hand over at the mess of records on the table. 'Mixed up. No matter how hard I try.'

'I'm sorry if this is difficult for you, brother, but I have to ask you about the murders of Brother Cuthbert and Brother Silvanus.'

Osmund nodded.

'Were you close to either of them?'

'No, sir. They were my brothers and I loved them. But they were both obedientiaries. They had been in those high positions for years. I was only a choir monk. I got to know them better once I became cellarer. They were very good, the very best. They knew their duties down to the last detail and never failed. Unlike me.'

'I'm sure they weren't perfect. And certainly not at the start.'

'Perhaps not. I don't know. I wasn't here then. They were a lot older than me.'

'Where were you the night Cuthbert died?'

'Asleep in the monks' dormitory. With the other monks.'

'And Silvanus, only yesterday morning?'

'I was with my lay brothers, giving them their work like you saw earlier. I was in church, with the other monks, before and after. In the cloister, with the other monks, at my devotions. Until I had to leave again for my own work. Inspecting the lay dormitories and the lay brothers' day room. And all the other things I mentioned.'

'Does that mean you leave the cloister whenever your duties require it?'

'I have to. Same as all the other obedientiaries. I have great responsibility now. I have to live up to it.'

'I'm sure you will, brother.' Stanton gave him the most reassuring smile he had.

It wasn't returned.

'Now that I've seen the store,' said Stanton, 'perhaps you could show me around everything you are responsible for?'

Stanton needed to see every nook and cranny of this place. He'd seen a lot of it along with Barling, but they'd yet to properly enter the lay brothers' areas. This would be a useful way in.

Stanton had been expecting the lay brothers' domain to be almost identical to that of the monks. Some of it certainly was.

Their dormitory on the first floor above the store room was the same size, but there the similarity ended. Even though it didn't have the sacrist's chamber, it was much more crowded, with the lay brothers' mattresses pushed in closer to each other. Instead of a covering of warm wool, each one had a worn-looking hide. The rough sacking that doubled as pillows may have held some personal items. There were no individual chests to store the brothers' belongings. A few larger ones were dotted about.

At Stanton's request, he and Osmund had come up to the dormitory via the lay brothers' night stairs. The stairs led up from the church,

137

but from the nave in the west rather than the choir in the east. As the lay brothers prayed separately, they slept separately. *A monastery within a monastery, if you will*: Abbot Philip's words as he had guided him and Barling around on the first morning. Now he saw what that meant. A lesser house.

'Were all the lay brothers asleep in here on the night of Cuthbert's murder?' asked Stanton.

'Yes,' replied Osmund. 'I had to rouse them from sleep as I had been, for there had been no bell. Their door was also locked.'

But Daniel said he'd slept in the stables that night. 'All of them? Are you sure?' He might have caught Daniel in a lie.

'Let me think.' Osmund chewed his lip again. 'Yes. No. No, not all. Daniel slept in the stables, looking after one of the animals. He sought my permission first. I'm sorry, it slipped my mind.'

'No need for apologies, brother.' Saints alive, the man was a ditherer. 'Should we move on?'

The day room below told the same story of a separate life. No grand Chapter House. No special refectory in which to eat.

'The lay brothers don't need as much space as the monks, as they're out working most of the time,' said Osmund. 'So everything happens in this one room.'

A room which held marked, chipped tables and worn-looking stools and little else, save a huge cross hanging from one wall.

Osmund went on. 'I hold the chapter meetings here but only once a week. It's where I lead them in prayer and then hear about and punish any breaking of the sacred Rule. It gets broken often, believe me.'

A room where Daniel, exhausted from his work, like all the others, could be made to sit on the cold floor and eat his dinner, day after day. For a reason like reading a book.

Stanton couldn't reply to Osmund and trust himself to be polite. Instead, he merely nodded and asked to move on.

Chapter Twenty-Four

Barling followed Brother Elias into the sacristy of the late Cuthbert and through the partition to enter the library proper.

'My apologies that there is nowhere to sit, sir,' said Elias.

'That is of no consequence, brother,' replied Barling. 'What is of greater importance is that we can speak privately without being over-heard.' Although the last time he'd stood here and had become aware of a listener, it had been Elias. The man moved quietly even for a monk. Barling had had no warning of the man's arrival in the cloister a few minutes ago, either.

'I shall keep an eye on the passageway, sir.' If the monk had realised that Barling's comment was directed at him, his polite expression gave no indication of it.

'Excellent.' Barling's gaze swept over the room in which they stood. A beautifully constructed one for the storage of books, and, more importantly, a dry one. Tall recessed arches in the stone walls had cupboards set into them, with stout locks keeping them closed. Other locked chests were stacked in the room. It struck him that this room was far more orderly than the books and manuscripts that were stored in the sacristy. 'I do not wish to unduly keep you from your devotion, brother.'

'I am at your command, sir.'

'You shared the space in the sacristy with the late Brother Cuthbert. In fact, you still use it. That is correct?'

'Yes, sir.'

'Was there any conflict between the two of you over how much you took of his room?'

Elias looked a little surprised. 'No, sir.'

'You are sure?' Philip had said that Cuthbert despaired of Elias and his books. 'No arguments, no tension?'

'None, sir. None at all. Cuthbert and I got along quite well.'

'Would you say you were his friend?'

'No. In truth, I don't think he had any special friendships. He was a very quiet man. He was devoted to his duties and his God. And he was very good at those duties. I admired that about him.'

'Then there was no issue of strife or upset between you?'

'Not between us, no. But he was upset about one thing. Very upset.'

'What might that be?'

'A couple of months ago, he lost a chalice.'

'How does one lose a chalice?'

'That was what Cuthbert kept saying. He was frantic. As I say, he was very good at his duties. He kept every item needed for the church in beautiful condition and order.'

'But he mislaid a chalice. The most sacred of objects.'

'Not only sacred. It was a particularly fine silver one, gilded inside. I knew which one he meant for of course I'd seen it so many times on the altar. He searched and searched: the sacristy, the church. Everywhere. I helped him. We went through everything in this room, every cupboard and chest. But we could not find it. The very next day, he confessed at chapter, when Abbot Philip made the usual request for any statements or witnesses of sin. Cuthbert prostrated himself on the ground at once and begged for forgiveness for his transgression. My lord abbot was deeply angry, as one would expect.'

'Could someone else not have stolen it? It would be a sinful crime indeed, but the chalice will have been worth a great deal.'

'Abbot Philip asked that very question. He demanded to know whether there were any witnesses to such a crime or other confessions. Nobody said a word and so Cuthbert was punished.'

'By Abbot Philip?'

'Yes. He gave Cuthbert a beating on the back with a stick and Cuthbert had to fast for a month.'

'A harsh response.'

'Not compared to our old abbot, Ernald. If it had been Ernald, he'd have taken the skin off Cuthbert's bare back with a switch. Ernald despised any and all sin. He believed punishment should be as severe as possible, for it was the only way to stop a sinner falling back.'

The old abbot again. The late Ernald cast a long shadow over this place. 'Was the chalice ever found?'

'No, sir. And Cuthbert's distress at its loss carried on. Carried on until the day he died, in fact.'

'I would now like to turn to that,' said Barling. 'Can you tell me where you were the night he was killed?'

'Asleep in the dormitory, with all the other monks.'

Barling had not really expected a different answer.

'What about yesterday, when Brother Silvanus was murdered?'

'I was in church, for the Offices and Mass. In the cloister for devotion and prayer. Also here in the library.'

'Do you know anybody who would have wished harm to Silvanus?'

'No, sir.'

'Did you?' Barling watched him carefully, as much for his expression as his words.

'No. Nor to any man.'

'In your movements as you described for yesterday, were you ever alone?'

'From time to time, yes. But never for long. I have a store of ink and other writing materials for the scribes. If any of those monks need anything, I have to fetch it for them to minimise disturbance in their work. If a monk asks me for a book, I will go and get it.'

'Like you did for Brother Reginald, the time I was in here with Abbot Philip and my assistant?'

'Yes, he does suffer very much with his joints. It's a sad affliction. He was an outstanding scribe once. Now he cannot even grasp the pen.' He shook his head. 'But I also fetch and carry because I don't want others in here if at all possible. People put things in all the wrong places.' He gave a small frown. 'After the disappearance of the chalice, I don't want any of my books to go missing.'

'Your books?'

Elias looked embarrassed. 'I mean the abbey's books, of course.'

'Of course.'

'I look after them as carefully as if they were mine. It was Abbot Ernald who started the collection when he set up this house three decades ago. Many have been written here. We have copies of the Bible and biblical commentaries. Collections of sermons. Writings of the founder of our order, the great Bernard of Clairvaux. Lives of the saints. Tracts on canon law. Medical texts for Brother William. Instructional texts for the lay brothers.' Elias's face lit up as he described his treasured library.

'It sounds wonderful.' Barling spoke from his heart. Books to him were a singular treasure.

'It is. I could go on. Some of them are the very finest manuscripts. They are worth even more than the chalice. I keep all of those secure in here, locked away.'

'Yet you have many stored next door in the sacristy, where anybody could take them?'

'Most of those are from the lady Juliana's recent donation.' He looked and sounded less enthused now. 'I am checking through them and examining them. Some are – how can I put this? – not the most suitable for a collection in a monastic house.'

'How so?'

'It is often the case with donations. Benefactors know how much a book is worth and think that is all that matters. But we make a careful choice of the books that we need and use. We may for instance receive a romance. Not only is the subject matter not suitable, but such a manuscript is likely to be lavishly illustrated. That is not how the manuscripts of the White Monks should be decorated. They should be without excessive adornment and have the plainest colouring.'

'Then what will you do with the unsuitable donations?'

'As I said, they can be worth a great deal, so we shall sell them. It means that the donation can be gratefully received and not turned down, which might upset a benefactor.'

'I see.' Barling thought that perhaps the murder of two monks might be far more likely to upset a benefactor. 'I will leave you to your sorting, Elias. You have much to do.'

'Thank you, sir.'

Barling went to the door. Then paused. 'One more thing.'

'Yes, sir?'

'Have you been teaching Daniel the lay brother to read?'

A shocked flush swept across the monk's face. He swallowed hard. 'Yes, sir.'

'Perhaps you need to consider a confession at chapter, Brother Elias. Always wise to unburden your conscience.'

With that, Barling left. He'd given Elias plenty to think about.

Chapter Twenty-Five

Barling made his way into the guesthouse, grateful for its warmth and shelter. The hail had stopped and it was snowing now, and a light powdery covering lay across the ground. The air felt colder than ever. The dawn would still be at least an hour off and he'd had to take care on ice that had formed underfoot in several places.

He went inside and made his way to his room. As he did so, he saw Daniel with a pail of hot water outside Juliana's chambers. The lay brother gave a polite knock.

'Your water, my lady,' he said, putting the pail down and turning to leave.

'Daniel?' said Barling.

The man paused. 'Yes, sir?'

'Has Stanton returned yet?'

'No, sir. I saw him with Brother Osmund not long ago. They were going into the forge.'

Barling nodded, more to himself than to acknowledge Daniel. Stanton would take as much time as he needed to take. Hopefully, he would not be too long. 'I shall require hot water for my room as well, Daniel. Please bring it as soon as possible.'

'Yes, sir.'

Barling entered his room and started to update his records on his latest enquiries. He could hardly get his hands to work, such was the cold gripping them. He rubbed them hard together to warm them. As he did so, he thought of Reginald's gnarled hands. No amount of rubbing would restore those to use of the pen. It must indeed be a painful loss for him.

A knock came from the door.

'Sir?'

Daniel.

'Come in,' said Barling.

As the brother did so, bearing the welcome sight of a large steaming pail of water and clean linen towels, Stanton entered the room behind him.

'God above.' Stanton's teeth chattered. 'Think it's colder than ever out there.'

Daniel plunked the pail down on the floor and left the linen next to the washing bowls. 'Do you need anything else, sir?' he asked Barling.

'No, thank you.'

'Sir.' He left, Stanton closing the door behind him after checking that the lay brother had gone about his business.

'Did your early rising pay off, Stanton?' Barling used a jug to pour some hot water into one of the bowls.

'It did.' Stanton gave him a displeased look. 'Although I'm sure that I could have got the same answers after a few more hours in bed.'

'You got answers, and that is the main thing.' Barling dipped his hands in the bowl, revelling in the warmth. 'And how was the quality of those answers? Was Brother Osmund forthcoming?'

'He was.' Stanton took another bowl and did the same as Barling with the water. 'My, that's good.' He splashed some on his face too. 'I'm not sure that his answers helped much, though. As we had already observed in chapter, the man's not really up to the task of cellarer. I

145

think Abbot Philip was right when he said to you he'd made a mistake in appointing Osmund to the position.'

'What of potential problems with Daniel?' Barling was careful to keep his voice low as he dried his hands on a piece of fresh linen.

'To be honest, I think most of the lay brothers have resentments against Osmund and against the rest of the monks too.' Stanton scrubbed his face and hands dry. 'And if they don't, they should.' He described the lesser circumstances in which the lay brothers lived and worked, compared to the monks.

Barling could tell such treatment of the lay brothers annoyed Stanton a great deal, which concerned him. One should never get caught up in personal opinions when one was in pursuit of the truth, he thought as he placed his used linen to one side. It clouded one's judgement.

Stanton threw his own bunched-up cloth on top of Barling's neatly folded one. 'As I say, I'm not sure it has got us very far, other than identifying a whole number of people who have bad feelings towards the monks.'

'But the lay brothers tend not to be alone or unsupervised,' said Barling. 'No matter how resentful they are, it is unlikely they would have had the chance to act on it. Except for Daniel, of course.'

'Perhaps,' replied Stanton. 'Did you get anything of use from Elias?'

'That this abbey has a magnificent library, though sadly that is not the purpose of my visit here. But, of more relevance, I had it confirmed that Elias has taught Daniel to read. So that was certainly one truthful thing the lay brother said to you, Stanton.'

Stanton gave a firm nod. 'See? I said I thought he was truthful.'

'As for the murders of Cuthbert and Silvanus, Elias also claims he knows nothing about them. When I asked him about tension between him and Cuthbert, he said that it did not exist. There were a few other things that stood out.' He outlined them briefly to Stanton. Juliana's many unsuitable donated books. The missing chalice and Cuthbert's punishment.

'I didn't know the sacrist,' said Stanton, 'but I can't help feeling sorry for him. Despite being surrounded by people here all the time, he seems to have led a lonely life.'

Feelings again, noted Barling. 'Not necessarily,' he replied. 'He may well have been an individual for whom his own company was the best company. I share such a fondness—'

A knock came at the door. 'Excuse me, sirs.' Daniel's voice.

Barling got up and opened the door. 'Yes, what is it?'

'I'm sorry to disturb you, sirs. But my lady has not taken her hot water in. She's not answering her door, neither. What should I do?'

Barling exchanged a look with Stanton.

'We'd better go and check,' said Stanton. 'She was very upset yesterday.'

'Agreed.' Barling led the way, stopping outside her closed door with Stanton and Daniel. He rapped on it loudly with his knuckles. 'My lady, it is me, Aelred Barling. Are you unwell?'

Silence.

He knocked again. 'Lady Kersley?'

Still nothing.

He looked at Stanton.

'Open it,' said Stanton.

'If it is locked, I shall need help from both of you.' Barling tried the handle. It was not.

The door swung open on a silent, empty room.

Lady Kersley was gone.

Chapter Twenty-Six

Stanton made his way along the claustral walk, hurrying towards Philip's carrel. The monks were deeply engrossed in their prayer. Hard to believe that they'd been doing that since the early hours of the morning. He knew he'd be face down in a prayer book. Snoring.

He reached the abbot's carrel. He didn't want to risk startling the man, who read in a steady hum, bent on his knees and with his cowl up against the cold. He gave a quiet respectful knock on the outside.

Philip looked around and his dark brows drew into a concerned frown when he saw Stanton.

'My lord,' whispered Stanton, 'Barling needs to speak to you urgently. He's in the warming room with Daniel.'

Philip nodded and got to his feet at once.

Stanton entered the warming room behind the abbot and shut the door. The air in here was the warmest he'd felt since he'd arrived at the abbey. He needed to find some more reasons for being in here.

'You needed to see me, Barling?' said Philip. 'What is it? Has something happened?'

'I am afraid that the lady Juliana has gone missing.'

'Missing? What do you mean?'

'Daniel here tried to rouse her this morning and got no response,' said Barling. 'He asked for my help. I also failed to get a response. I entered her room in case something untoward had befallen her. But her room was empty.'

Philip let out a long breath of relief. 'Barling, with all due respect, I fear you are being caught up in the panic of many here. She will have gone riding. She does that in the morning.'

Barling looked at Daniel. 'I said the same to you, did I not?'

'Yes, sir.'

'Then tell your abbot what you told me, boy.'

'It's too early for my lady to be out, my lord abbot.' Daniel kept his gaze well down. No insolent looks for his abbot. 'And she never goes out in the morning before she has washed. Brother Silvanus warned me about being late with the water for her.'

'I am most concerned, Philip,' said Barling. 'We need to find her.'

'We can help with the search, my lord abbot,' added Stanton. 'I'm quick on a horse.'

'One moment.' Philip held up a hand. 'Daniel, please return to the guesthouse. At once. You need to be available for the lady Juliana's return. At once, I say. Do you hear me?'

'Yes, my lord abbot.' Daniel went without a backward glance.

Stanton saw Barling's look. It wasn't a happy one.

Once the door was shut, Philip spoke again, lowering his voice still further. 'Barling, thank you for your concerns about the lady Juliana. But the likelihood is that she has gone for a walk or is in a private Mass with one of the monk priests. Were I to start a huge fuss in tracking her down, what would that say? It would suggest that I, abbot of this abbey, believe that some harm has perhaps come to one of our most generous benefactors. That's what. What would she think of us once she has been safely located?'

'Philip,' began Barling.

'I'll tell you what she would think,' said the abbot with a frown. 'She would think that this abbey is no longer a place of order and prayer but a place of utter misrule. Presided over by me. She would take her generous gifts and move them elsewhere and we would never again be the beneficiaries of her generosity. I will ask Maurice to discreetly locate her. He knows her of old and she him. I'm sure he'd be able to carry this out with the necessary tact.'

Stanton wasn't sure about the tact. Maurice could have sudden flares of real temper.

The deepest of the monastery's bells sounded.

'Now, if you'll excuse me,' said Philip, 'I need to send Maurice to his task before I begin Lauds.' He walked out, his long strides showing his ire.

Stanton looked at Barling. The clerk wore the irritated look that he always did when he was thwarted, abbot or no abbot. 'He's probably right, Barling. At least, I hope he is.'

'I sincerely hope so too. Daniel is the one who raised concerns that the lady Juliana was missing. Daniel is also the one who found the body of Silvanus. And yet Philip allows me no opportunity to put my case to him. He shows me his back and walks away.'

Stanton said nothing.

'Nevertheless, it is his abbey. Things are tense enough here as it is. I do not wish to add to his troubles.' Barling gave a sharp sigh. 'But Philip has also disrupted my plan for today. I was going to speak to Maurice. Now he, just like Reginald, is unavailable. I shall accompany you to the gatehouse, Stanton, where Brother Lambert is no doubt ensconced. At least our time will not be utterly wasted.'

Stanton thought it probably would. And he'd far rather stay in the warm. Not that he was about to say so to the prickly Barling.

Chapter Twenty-Seven

'Brother Lambert!' Barling knocked hard on the door of the gatehouse, the bitter wind that carried powdery flakes of snow whipping into his face. 'Show yourself, please.'

The main gate stood open, presumably to allow the carts of the lay brothers to pass in and out quickly at this busy time of day. He could see one heading off on the road now, four bearded brothers in it. The gate was otherwise deserted. No beggars crowded around it as they had the other morning.

The door opened a crack and Lambert's scarlet, fleshy face appeared. 'What do you want? The gate is open.'

Barling could smell the ale on him, despite the clean, cold wind. 'Let me in, brother. My assistant and I wish to speak to you.'

'Perhaps later, sir. I am not well.' The monk went to close the door again.

But Stanton shoved his foot in the crack. 'Now, brother.'

Lambert took a stagger back and Stanton forced the door wide on to Lambert's cosy little lair. The stink of ale and stale flesh came heavy on the air.

A sleepy female voice. 'What's happening, Lambert?'

For a moment, Barling thought it must be the lady Juliana. But no, the voice was far too young. And it was not Juliana that looked back at him.

A wooden partition that reached halfway to the ceiling cut off about a third of the room. Peering over the top was the face of a tousle-haired young woman, her shift slipping from her naked shoulders. She met Barling's eye and her face stiffened in surprise. Then she ducked out of sight with a stifled oath.

'Agatha?' Stanton's question was a mixture of recognition and amusement.

Agatha. Barling frowned to himself. The impertinent beggar girl who had accosted Stanton so boldly on the ride out to Gottburn. 'Come out, girl,' ordered Barling. 'At once.'

'Nothing is happening.' Lambert made his ridiculous declaration as he swayed on his feet.

Barling caught Stanton looking away to hide a smile and his irritation grew even further. None of this was a laughing matter.

Scuffling noises told of Agatha's haste in getting dressed. 'I'm very sorry, sirs, I was simply sheltering here from the cold.'

'I should think so. Dreadful weather.' Lambert nodded to Barling and Stanton as if somehow that would lend weight to his nonsense. 'Are you warmed up now, girl?' Lambert turned to speak and almost lost his footing. Only a grab at the partition saved him. He let go a stream of curses.

'This is intolerable,' said Barling in a low voice to Stanton. 'You take the girl into that room at the back. See if you can get any useful information from her.' He fixed his assistant with his best glare. 'And do not allow yourself to become side-tracked in any way. Do I make myself clear?'

'As always,' replied Stanton, his features perfectly solemn.

Agatha stepped from behind the partition, not as modestly clad as Barling would have liked. But at least not as shamelessly unclothed as she had been a few minutes ago.

'Agatha, I need you to come with me,' said Stanton.

'I'd be happy to, good sir,' she said with a dimpled smile.

He did not react in kind, simply held a hand out for her to go into the next room.

Good.

The door shut, leaving Barling alone with a Lambert who was looking just as confused and unsteady as previously, but who now also appeared very annoyed too.

'Where's she gone?' asked the monk.

Barling ignored his question. 'Brother Lambert, as you know I am here on the business of the King. That business concerns the murder of brothers Cuthbert and Silvanus. I wish to ask you about them.'

'Me?' The man gaped at him, a new wave of stale ale coming from his slack lips. 'What would I know about them?'

'Where were you on the night of the eve of Christmas, the night Cuthbert was murdered?'

Lambert screwed up his face as if Barling had asked him a challenging question. 'Round and about, I would say.'

'Round and about?'

The monk gave an extravagant nod. 'Definitely.'

'Yesterday morning?' The morning when Barling had seen this drunkard of a monk give out bread to the beggars while shouting insults at them.

'I'd say the same.'

'Round. And about?'

'Yes, that's it.' Lambert gave a long, low belch.

Barling would keep trying. And he hoped Stanton was getting a little more sense out of his interviewee.

153

Brother Osmund sat at his table in the store room and went through the same pile of written accounts for what he guessed was the fourth time. The shortening candle told him how long he'd spent at it. Hours, though he wished he'd had longer. He'd had to waste so much time with the King's man.

The notes that he had made about the latest sacks of wool sent to York must be here somewhere. They must be and yet he couldn't find them.

He'd been fretting about their loss for the last two days. He remembered writing them so clearly, remembered where he'd left them.

Then they were gone, and he'd not found them yet.

At Vigils, he'd prayed so hard that he might find them. Begged God that he would not have to face Abbot Philip with such a loss. Again.

Philip had been kind at first when he'd made him, Osmund, cellarer. Osmund had hardly been able to believe his own appointment. He knew that others had shared that disbelief, especially the older ones.

It hadn't been long before their disbelief had turned to open scorn. His lord abbot's kindness had changed to a testy patience. Then irritation. Then, a few times, to outright anger.

Before his appointment, Osmund had had no idea how important the cellarer was to the abbey. When he'd joined as a novice, he'd thought, somehow, that the abbey just . . . was. That all he needed to do was read and pray and sing to the glory of God.

And he did. And he loved it.

He wasn't the best at some of it, especially the reading. Brother Maurice, trying as his novice master to instruct him yet again in a passage of the Bible, would shake his head.

Oh, Osmund, Osmund. You, I fear, will be one of those novices that acquires years far sooner than understanding.

Osmund hadn't quite understood what Maurice had meant. Now he did. Maurice thought, Abbot Philip thought, everyone thought, that he was slow-witted. Even some of the lay brothers did. He could tell it from their pitying looks whenever he had to address them or allocate their work.

But he wasn't slow-witted. He was perfectly aware that there were things he was good at, such as singing. He knew he had the best voice in choir. 'That of an angel,' Maurice had said. And other things he'd excelled at before he came here. Like playing the fiddle.

He was equally aware that there were things for which he had no talent, like this pile of accounts and records before him. So many covered in numbers that swam before his eyes. Records that he tried and tried and tried to keep in order, but never could.

An unexpected pulse of temper went through him.

'By Saint Peter of Rome! Where is it?' He flung the documents he held across the table.

'Brother?'

He froze at the deep voice behind him.

'Are you all right?'

Osmund turned to see Daniel two steps behind, the tall lay brother looming over him as he sat here at his desk.

'Yes, I am fine, Daniel.' He fought to compose himself. 'What is it? I am very busy.' He heard the sharpness in his tone and hated himself for it. He was speaking to the lay brother exactly as Abbot Philip spoke to him.

'There's a problem with the pipes, brother.'

'Pipes? What pipes?' Oh, no. If Osmund was bad at numbers, the workings of the monastery's water were an even bigger mystery to him. But he oversaw the lay brothers now and the lay brothers oversaw the pipes.

'The guesthouse, brother,' said Daniel. 'I've not looked properly yet. But I think there's some sort of blockage.'

'The guesthouse? Then can't you ask Silvanus to—' The words were out of Osmund's mouth before he could stop them. May God strike him down. He'd forgotten in his anxiety over his lost account.

Daniel didn't answer. Gave him the look that told him his foolish, unforgivable remark would be a huge joke among every one of the lay brothers within a couple of hours.

'Then show me.' Osmund got to his feet, aware that his face was hot with his embarrassment. 'And quickly, as I have much work to do.'

He followed Daniel outside into the bitter cold of the bleak morning, with snow coming down fast and hard.

Only the heavy clump of Daniel's boots on the snow as the brother walked beside him broke the muffled silence.

As they approached the guesthouse, Daniel pointed to the latrine block. 'I reckon the problem could be under there. The flow's not good inside. Hardly anything. If not there, we can try further upstream.'

Osmund's spirits sank even further as they walked up to the tunnel that carried the spoil away and the whiff of that waste met him. He had no idea what to say or do. All he could think of was his missing papers.

'You need to take a look, I think, brother.' Daniel's bearded face was an impassive mask.

Osmund knew full well he needed to do so. He knew with even greater certainty that it would be of no use whatsoever. And he knew Daniel knew it as well. He took a last gulp of fresh air and squatted down before the large pipe, aware that his shoulder was about the height of Daniel's knee.

'Can you see anything, brother?' rumbled the deep voice from above him.

Osmund didn't expect to. But he could, Jesu Christus, he could. The world seemed to lose air and he was losing sight, losing reason.

For bobbing in the pool of spoil were not twigs. Nor grass. Nor branches.

But the unmistakable form of a human corpse.

And it was one he recognised. Immediately.

Chapter Twenty-Eight

Stanton shut the door on Barling and the drunken Lambert and turned to Agatha.

All things considered, he'd definitely been given the more appealing task.

Her thick chestnut hair fell around her shoulders and though she'd laced her shift, her deft fingers tweaked at it to loosen it as she stood before him.

By all that was holy, it was good to see a woman's flesh again. He'd had his fill of living among monks and brothers.

'Well, Stanton. Or, if you'd prefer, I can call you Hugo.' Her dark grey eyes met his as her mouth curved in a knowing smile. 'Who would have thought that you and I would end up alone so soon?'

Much as he'd have liked to, he wouldn't let her divert him from his task. Barling would have his head if he did. 'Agatha, we're alone for me to question you. No other reason.'

'That's a shame.' She took a step towards him and placed one of her hands on his chest. 'Hugo.'

He caught the scent of her: warm and sweet and inviting. 'It is,' he replied, willing himself to ignore the surge of his own blood. He slid a hand over hers, as much to feel her smooth skin as to break her touch.

'But we can't do anything.' He made his tone as firm as he could. 'Not now.'

'Why?' She looked confused and hurt, still hadn't stepped back, grasped his hand tightly so he couldn't break away. 'Don't you like me?' Her lips parted. 'I like you.'

Saints alive, he wasn't made of stone. A kiss, that was all, it wouldn't hurt. He went to lower his mouth to hers. And then he heard it.

A tiny clink.

His free hand shot to hers, closed around her small fist that held his purse. 'Give it back, girl.'

'Take it, then.' She shoved it at him with a filthy oath and stepped back from him, pulling her clothing closed. Her small, round face, which had been filled with lust only a moment ago, could now be that of an angry cat.

It made her even more desirable, though he knew she'd scratch his eyes out if he went near her. To his regret, his purse had been her prize, not him. And he'd not only nearly fallen for her tricks, he'd wasted valuable time. 'So if you've finished trying to steal from me, I need to ask you some questions. Aelred Barling, the man in the next room, and I are—'

'The King's men. I know. I know all about why you're here.'

'How?'

'Gossip at the gate. I hear everything there.'

'Then as you know it,' said Stanton, 'you'll know the seriousness of our business. But why are you here?'

'I come for the charity.'

'Agatha, I'm not a fool.'

She arched her brows at him as if she disagreed.

Stanton put his hand to his purse to make sure he still had it.

'I've been here since yesterday,' said Agatha. 'And it's true about the charity. Well, nearly true. Brother Lambert can be very generous. He even lets me sleep here in the warm with plenty of bread when the weather gets bad, so I don't have to make the journey home. I can be generous too.' She raised her chin to meet his gaze. 'If I am allowed.'

Stanton ignored the call of his own flesh, trying to remember what the priest Theobald had said about snow and the valley. 'The weather was very bad around Christmas time, wasn't it? Very deep snow, I've heard. Did you stay here then?'

'You mean on the night that Brother Cuthbert was murdered?'

Her brazenness was remarkable. 'The very one.'

'Yes, I was. It was a special favour by Lambert as it was Christmas time.'

'Then you didn't go back to the village of Gottburn?' Theobald had said that all his parishioners were accounted for.

'Why would I go there?'

'Don't you live there?'

'Me? No. My older brother and I have a small cottage a few miles outside it. There's only him and me. Our parents are dead, our other brothers and sisters too.' A brief sadness clouded her face. 'We never go in the village, we're not welcome there. My brother drinks more than Lambert. Then he gets into fights and brawls. The folk of Gottburn don't let him come anywhere near, haven't done for a few months. They don't like me, neither. Especially the women. Jealous mares, the lot of them.'

Stanton could well understand why Agatha might raise hackles, but it still seemed harsh for a young girl to be completely shunned like that. But importantly for his investigation, it would appear that Theobald hadn't allowed for two of his parishioners in his account because he never saw them in his church. 'Yours must be a hard life,' he said gently.

She shrugged. 'Like I say, I get looked after here.'

'Did you know Brother Cuthbert?'

'I might have seen his face, when he'd come in to look after the gatehouse for a little while. A few of the monks do, so that Lambert can go to their meetings and such like. But I don't know who they are.'

'What about Silvanus?'

'That vicious guestmaster?' She shuddered. 'No. He was horrible to me, to all the beggars, even when people came on feast days. I think he thought we made the entrance look untidy.' She smirked. 'Well, he can't complain any more, can he?'

'That's certainly true.' Stanton looked at her hands, trying to guess if they'd have the strength to wield a pitchfork. She'd certainly be able to plunge a skewer into a man's throat. Or pour wood tar in his mouth once he was dead. 'Did Lambert say anything about—'

A tremendous banging on the door interrupted him. A male voice came from outside, raised in panic.

'Lambert, are you in there? Open up, in the name of God. Lambert? Anyone? Answer!'

Stanton opened the door of the inner room just as Barling answered the outer door.

Osmund the cellarer stood there, his eyes wild with terror.

'What is it, brother?' demanded Barling.

'It's the lady Juliana, sir,' said Osmund. 'Come quickly, I beg you.'

Chapter Twenty-Nine

The lady Juliana was dead. Drowned, in fact. A bad enough death to perish in water, thought Stanton, but this was different, and far worse.

'Can you see her, Stanton?' Barling was peering into the dark tunnel that carried the waste from the latrine block in the guesthouse.

'Yes.' Stanton crouched down to get a better view. There wasn't much daylight this morning, with the snow coming down more heavily and even less light in the shadow of the pipe. His stomach turned over. Not only at the foul stench. But at the curve of a back, a hip in a robe of red and blue. 'Brother Osmund is right. It's her.' He straightened up again.

A disgusted gasp came from Agatha, who'd followed them as they'd hurried over here.

'How . . . How can this be?' puffed Lambert, who'd done the same, breathless from his haste.

'Oh, dear God, sir.' Osmund was deathly pale. 'Daniel and I thought so too. But I prayed it wasn't so. Oh, dear God. How could such a terrible accident have happened?'

Accident? Stanton blinked hard. The monk really didn't have the sharpest mind. At all.

'It is no accident, brother,' came Barling's clipped response.

'But . . . But,' said Osmund, 'could my lady not have fallen in?'

'It is not possible to fall into a cramped tunnel,' said Barling. 'Had my lady fallen in the water outside of the tunnel, she would not have been washed into it.'

Osmund still looked unsure.

'Water doesn't flow upstream, brother,' added Stanton.

Osmund's hand went to his mouth. 'Oh, dear God.'

The clerk's shrewd glance went from Osmund to the bearded lay brother. 'It was you who found the body?'

Barling had left out the word 'again'. But it hung in the air like the smell from the latrine.

The glower on Daniel's face told Stanton the lay brother had picked up on Barling's barb only too well. 'Brother Osmund and I found her together, sir.'

'Is this true, Osmund?' asked Barling.

'Yes, it is. Daniel came to me and told me that there was a problem with the water flow from the guesthouse. He'd noticed it was slowed right down.'

'When I was cleaning up, sir.'

'And it's not a good sign if the water slows, is it, Daniel?' said Osmund.

It didn't surprise Stanton that Osmund had to ask Daniel about this. It seemed the monk had very little sense of any kind between his ears.

'Lots of pipes here, sir,' said Daniel to Barling. 'They run through the whole monastery. Our river never lets us down. It brings us our fresh water and carries the spoil away. If the flow slows or stops, it means we have a broken pipe or a blockage. We have to find it. Quickly. So we can fix it, like.'

'And we found the cause of the problem.' Osmund glanced over at the pipe and away again at once.

'I see.' Barling looked at Stanton. 'We will need to get my lady's body out.'

Stanton nodded. They did, though it would be a horrific undertaking. 'Have you got any sticks or poles, Daniel?'

'Yes, sir.' Daniel hurried off.

'Brother Osmund,' said Barling, 'while we are occupied, can you please fetch the abbot?'

'He will be in chapter, sir. With all the other monks.'

'Then get him out of chapter, brother.' The clerk's voice rose enough to send Osmund running off.

Daniel returned, carrying a couple of stout sticks and a long-handled baling hook.

'Better you let me and Daniel do this, Barling,' said Stanton. The slightly built, clumsy clerk would be no help.

Barling nodded and stepped out of the way as Lambert immediately began to gabble at him a jumble of questions and confused remarks. Barling silenced him with a hand.

An unusually quiet Agatha simply stared.

Stanton set about his task with Daniel. The lay brother wielded the baling hook with great accuracy, despite the awkward angle, and with deft skill and strength, while Stanton used one of the poles to help guide him.

As they hauled the filthy, soaked body of Juliana on to the muddy ground on to which snow was steadily settling, the abbot arrived with Maurice and Osmund.

'By Saint Peter of Rome.' The abbot gave an appalled look at the sight before him, Maurice uttering his own shock. Lambert launched into an account of what had happened, every one of them talking over the others.

Barling paid them no heed, but came over to squat next to the body, motioning for Stanton to do the same. 'You can step away now, Daniel.' Barling lowered his voice to a murmur to speak to Stanton.

'You can see she is dressed in her linens. No dress, though she wears her robe. No veil.'

Barling continued to move his gaze over every inch of Juliana.

Stanton kept his fixed on the blues and reds of her robe. He couldn't look into her face. He knew they had to do this but he hated it to the depths of his soul.

'And what have we here?' Barling picked up a few snow-covered dead leaves. He dabbed gently at Juliana's stained forehead, revealing a huge bruise on her right temple.

'Barling,' called Abbot Philip, 'I need to see you in my hall. At once.'

The clerk met Stanton's eye. 'I have seen enough,' said Barling.

They both got to their feet.

Philip carried on issuing orders as he started to walk away. 'Maurice, make the necessary arrangements to have the lady Juliana taken from here. Daniel can help you.'

As Stanton set off behind the quick steps of the abbot, Barling with him, he turned to see an angry-looking Maurice speaking to Agatha and Lambert and pointing at the gatehouse.

Osmund just stood there as the snow continued to fall. He looked more lost than ever.

Chapter Thirty

Barling sat in his usual place at the bare table in the abbot's hall, Stanton opposite him. Though they were back inside, the wind outside had risen, sending the whistle and moan of draughts through the building.

Philip did not sit. Instead, he paced. 'The lady Juliana's head was struck, you say?'

'That is correct,' replied Barling. 'I would have hoped hard enough to have caused her immediate death.'

Philip paused, aghast. 'Why would you hope for such an appalling act to be carried out upon her?'

'For it would mean that she was dead when she was submerged in the sewer. Otherwise . . .' He did not need to finish his sentence.

Philip's pale face went even paler and he began to pace again. 'Who would carry out such an assault, Barling, on a defenceless woman?'

'I do not know, Philip.'

Stanton did not look at the abbot but shook his head wordlessly too.

Barling knew how he felt. The violence and degradation inflicted upon Lady Kersley was sickening.

'But why?' Philip paced on. 'I cannot believe this has happened. Cannot. The lady Juliana was a cherished friend of this monastery for the last ten years. This abbey was her refuge, her comfort after the loss of her husband. For her to have met her end with such horror? Here?'

'I agree, Philip,' said Barling. 'It makes no sense.'

'This horror that has been visited on Lady Kersley,' said the abbot, 'would be shocking enough had it been a unique event. But it is not the only one. It is yet another murder. The third. Two of them a day apart! In a house of God. The house over which I preside.' He flung himself into his chair and ground at his face with his palms. 'Such evil. It makes no sense. None.'

'It will make sense, Philip,' said Barling. 'We will get to the answers.'

Stanton cast him a dubious look.

Barling was aware of how inadequate his own response had sounded. With this latest discovery, inadequate was indeed how he felt.

'As you keep telling me, Barling,' said Philip. 'Yet you have not got to the answers. Or any answer! And the deaths are not stopping, are they? Are they?' An edge came to his voice, an edge that told Barling the man was close to panic.

'I am fully aware of that, Philip.'

The abbot dropped his hands. 'I am sorry, Barling. I do not mean to rail at you. But I think the time has come for us to seek more help. When I asked for you, it was only Cuthbert's death.' He shook his head. '"Only"? What insult have I just uttered to my sacrist's memory?'

'Not an insult at all,' replied Barling. 'What you mean is that since we arrived to assist you, there have been two more murders. And as matters have worsened, you believe extra assistance is needed.'

'It is.' Philip cast him a grateful glance.

'I have no quarrel with that view,' said Barling. 'And I am sure that my assistant holds it also.'

'I do,' said Stanton.

'Then we are all agreed,' said Philip. 'We need help and we need it quickly.' He looked at Stanton. 'You're a fast rider, aren't you? A skilled messenger?'

'Yes, my lord abbot.'

'Barling,' said Philip, 'we shall prepare letters to other holy houses—'
A knock at the door interrupted him.

He raised his voice. 'Who is it?'

'It is Elias, my lord abbot. May I speak to you?'

'Come back later. I am occupied.' He looked to Barling again. 'As
I was saying—'

Another knock and the door opened without Elias waiting for a
response. 'My lord abbot, I really need to speak to you.'

'Elias.' Philip's brows drew together. 'I do not know why you would
choose to behave in such—'

Another interruption from Elias. 'It's about the murders, my lord
abbot.'

Philip's look shifted to one of surprise, the same look shared
between Stanton and Barling.

Barling nodded at the abbot.

'Then come in, Elias,' said Philip.

The red-haired library monk entered the room and Barling saw that
he carried a finely bound book with him.

'I am very sorry to have had to interrupt you, my lord,' said Elias.
'But I think I have found a link between the murders that have taken
place here. Although it might seem a strange one. The link is this book.'
He held it up. '*The Vision of Tundale.*'

'A book?' Philip stared at him. 'Have you lost your reason, Elias?'

Barling doubted that was the case. Elias seemed to him a man of
the utmost seriousness and quite sane. 'We should hear him out, Philip.
At the moment, we are lost.'

'If you must.' Philip waved Elias over. 'Though I wait to be
convinced.'

Elias made his way over with his usual quiet steps. He placed the
large book on the table and remained standing. 'I realise that you know
Tundale's story well, my lord abbot.'

'Of course I do,' said Philip. 'It is one much favoured by our order.'

'Have you heard of Tundale's story, sirs?' asked Elias of Barling and Stanton.

'I have heard of it,' replied Barling. 'But only in its broadest outline.'

Stanton shook his head. 'Never.'

Elias looked at Philip. 'My lord abbot. If I may?'

'Go on,' said Philip. 'But be quick. Do you hear me?'

Chapter Thirty-One

Barling listened intently as Elias began.

'In the *Vision*, Tundale is a knight,' the monk said. 'A man who is guilty of many sins but who has never repented. He is having dinner with another man, whom he has wronged. Suddenly, Tundale is struck by the most violent fit. He dies and finds himself in a place of terrifying darkness. But then Tundale's guardian angel appears. The angel reminds the knight that he has spent his life ignoring his angel's guidance. Tundale admits this and confesses his guilt for all his sins. Then Tundale's journey begins. The angel brings him down into the darkness, showing him the torments and punishments that await every kind of sinner. Down and down, until he reaches the very depths of hell, where he witnesses the arrival of the Prince of Darkness himself: Satan.'

The abbot took up the story. 'But for those who reject sin, there is hope, just as the angel brings to Tundale.'

Elias nodded. 'The angel leads the knight back up from the depths where sinners are lost, showing him the rewards of the virtuous. Tundale is rewarded for confessing his guilt. The angel returns his soul to his body. The knight awakens, to the astonishment of those who witness this miracle. Tundale gives all of his wealth away. He spends the rest of his life devoted to God, telling of his journey and preaching the need to repent.'

'A fascinating tale,' said Barling, 'and no doubt most suitable for devotional reading.'

'It is,' said Philip, 'and it was one of Abbot Ernald's favourite texts. He based many of his sermons on it. The copy that Elias has there was scribed by Reginald at Ernald's special request.'

'But,' said Barling, 'how does it have any bearing on the murders here in the abbey?'

'Let me show you.' Elias opened up the book. Its script was expertly and beautifully composed: Reginald had been most talented when his hands had the suppleness and dexterity of youth. Elias turned to a section near the beginning. 'This passage talks about the punishment of sinners over hot coals, where they are burned so badly that their flesh becomes as molten as wax in a pan.'

Barling met an equally stunned Stanton's look. What Elias had just said had a terrible, terrifying resonance.

Elias turned to another section. 'This, the next passage: the sinners are tormented by evil fiends with pitchforks in their hands. Glowing skewers too. And the sinners are on a great mountain that stinks of brimstone . . .' He took in a breath. 'And pitch.'

Wood tar. Barling saw Stanton's lips form the words even as he thought them.

Elias went on. 'The third passage has the sinner in—'

The abbot finished his sentence for him. 'A stinking pit.' He stared at the page, his dark eyes glazed, paler than ever.

'Links, then, to the murders of Brothers Cuthbert and Silvanus and of the lady Juliana,' said Elias.

'It would certainly seem that there are links,' said Barling.

'I'll say,' said Stanton, eyes wide.

'But,' added Barling, 'it is easy to see links when often there are in reality none. A fearful mind will see the pattern of tree branches in the moonlight and believe them to be the claws of a monster. But they are no such thing. Given the recent events here, this is indeed a fearful place.'

A bit of colour came back to Philip's face. 'A good point, Barling.'

'It is, sir,' said Elias. 'But I fear there are other links to the murders.'

'More weapons that were used?' asked Stanton.

'No,' said Elias. 'The sins that were being punished. The first, with the fire and melting flesh, was the punishment of murderers.'

'Then it does not fit,' said Philip. 'In the slightest. Cuthbert was no murderer.'

'But, my lord abbot,' said Elias, 'the second sinners are those who utter falsehoods, beguile others, cheat them of their wealth.'

Barling took in the words. The man could be describing the late Silvanus.

'And the third group of sinners, those in the stinking pit, are the proud,' said Elias.

A heavy silence greeted his words, broken only by the moan of the wind outside and the crackle of the fire in the grate.

The proud. Juliana, with her insistence that she be buried with the monks. Her disgust at the idea of being laid to rest with common people, her delight at being with men of the court.

The abbot spoke first. 'What do you think, Barling?'

'I think that we should discuss this in private.'

'Of course.' Philip looked at Elias. 'Thank you. You may go.'

'Yes, my lord abbot.' A disappointed-looking Elias went to pick up the book.

'May I ask that you leave that behind?' asked Barling. 'I would like to read it.'

'Yes, sir.' Elias gave a bow. 'Sirs. My lord abbot.' He left at once, closing the door softly behind him.

'I ask again, Barling, what do you think?' said Philip.

'I am making the assumption that Elias is of sound mind. He certainly seemed so when I spoke to him earlier.'

'He is,' replied Philip. 'And the similarities he describes with the *Vision* worry me deeply. This book does indeed have a great importance for our house, but, like I said, Cuthbert was no murderer. And as you said so wisely, Barling, we do not want to start a panic by making links where there are none. What I – what we – need is more help. Help from other houses in the order to find out who is doing this, and we need it as soon as possible. Monks may speak more freely to other monks. Should we start the letters while Stanton packs and gets his horse ready?'

'We should.'

Stanton got to his feet. 'The moment they're done, I'll be off.'

Barling took the writing materials that Philip passed to him and thanked God for the skilled horsemanship of Hugo Stanton.

Chapter Thirty-Two

Barling stood in the courtyard in front of the stables as a heavily cloaked Stanton prepared to mount up. The snow continued to fall: relentless, unceasing. While they'd been in the abbot's hall, the whole world had turned white.

The horse that Stanton had readied wore a trapper as protection against the weather but bowed its head beneath the onslaught.

'Hard to believe the middle of the day isn't long passed.' Stanton squinted up at the sky. 'It feels more like evening.' He looked at Barling, flakes settling on his hat and lashes. 'Mind you, we've already been awake for twelve hours. Maybe that's why.'

'You have the letters?' asked Barling.

'Safe in here.' Stanton patted his satchel with a thick-gloved hand.

'I think the snow is getting heavier. Much heavier.' Barling knew he sounded somewhat fretful but he could not help it. He hated sending Stanton out to travel in such weather.

'I know.' Stanton grinned at him. 'But I've gone through worse. Well, nearly worse.' He took a quick look around to make sure they couldn't be overheard. 'Did you get anything of use earlier from Lambert, by the way, before hearing about the lady Juliana?'

'Not a great deal. He favours wine and ale far too much and made little sense. But of interest was how much time he spends in the gatehouse alone and unsupervised.'

'He's not alone as often as you might think,' said Stanton. 'We found Agatha with him today. That's not unusual, by her account, and the rest of her story was interesting.'

Barling listened as Stanton gave him a quick summary.

'Then she was here in Fairmore on the night Cuthbert was murdered?' said Barling.

'Yes. Though she says she knows nothing about it – nothing about Silvanus, either. She really disliked him.'

'Did she have any dealings with the lady Juliana?'

'I don't know. My lady's body was only discovered when I was talking to Agatha so I wasn't concerned about her at the time. I did notice that Maurice seemed angry at the girl, although I couldn't catch what he said.'

'Interesting. I will try to speak to Agatha again while you are away.' He cast a glance at the sky. 'Stanton, you must be off.'

'I know.' Stanton hesitated. 'Do you really think somebody is following the punishments in that book, Barling?'

'I honestly do not know. As the abbot says, Cuthbert was no murderer, so that does not fit. The book is in my room. I shall read it as promptly as I can, though it is of substantial length.'

'Why would somebody do all this? It makes no sense.'

'It is just as it was last summer, Stanton. It will all make sense once we have the complete picture.'

'But what if the murderer is planning to strike again? I'm a bit bothered about leaving you here, Barling.'

'You have no need to fear.' Barling nodded at the horse. 'I would be in far greater peril on the back of that animal in conditions like this and I would slow you down far too much. You would have to keep stopping to dig me out of snowdrifts.'

'I'm serious, Barling.'

'So am I. I will take every precaution. But you will not be gone long and you can fetch those who will help to make this place safe.' He handed Stanton another letter. 'Take this with you also. I know you already have those from Philip that I helped him compose for other holy houses. This one is from me and bears my court seal. It is private and it needs to go to my lord de Glanville. I did not want Philip to know I was writing to him. But de Glanville needs to know what is going on.'

'You want me to go all the way to Westminster?'

'No. You can arrange for it to go from York. And make sure that you alert the folk of Gottburn as well. Who knows where the killer might decide to strike next?'

'We'll find whoever is responsible.' Stanton reached both hands up on to his saddle. 'Just like before.'

'Are you sure about travelling in this weather?' asked Barling for a final time.

'Yes.' He pulled himself up into the saddle in one easy movement. 'I'll be fine. But you be careful while I'm gone.'

'I will,' said Barling. 'I know the rhythms of this place well enough by now to avoid danger.'

'If you say so.' Stanton flashed him a grin. 'I'll see you soon, Barling.' He clicked to his horse and was gone in a spray of flying snow.

'Godspeed.' Barling watched him go, offering up a brief prayer for Stanton's safe return.

He saw Lambert swing the gate open. Then Stanton was gone.

Barling set off for the inner precinct of the abbey. He knew who he had to see next.

One who he guessed would be most displeased at having to speak to the King's man, let alone answer his questions.

But answer he would: Barling would make sure of it.

Chapter Thirty-Three

Barling entered the infirmary, stamping the snow from his boots. A separate building to the rest of the monastery, it was located east of the cloister. Unlike the other buildings, it comprised a single storey, no doubt to ensure that a sick or lame monk could easily access it. He closed the door behind him at once to keep out the chill wind. Directly in front of him was a wooden partition, erected to keep the room as free from draughts as possible.

The partition was open on both sides. Barling chose to enter via the left, assuming correctly that it would make little difference.

As he turned the corner into the candlelit room, he was greeted with rows of beds similar to those in the dormitory, but far fewer in number. The beds were of a more comfortable design, being the same as those in the guesthouse, with deep straw mattresses in a wooden frame and thick blankets. The smell of food in there told of a better diet than the monks' usual fare. A fireplace on one wall brought heat and comfort to the room. Towards the back of the oblong room, he could see a number of small chambers similar to those in which Cuthbert the sacrist had slept, although they did not have any doors to them. A large cupboard was tucked into one corner. Its open shelves were neatly stacked with bottles, dried herbs and various instruments.

Many of the beds were occupied and a few curious faces turned towards him. The occupants of other beds lay still, either in slumber or pain or oblivion, it was impossible to tell. One ancient monk sat bolt upright in his bed, rocking back and forth and humming the first two lines of a hymn, over and over again.

'What brings you here, sir?' A familiar voice. William, the bald infirmary monk, came bustling towards Barling, a black scapular worn over his clothing to keep it clean. 'I hope you are not ill?'

'No, I am hale, thank you, brother. I am here because I wish to speak to Brother Reginald.'

'I am afraid that's not possible, sir. He is still resting after his bloodletting.'

'And I am afraid that I must insist, brother. Please tell me where he is or I shall be forced to disturb every one of your beds looking for him.'

William shot him a displeased look. 'I would rather you didn't do that, sir.' He pointed to one of the partitioned beds. 'He's in there. But, I implore you, please don't take too long. He needs to build up his strength and if he gets agitated, it'll set him back.'

'I will be quick, I promise.' Barling made his way to the bed and found Reginald already sitting up as best his stooped spine would allow. The linen on which he lay was as white as his hair. Instead of his cowl, he wore a tunic, which seemed to greatly diminish him in size. Tiredness was etched into his face. Nothing, however, could diminish his deep voice.

'I could hear you from here, sir.' Or his piercing grey eyes. 'I have little desire to speak to you. But this is how you conduct your enquiries, is it not? Going from man to man, questioning, testing out each story with the next, before you put it all together like the tiles on the church floor and make a coherent pattern.'

'You make it sound very simple, brother. I wish it were as easy as that.'

'But it is not, is it?' His brows lowered. 'I heard about the lady Juliana.' He shrugged, which made him slip down a little but he made no effort to raise himself up again.

Barling would have to make sure he got his information as quickly as possible. He had no doubt that William would banish him from here soon. 'It is indeed a shocking thing to have happened.' There was no point in asking Reginald about his whereabouts. He would have been here, ill and tucked up in bed. 'Yet I am sure the murders of Cuthbert and Silvanus will have been of a greater shock. Can you tell me anything about them?'

'As you know, sir,' said Reginald, 'I have no desire to speak to you. I can assure you that would be the case even if I were well. As I am not, I have even less interest in wasting my strength on you. In order to preserve it, I present to you my tiles.' The prior gave him a hard smile. 'When Cuthbert was murdered, I was asleep in the monks' dormitory. When Silvanus was killed, I was worshipping my God: I was at my devotions in the cloister and in the church for Mass and the Office.'

'I see,' said Barling.

'As for the remainder of my tiles, you know that I am the prior of this house and have been for the last twenty years. I have been here since its foundation by Abbot Ernald, thirty years ago. He made me his prior, his deputy, and I continue to be prior under Philip. I assign work to the choir monks every morning that is not a feast day. Boot greasing, painting: whatever needs to be done. I have no wish to murder anybody and I do not know anybody who does.' Another smile, devoid of any warmth. 'Is that what you came for, sir?'

Bustling steps behind him announced the arrival of Brother William. He took one look at Reginald and turned to Barling. 'I'm afraid you must leave now, sir.' He moved to the prior's side, helping him to adjust his position in the bed.

'Of course.' Barling got to his feet and went to leave. 'I do have one more tile for which I need to find a place, brother.'

'Oh?'

Barling ignored William's gestures to leave.

'Did you copy *The Vision of Tundale* for Abbot Ernald?'

It was clearly not a question that Reginald was expecting. He took a moment before replying. 'Yes, I did. I laboured over it for more than a year. Why?'

'Only that I look forward to reading it, brother.'

'Then I hope you enjoy it. There are many valuable lessons to be learned from it. It was the finest work I ever produced.' He held up his gnarled hands as much as he was able. 'Alas, work I can do no more.' He dropped his hands and his voice. 'My gift has been taken from me.'

Chapter Thirty-Four

If Stanton thought the snow had been coming down hard in the courtyard, it was as nothing now that he was outside the shelter of the abbey's roofs and walls and in the full force of the storm.

As he rode away, the hooves of the horse beneath him made little sound on the thickening carpet of white. He took a quick look back over his shoulder. At this time of day in the middle of January, he would expect to see the lamps of the monastery shining out into the dusk.

Now, with the snow that was falling, he couldn't see the lamps. He could barely even see the bulky buildings of Fairmore.

He faced forward again, his feet and hands already numbing, despite his thick boots and gloves.

The wind blew in a low, ceaseless roar as it whipped through the trees and buffeted icy clouds of snowflakes into his face. And such flakes. They were nothing like the powdery fall of the last couple of days. Each one was like a large, square feather that settled on and stuck to him. Not only on him: on to his animal, the ground, the trees.

The world was whitening before his very eyes, the darkness of trees and bushes fading away like mud did from linen when it was put in water. Even his face wasn't spared, the cold sting of the flakes blinding him and settling on his cheeks. He buried his face in his cloak against the chill and pulled his hat down further over his eyes to try to shield his vision.

It worsened now that they were climbing higher out of the valley.

He could only tell because of the altered angle of his horse's legs under him. He was riding almost blind now. He leaned forward in his saddle, wary of losing his balance. Any injury from falling from his animal in these conditions could mean death. For both of them. His horse seemed to sense that too, and had slowed right down, head bowed like Stanton's against the battering of the weather.

At this rate, getting out of the valley would take four times as long as it usually did.

And the weather was worsening still.

And it was the very beginning of the night.

And he was getting colder. Much colder.

Maybe Barling had been right to question this journey.

Stanton remembered the priest Theobald saying how Fairmore could get completely cut off in the snow. Stanton had understood what the priest had meant. What he hadn't fully appreciated was how fast and completely it would happen. Probably just like the old abbot, Ernald, hadn't. Ernald, the man who'd insisted on building his abbey in such a remote place, who had taken no notice of the warnings of the people who'd lived in the place for generations. And it was thanks to Ernald's pig-headedness that Stanton was having to try to battle his way out, a battle he was losing fast.

He managed to keep on going, the climb steeper now.

His animal stumbled beneath him. Stanton clung on with an oath and saved himself.

He raised his head as much as he could. Damn it all, he couldn't even tell if he was on the roadway any more.

His horse lurched again, almost fell into a deep snowdrift. That did it. This was impossible.

Curse this snow and curse it a hundred times. He knew how important it was to get help. He wouldn't have insisted on riding out in this otherwise. But he couldn't make it. To his shame. He'd have to turn back.

He looked around and swore again. Back to what? The storm was so fierce now, he could see nothing at all of where he'd come from. The only thing that was of any help was the downward slope of the ground.

He tried to bring his animal round, but the horse stopped dead, unsure. He didn't blame it. He was asking it to make a move where it could neither see nor balance properly.

'Come round, come round.' He tried a call and a kick, pulled hard on the reins.

Nothing.

He tried again. But got a snort and a frightened eye roll. If he wasn't careful, the horse would throw him.

He was going to have to dismount.

Stanton slid from the saddle, careful to keep a tight hold of the reins. Though he sank into the snow above his knees, his boots still didn't meet solid ground but more snow underneath. Or at least he thought so. He hadn't much feeling in his feet.

After a lot of gentle persuasion, he got his horse to turn and start walking back down.

Walking initially made him a little warmer. Then the wind won the battle again and the chill seeped through every inch of him.

Around him the snow swirled thicker than ever. He had to keep moving, keep his mind on following the slope that would take him to the valley floor. From there, he'd be able to get to the abbey. He hoped.

And then, through the noise of the storm, he heard a scream.

A female scream. For help.

Chapter Thirty-Five

Barling knocked to announce his arrival at another partitioned room. But this was not one in the infirmary. This was the one belonging to the late Brother Cuthbert in the monks' dormitory, which was now occupied by Brother Maurice.

As he'd crossed from one building to the other, Barling had been struck by the full force of the snowstorm that now raged. Anxiety gnawed at him. He should never have allowed Stanton to set off today.

Maurice paused from his task of folding some clothes. 'Yes, who is it?' He looked around and squinted at Barling with his less bad eye. The other, sightless and white as milk, seemed to stare right at him.

'It is me, the King's man. Aelred Barling. May I have a word with you?'

'So long as you don't mind me carrying on with my work. Well, Cuthbert's work at the moment.'

'Not at all, brother.' Barling walked in. He knew he would have to exercise caution with Maurice. The man seemed easily roused to fits of emotion, be it anger or sadness. Were Maurice to be overcome with either, his answers would be of little value. 'You are still doing his duties as well as your own?'

'I am. It isn't a bother. I can't do much reading now. God may have taken most of my sight, but He has left me my health and my strength. And what kind of man would I be to complain about extra work when Cuthbert was taken from us in such circumstances?'

'Indeed,' said Barling. 'It was you that found him, was it not?'

'It was.'

Barling listened as Maurice carried on his folding and gave his account: a wakeful night, as so often happened to him. Rousing the novices and monks. The locked stairs. The search. The stench. The discovery. Nothing the monk said was any different from what Barling had previously heard.

'An unimaginable discovery,' said Barling.

'I can imagine it only too well,' came the tart reply.

'A harsh burden.' Barling nodded, annoyed at himself for his poor choice of words. 'May I ask if you were close to Cuthbert?'

'If you mean close as a friend? No. He was a very quiet man. But he was a monk of virtue and holiness.'

'Then you did not know him well?'

'I knew him as a man very well, like I do so many here. As the novice master, I know all their sins and flaws. They come under my care and instruction, you see, when they first enter the abbey as young men. They are raw and unformed. They behave in all sorts of ways that need constant correction.' Maurice sucked his few teeth in displeasure and set to folding a blanket.

'Such as?' asked Barling, keen for him to continue with what could be some very useful revelations.

'Take Philip,' replied Maurice. 'He is abbot now, but he had brought with him all sorts of unacceptable behaviour from his time studying in Paris. William, a monk who can watch over a dying man through the night, used to fall asleep the minute he opened a prayer book. Elias had no manners and a shocking tendency to swear. I could go on, but you can see what I mean. They have to be moulded, shaped. Endure the fire of God's kiln. It is not an easy process. Our life here is harsh and it comes as a shock to them when they first arrive. They expect a life of prayer and devotion. What they do not expect is a life of hard work, little food and even less sleep.' He sucked his teeth once more.

'How do they react to such demands?'

'Some of them run away. I have tracked many down over the years. Brought them back too. And they all have thanked me for it. But they should not be thanking me, they should be thanking God, for it is God, not me, who protects them from Satan's relentless assaults.'

'They are assaulted by the devil?'

'Of course.' Maurice gave a definite nod.

Barling chose his next question with care. 'In what way does this happen?'

'The devil can assail their souls, especially at night. There have been instances in the monks' dormitory where novices have called out that they can see the devil. They have left their beds shouting in fear, trying to fight off Satan. They have seen the devil stand over them, or one of his agents in the form of a black dog, skulking amongst the shadows.'

Barling thought that perhaps the lack of sleep might have been doing some of this work and not necessarily the devil. After having himself kept some of the same hours as the monks today, he could understand it.

Maurice went on, clearly warming to his topic and beginning to work himself up, his folding task abandoned. 'As well as inspiring terror with visitations and evil visions, the devil can also possess men of God and make them violent. A monk once flew at Abbot Ernald, striking him in the face and neck and injuring him quite badly. The monk had to be punished, of course. He was flogged and spent many months in the abbey's cell. He did penance during that time and, through his punishment and his repentance, the devil left him.'

'Oh.' This sounded promising. 'Which monk was this?'

185

'One who died many years ago,' he replied, to Barling's disappointment.

'I see. Are any other monks currently being troubled by the devil?'

'Every day,' said Maurice. 'For this is the battle that is our life. The only battle. Where there is temptation, there is Satan. We must overcome him.' He clenched his fists for emphasis. 'At all times.'

'Was Cuthbert ever possessed by the devil?' This was easier to ask than whether Cuthbert had been a murderer.

'Cuthbert?' Maurice shook his head, his hands relaxing again. 'No.'

'He had no secrets or flaws that you discovered when overseeing him as his novice master?'

'I do not think this is a suitable question, sir.' Despite his ruined eyes, Maurice could still deliver a fierce glare. 'Cuthbert was murdered. I do not see how prying into his past sins could help.'

'I am sorry, brother. I am just trying to get an overall picture of him as a man.'

'He was a far better novice than many. I had no serious cause for concern.'

'That is good to hear.'

'I think it might have been because he was a few years older than the usual age when he joined. He had a much greater maturity.' He pointed a finger at Barling. 'Maturity is also a great virtue, you know. Though not many think it.'

'It is indeed.'

'If there were more respect for a mature mind, then Reginald would have taken over as abbot when Ernald died. It would have been far more fitting. Silvanus thought so too. He was a great admirer of Reginald's wisdom. But no. Instead we elect young Philip.'

Barling could not help a smile inside. Abbot Nicholas, the abbot who'd carried out the visitation to Fairmore, had spoken to Barling and de Glanville of petty jealousy and resentments behind Philip's election, and here it was out in the open. Philip was the same age as Barling, which was young, perhaps, compared to Maurice and Reginald, but by few other measures. 'Perhaps we can now talk about Silvanus. Can you tell me where you were the morning he was killed?'

'I would have been in the cloister or with my novices in the monks' day room. Or possibly up here checking the dormitory. I have many duties.'

'Forgive me for bringing this up, but when I saw you, you were most distressed about Silvanus.'

'Of course I was. I'd trained him as a novice.'

'And the lady Juliana?'

His look darkened. 'Women have no place here.'

'The lady Juliana was most generous.'

'Still no place. Like that girl who was with Lambert.' His look darkened more. 'Again.'

'Agatha is her name, I believe,' said Barling.

'Her name matters not. A sinful, lustful little temptress is what she is. Ensnaring Lambert with her wiles. I have told her that she is to be gone. Gone.' His hands balled into fists again. 'I do not wish to see her here again. Ever.'

Chapter Thirty-Six

Heart racing, Stanton looked to where he thought the source of the scream might be. He could see nothing except driving snow and the outlines of the closest buried bushes and rocks. The rest was a white, whirling wall.

'Where are you? Hello!'

Stanton tried to shout above the noise of the storm. It was no good. The sound of his voice was lost, carried off by the gale.

He looped his horse's reins around his forearm, cupped his gloved hands and tried again. 'Hello!'

Nothing.

'Can you hear me?'

Still nothing except pelting snow and the howl of the wind, which blasted in a sudden gust that could almost be a shriek.

His heart began to calm again. Maybe he hadn't heard a scream at all. He'd heard the wind. It died down for a few moments, as if exhausted from the pitch to which it had built.

He set off again, his reins firm in one hand, watching where he put every struggling step.

And there it came again. Another shrill cry. A cry of terror. And another. 'Help me!'

His pulse hammered again. This wasn't the wind. 'Hello?' As he started to move towards the sound of the voice, he caught another sound in the wind's brief lull. A deep rumble. The rumble of fast-flowing water. He was nearer to the abbey than he thought.

'Please! Somebody!'

And so was whoever was screaming.

'Where are you?' He tried to break into a run, floundering in the deep drifting snow.

'Help me!'

The river. He let go of his horse – the animal was only slowing him down. 'Hold on, I'm coming!'

The wind built again, drowning out his call and masking the sound of the river.

But he knew where he was now, recognised the thrashing white-covered shadows of the tall stand of trees.

He forced his way through the low branches, sending clumps of snow falling on to his head and shoulders. He was there, he was in the steep, rocky clearing with the snow still hammering down, where the river roared and boiled through the narrow rocky channel.

And on one of the snow-covered rocks, right next to the torrent, lay Agatha, face down, arms and legs spread-eagled under a cloak that was being covered in falling snow.

His guts turned over. 'Agatha!'

She raised her head to meet his gaze. Just. 'Hugo!' Her cry was shrill with terror.

'Are you hurt?'

'No. But I can't get up. I couldn't see where I was going and I fell. It's all slippery.' Her voice choked on her terror. 'If I move, I'll fall in.'

'I'll come and get you.'

'Now. Now! Do you hear me?'

He moved towards her, mindful that this snow lay on wet, mossy rocks. If he wasn't careful, he'd be in the water. And that would be the end of him. The snow under his right boot shifted and moved, breaking off and collapsing into the river. Stanton went down on one knee with an oath, steadying himself.

'I can't get any closer, Agatha.'

'You must. Oh, you must.'

He moved a couple of steps back to more solid footing and grabbed for a snow-covered branch. He broke it off. Then edged his way back towards Agatha as far as he dared.

'You need to grab this,' he said. 'And hold on tight.'

'If I have to grab it, I'll fall!'

'Don't think about falling. Just grab it, grab it when I say. Tight. Tight as you ever held anything. And don't let go. Do you hear me?' He pushed the branch to her, holding it firm in both his gloved hands.

'I'll fall, damn you!'

He pushed. Pushed. 'Now!'

She grabbed at it. Slipped towards the water with a scream.

Then stopped. She had hold of the branch.

Stanton's gloved hands were slipping from it. 'Curse it all.' He braced his knees, praying his footing was sound. Gave one mighty haul.

Then she was up, out, a couple of feet from the edge in a pile of soft snow, screaming and thrashing her way from the deadly water's edge on her hands and knees.

Stanton sat down hard. Hell's teeth. She was safe. He might have lost one woman to an untimely death. But not this one.

He righted himself in the snow and moved to help her get as far away from the water's edge as possible. 'Here, take my hand.' He bent to her, pulled her to her feet.

She looked up at him, shaking hard from cold and shock. 'You came looking for me, then?' Her question was a thin echo of her usual bravado. 'I can say thank you, you know. I know how.' She shuddered from head to foot, her wretched clothes plastered to her thin frame. 'I do it all the time.' Tears pooled in her grey eyes and she scrubbed them away.

He'd no doubt that even half-frozen and distressed as she was, she'd let him use her. It was all she knew. He'd no appetite for it – not out here, not now. 'Hush,' was all he said. He drew her to him, pulled his own cloak around her to try to warm her. 'There's no need.'

Her cheek pressed against his, her flesh cold as stone. 'God help me: I was so afraid.' The last word came out on a choked sob.

'But you were brave, Agatha.' He held her tighter. 'So brave.'

'Hugo, I nearly died.' And then her tears came, broke from her as she sobbed and sobbed, clinging to him as if she clung to life itself.

'You didn't, Agatha. You're still here.' He held her tighter still, the better to drive the cold from her.

———

Stanton made his way into the guesthouse, numb with cold. He'd left his retrieved horse in the stables and Agatha with Brother Lambert. She'd told Stanton as they made their way down to the monastery gate that she'd been ordered away by an angry Maurice. But she'd left it too late and had become lost in the snowstorm. Lambert had been pleased if somewhat surprised to see her return.

Whether they got up to sin or not, Stanton didn't really care. Agatha had worn her brazen look again, a look that he now knew to be a mask, but she wouldn't be swayed by Stanton. She'd insisted that Lambert's gatehouse was where she wanted to be. At least she'd be safe and warm in there and that was all that mattered. As for him, he was hugely relieved he'd saved her. Proud, too, of his actions. But devastated that he'd not succeeded in the task given to him by Barling, a vital one. He knocked on Barling's door to tell the clerk of his failure, but the room was empty.

Forget drying off. Barling had assured him he'd be fine while Stanton was gone, but even though he was back so soon, he needed to make sure that he was. He needed to find the clerk.

Stanton hurried back out and over to the main cloister. To his immense relief, he saw Barling walking towards him, the clerk's black robes standing out against the snow.

'Stanton!' said the clerk. 'Praise God you are safe.' He took in Stanton's appearance with a swift glance. 'I feared for your life as the weather worsened so badly.'

'I'm sorry, Barling.'

Barling held up a hand. 'There is no need for apologies. It is I who should be apologising for asking you to try to make such a perilous journey.'

'It wasn't only me out there.' He explained what had happened, about turning around in the snow, returning to the valley and finding Agatha.

'Then the girl was indeed fortunate that you happened to be nearby,' said Barling. 'Maurice will be very displeased that she has returned. He told me that he ordered her away.'

'Better an angry Maurice than her drowning or freezing to death.' Stanton could hardly control his own shudders.

'We need to get you warmed up, my boy.'

'I don't care. What I care about is what I've seen of the conditions further up the valley.' He swallowed hard. 'We're trapped here now, Barling. Trapped with whoever has committed these murders. And no one will be able to help us.'

Barling nodded slowly. 'Then we must gather all the monks together at once. They need to know of the danger they are now in. That we are all in.'

Chapter Thirty-Seven

Barling hurried along the claustral walk with Stanton.

He could hear a single voice, reading loudly, steadily and calmly: that of Abbot Philip.

Barling turned to Stanton. 'Good,' he murmured. 'The monks are still gathered at collation. We will not have to waste time bringing them together. He raised his own voice as they walked up. 'Abbot Philip. My apologies for breaking the silence of the cloister. But I must disturb you and the brothers from your prayer.'

The other cowled monks turned unsure faces towards the arrivals as Philip looked up from his book with an irritated frown at being inter-rupted. His face fell when his gaze lit on Stanton. 'What's happened, Barling? What's going on?'

Barling lowered his voice again, his words for Philip's ears only. 'The weather has closed right in. Stanton had to turn back. He would have frozen to death otherwise.'

'Then thank God you are safe. This valley can be treacherous.' His troubled look met Barling's. 'We should not have been so insistent. I fear our decisions are becoming ill-thought-out and dangerous.'

'It was worth a try, my lord abbot,' said Stanton. 'It got a lot worse very quickly. More than I'd have expected.'

'Yet if we had not sent him,' said Barling, 'someone else would have lost their life.' He related what had happened to Agatha.

'Then you were sent by God's hand,' said Philip.

'However,' said Barling, 'I think you need to speak to the monks about being particularly vigilant. The extra help you and I sought is not available. We are no nearer to identifying who the killer is. It may be that the snow is actually protecting us and stopping anyone who had murderous intent from coming here. But the very opposite may be true. We are effectively trapped in this place now.'

Philip's pale face blanched further. 'May God protect us.' He turned to his monks and raised his voice. 'Brothers, I need to inform you that our abbey has been cut off from the outside world, as has happened in the past.'

A low, unsurprised murmur met his words.

The abbot went on. 'Because we are blessed with good fortune, we need not fear starvation or want. Our cellars are full and our supplies can last us for many weeks. I would ask that you further temper your appetites to make sure that is the case.'

All cowled heads nodded in instant obedience. 'Yes, my lord abbot.'

'There is one more thing that I would ask you to be mindful of. As you know, the greatest of evil has visited this house three times now. I would ask that you remain alert at all times and advise me or the King's men at once, should you see anything untoward.'

Anxious looks stole across many faces.

'We need to inform the lay brothers as well,' continued Philip. 'Osmund, can you do that, please?' His gaze sought out the cellarer.

Silence met his question.

He frowned. 'Osmund?'

Still no reply, just the whistle of the wind and a sudden whispering amongst the monks.

Barling's frown met Stanton's.

'Where is Brother Osmund?' asked Philip.

The whispering got louder.

Philip tried again. 'Does anybody know?'

'No, my lord abbot, no.'

'Not I.'

The answers were many and all the same. Nobody knew.

'Perhaps he is already with the lay brothers, my lord abbot?' This from Elias.

Maurice got to his feet. 'I'll go and ring the bell for Compline, my lord. For it is already time. I am sure the bell will summon him from wherever he may have got to.' The novice master headed off towards the door of the church, shaking his head. 'Probably got lost in his own cellar,' came his audible remark as he left.

The abbot ignored the old monk's open rudeness. 'Then let us go and pray the Office at the close of this day.' Philip raised a hand in blessing and the monks started to file off to the church. He turned to Stanton. 'Thank you once again for your courageous endeavours. I bid you both a good night.' He hurried off after his monks.

Barling looked at Stanton, who was shuddering hard. 'Thanks will be of little good unless you get warm and dry. Otherwise you will catch your death.'

'In truth, that doesn't feel so far away,' said Stanton, his teeth chattering hard.

As they headed back into the snow towards the guesthouse, the deep bell rang out its usual regular toll for Compline.

But only a few yards further on and Barling could hear it no more, swallowed up as it was by the howl of the storm.

Chapter Thirty-Eight

Barling sat at his little table in his room in the guesthouse as the storm raged on outside. Stanton had gone to bed, the young man's face etched with the exhaustion of his battle with the snow and wind. Tiredness threatened to consume Barling too. But he needed to make notes on all their findings to this point. He and Stanton had found out a great deal. But, to Barling's rising consternation, none of it was making sense. Worse, the deaths were continuing. Updating his written record might help to reveal some answers. He held a fervent hope that it would.

As ever, the smoothness of the wax on his writing tablet helped his thoughts and his written words to start flowing.

He listed the three people who had been murdered:

Cuthbert, the sacrist – strangled and burned.

Silvanus, the guestmaster – pitchfork through the chest, skewer in the neck. Wood tar in mouth.

Juliana, a benefactor – blow to the head. Drowned?

He looked at the names on the tablet for some time, thinking about any possible reasons for their deaths or connections between them. But his eyes kept going back to the copy of *The Vision of Tundale* that was on the table to one side. He hauled his mind back from Elias's theory. He needed to have his own.

Next, he moved on to consider what he knew about those who were alive. First, the monks:

Philip, the abbot. A man who was bending under the huge weight of the office of abbot, an office that carried great loneliness as well as great responsibility. And a bending branch could snap suddenly and without warning.

Reginald, prior to Philip. Advanced in years and no doubt suited to the post of abbot, and yet now that opportunity had passed. His eyes went to the book again. Scribe of the late Abbot Ernald's copy of *The Vision of Tundale.*

Vision. The word stared back up at him.

Maurice, the novice master. Maurice had spoken at length about monks being assailed by visions. Maurice was also advanced in years and a very close friend of Reginald's.

Elias, the library monk. A learned, intelligent man. One with no obvious close friendships. Shared space with Cuthbert. One who also had a link to the book. Not only had he brought it to Barling's and the abbot's attention, but Elias was also the keeper of the book.

Barling's pulse went a little faster. Written down like this, it looked as if the book was indeed linking them all. His eyes went back to Philip's name. So what was Philip's link? Yes, he knew the book well from the old abbot's enthusiasm for it and his many sermons which took its contents as their theme. But so would most if not all of the other monks. Barling hauled himself back to his list, scolding himself for getting distracted. Order, always order. That was the way to proceed.

William, the infirmarer. A man skilled in his profession at tending to the living and who prepared the bodies of the victims for the grave.

Lambert, the gatekeeper. A drunkard who lusted after a young woman. He wrote her name down, just in case.

Agatha, a beggar. Most likely a prostitute. A woman who needed the abbey for her well-being, if not her very survival. A sad existence for one so young, and, truth be told, so fair.

But no links to the book with these last three names. Barling gave a frustrated sigh.

Osmund, the cellarer. A man who wore the burden of his office even more heavily than Philip. Mocked by his peers and his subordinates. Again, there were no links to the book. At least, none that he knew of.

Daniel, a lay brother. A man who worked like a plough ox. A man who despised the monks. A man far too close to the murders for Barling's liking, though Stanton had argued against that. A man who could not read or rather was not allowed to read. So had he been reading the *Vision*?

Barling was back to the book again.

He looked at his notes once more. It seemed so difficult. In such a confined community there were so many links and connections between all the names, including the victims. The lady Juliana had been fond of Silvanus, for instance, and his endless flow of flattery.

Wait. Juliana. She had donated a valuable collection of books.

And there it was – books. Again.

There was only one thing for it.

Barling pushed his notes away.

He would have to read *The Vision of Tundale* for himself. Even if it took all night.

Reginald lay in his bed in the quiet of the shadowed infirmary, listening to the relentless noise of the storm outside as he waited for the relief of sleep. Pain coursed through every bone and joint in his body and would do so for every moment he was awake. Usually, after a bloodletting, he would have slipped into slumber by now. All of the other patients in the infirmary seemed to have managed it.

But his disagreement with Philip about the King's men continued to play on his mind, making him fretful and unable to settle, no matter how much he needed to. He could not agree that Philip's actions were the right ones, despite the abbot's insistence.

He thought back to what Philip's predecessor, Ernald, would have done in these circumstances. Reginald reckoned that Ernald would probably have kept them all in chapter till the crack of doom, waiting for somebody to finally confess. Yet Philip did not have the same authority, nowhere near it. The man was a poor father to this house.

A new spasm of pain shot down Reginald's back and he shifted a little beneath the coverlet with a stifled groan to try to ease it.

He tried to picture Abbot Ernald's face at being told he needed outside help to run his abbey. Despite his pain, he smiled. The sooner they saw the back of the King's men, the better.

If only Ernald had outlived him. Then his world could have carried on as before. He would not have had to get used to new ways, new methods, different approaches to doing things. It made him weary, weary in a body that was already exhausted from pain, from joints that ground against each other and sent agonising pulses through his limbs even when he barely moved.

On many days and nights, it could be demons stabbing him with knives.

Just like one of the fates in *The Vision of Tundale*. He scowled to himself. What had prompted the King's man to ask about the book, one of which Abbot Ernald had been particularly fond? It seemed as if nothing at Fairmore, past or present, was exempt from Barling's unwanted intrusion.

Producing a copy of Tundale's story had been one of the high points of Reginald's scribing days. Not only had it been a privilege to scribe a copy by special request of Abbot Ernald, but the story of the knight had enthralled Reginald.

His one regret was that he had not been able to embellish it with pictures. He'd come to this abbey from a Benedictine house, already not only a talented scribe but also an even more talented artist. He'd

199

been able to bring the first of those talents to Fairmore but alas, he'd not been able to use the second. Ernald had been a close follower of the rule that the White Monks should not insert lavish illustration nor colour into their manuscripts. Though it had almost broken Reginald's heart, he knew he would have to accept it. And accept it he did, though with every word he wrote of *The Vision of Tundale*, he'd thought about how he would have shown the story and its lessons for sinners in the vivid way that he could.

Tundale, the sinful knight: he knew how he would have drawn him. A man with a face like any other, the better to show the reader that sin could be hidden deep within a man or woman, that hiding misdeeds did little good. His depiction of the feast would have been sharp and clear. The knight apparently safe in this world, sitting at table in company as people did every day. Yet, like so many, Tundale did not realise that his hour had come, and he would be struck down.

Then would have come the angel, appearing before the stricken Tundale: a being with sweeping wings and a halo picked out in the glow of gold. A being that would bear him away to the depths of hell. A great challenge, Reginald knew, to show those depths on the page. The colours used would have been very dark: shades of black and grey that might have become an indecipherable murk. But he knew that in his hands, his younger hands, he could have shown the abode of evil in all its foul, terrifying darkness. He had always mixed his own inks, the better to get the effect he desired. Anyone who looked upon it would have trembled at the sight, as Tundale himself did in the words of the tale.

Reginald lifted a throbbing hand slowly and carefully to push one of his pillows back into position.

And then would have come the fates of the sinners, nine in all, each one deserving of the most careful illustration to hammer the lesson home.

The first, the fire that melted the murderers. He would have painted it in the fiercest, brightest yellows, the flames leaping from the page so vividly that the reader would swear that boiling heat came from it. For the punishment of the next, the souls of the false and the treacherous, he would have assembled a demon army. Every face of every devil would have been individually contorted with evil and each taloned hand armed with the sharpest trident, that they might pierce the bodies of the sinners and inflict the greatest of agony upon them.

It would have been more difficult to show the revolting pit of ordure into which the third group, the proud, were cast. But he could have shown the terror of those falling in, convey by the twisting of their bodies and horrified expressions the awareness of their suitable, unspeakable fate.

The image swam before him and he could almost hear the cries of the damned on the wind outside.

Yet the punishment of the fourth, the covetous, would have given him even greater pleasure to depict. The mouth of hell, opening wide in the manner of a great beast, with savage jaws ready to crush the sinners who were being driven in by more demonic hordes. The huge, dark beast would have loomed above all, sinners and demons alike, while deep red flames would spurt from its vile jaws. Ravenous creatures waited inside the mouth, each one with sharp teeth to consume those who had sinned.

The fate of the thieves, the next group, would have required a smaller scale, but would have been no less of an instruction. The *Tundale* sinners would have carried their spoils – a sack of grain, a stolen animal – across a perilous narrow bridge, which would not perhaps have been able to convey the severity of what awaited them. But the many metal spikes that drove into the feet of the sinners, bringing forth streams of blood, most definitely would.

His own feet pulsed in pain, as if spikes pierced them too. He changed their position as much as he dared but it was of little use.

As for the sixth, the fornicators, men and women alike: he would have had no difficulty in conveying what awaited them. Demon executioners would stand in bright, leaping flames, holding in their malformed hands the weapons of their art: coulters, axes, scythes, sickles, and every sort of the sharpest blade, that they might rend the sinners limb from limb. Yet there was more: vermin would be gnawing at the very site of the fornicators' sin, showing Tundale and the reader what awaited those who indulged in wicked pleasures of the flesh. The worst fornicators made up the seventh: the clergy who committed sexual sin. Their bodies would flail as they drowned in an icy swamp, while vipers gushed from their privy members.

Next, those who added sin to sin, cast into a horrible furnace, and burned away to nothing by the devil's horned smiths. Reginald would have had them twisting upon the heated anvil as they were struck with hammers and burned to ash.

The ash swirled up before him and he blinked hard. The shadows of the storm-battered infirmary returned. Of course there was nothing there. He'd begun to drift into sleep, the sound of the storm finding its way into his dream, that was all.

God be praised. Rest must not be that far away. He gave a deep yawn. Soon, he'd slip into dark oblivion.

Dark, like the last fate of Tundale, where the knight descended down and down into the deepest depths of hell, down to where the worst of sinners would be cast, where there was no light, and complete blackness enfolded him like the grave. Down to where the sinful knight would dwell for all eternity.

And there was one who awaited the knight, one whom Reginald could have shown in terrifying detail. He wondered if his desire to do so was what had brought the punishment of his painful affliction upon him. For in the depths was Satan, the Prince of Shadows himself, waiting for Tundale. Satan's huge body, dark as pitch, a long, thick, spiked tail trailing behind him. He would have had many arms and hands, a thousand as described by Tundale. And every one huge, with iron nails, ready to grab for sinners and crush them as easily as a man's hand could crush ripe grapes, scattering the wet, glistening pieces to the corners of hell with his fiery, reeking breath.

Reginald started.

Breath. On his face.

Along with a whisper: 'You will feel no more pain this night.'

Chapter Thirty-Nine

Stanton had slept deeply, exhausted by his unsuccessful battle to get out of the valley. He'd had a night of undisturbed rest, one in which he dreamed not of cold and winter, but of warmth and sunshine and meadows full of bright flowers. He'd lain in them, blissful, with his Rosamund in his arms. On waking, his drowsy mind had held his happiness for a few moments before his loss snatched it away once more. He'd saved Agatha, but he hadn't saved Rosamund.

Rosamund was dead and this day had no meadows and certainly no sunshine. The tempest had passed and the snow had stopped overnight but in its place a freezing fog had come down, so dense he could only see about twenty paces. Such was the gloom, the daybreak might as well not have happened.

Yet, as he stood in the churned-up snow outside the infirmary, he still wondered if he slept, for he was looking at a nightmare.

Half in, half out of the small storage shed next to the infirmary lay the body of William the infirmarer. His snow-covered legs lay outside in a wide scarlet stain in the pristine white. The rest of his body lay inside.

Philip knelt next to the body, an unsteady hand extended over William, murmuring a prayer for his soul.

'Who found him?' Barling's question was directed at the large group of monks and lay brothers who crowded round.

The clerk was out of breath, Stanton too. They'd been in the guest-house when the abbey bell had sounded a jangling alarm, over and over. They'd run outside and followed the sound of the shouts of horror.

'I did,' said Maurice. 'I was going across to the infirmary to see how Reginald was this morning. I saw poor William. So I ran for the bells.'

Philip finished the prayer and stood up. 'The bells brought me as well.' His voice shook.

Reginald was also present, bent over his stick, a cloak thrown over his tunic. 'I heard the commotion,' he said. 'I left my sickbed and came to see what it was about.'

'Did you hear anything before that, Brother Reginald?' asked Stanton.

'How do you mean?' Reginald looked at him in distaste, that he would dare to ask him about this.

Stanton didn't care about the old monk's pride. 'You'll have been close by in the infirmary.'

'No, I did not hear anything,' he replied. His sharp gaze fixed on Barling, obviously ignoring Stanton. 'I was in a lot of pain last night. William gave me some of his most powerful herbs to help me sleep. That was the last time I saw him.'

'I see.' Barling went to examine the body, motioning for Stanton to assist him.

Stanton stepped with caution, trying not to tread in the stained snow.

'What has happened to him, Barling?'

William's kind, round, dead face was dark and suffused with con-gealed blood.

'I would say suffocation.' Barling looked over his shoulder. 'Brother Maurice: did you touch or move anything?'

'I did,' said Maurice. 'William's face was under that full grain sack, the one next to him. I pushed it off, thinking he might still be alive. But it was useless.'

Barling lowered his voice again and looked at Stanton. 'Then he was suffocated. Somebody took that sack off that pile in the side of the shed. Either pushed or knocked him to the ground. And then held it over his face.'

'What about the blood near his legs?'

'We shall have to see.' Barling bent to scrape away the snow.

Stanton thought he might lose his meagre breakfast.

William was barefoot. Into the soles of each of his feet, half a dozen nails had been hammered.

Cries of horror broke from all of the monks and brothers.

'Dear God! It's the fifth punishment of Tundale.' Elias's voice cracked as he put his hands to his face.

A plea to the saints broke from Philip.

Stanton looked at Barling. 'You know what they mean, don't you?'

The clerk didn't answer him directly. 'Stanton, with me.'

Barling led the way past the horrified monks and into the infirmary. He walked straight over to the cupboard where William had kept all the items he needed for curing the sick.

To Stanton's bemusement, Barling started a careful, methodical search of it, pulling everything out and emptying boxes and baskets.

'And here we are.' The clerk drew out an object from a tightly knotted bundle of linen bandages.

Stanton could only stare. It was a chalice. A silver chalice, gilded on the inside.

'Then it is true,' said Barling. 'The murderer is bringing *The Vision of Tundale* to life.'

Stanton noted the shadows under his eyes. 'You read it? When?'

'Last night.'

'What? Are you mad, Barling?'

'Of course I am not. I looked carefully at the evidence we had collected so far and I realised it had to be done.' Barling lowered his voice. 'As for what I have gleaned from my reading, I now believe there may not be just one killer. There are certainly many monks and others associated with these murders who have links to the book.' He shared with Stanton the reasoning he had gone through whilst compiling the list of names on the tablet.

Stanton listened, appalled.

'I think,' said Barling, 'the way to put an end to what is happening here is to let the man or men responsible know that we are almost on to them. I will address the monks in the Chapter House with Philip. The lay brothers can listen from the doorways. Right now.'

'Shouldn't you ask Philip first?'

Barling held up the chalice. 'This will be more than enough persuasion. A sacred object found.' He went to walk out. 'Watch the faces, Stanton. Watch them all. For anything. Anything at all. Lives may depend on it, including our own.'

Chapter Forty

Barling stood next to Philip in the Chapter House, the voices of the monks a shocked chorus of horrified chatter.

He checked to see that Stanton was in position by the door. Good.

'Brothers!' Philip raised his voice. 'Pray silence.'

He received it instantly from the monks sitting on the seats that lined the walls, the lay brothers crowded in the doorway, every face rapt.

Philip went on. 'I share your revulsion of what has happened again this morning. Yet another of our beloved brothers, William, taken from us by an evil hand. However, the King's man believes he has found a link, which he will now describe to you.' His gaze went round the room, making sure that he made his point. 'I would like to remind you that we owe Aelred Barling every courtesy and that we allow him the freedom to speak without hindrance in this room. Do I make myself clear?'

'Yes, my lord abbot.' The rumble of voices that came back was not the most unwavering of assents. Never mind. It would have to do.

'Thank you, my lord abbot,' said Barling. 'I would like to give much credit to Brother Elias for what I am about to say, for it was he who first came up with the link.' He gave a nod of acknowledgement to the red-haired monk, which was returned. 'I believe you are all familiar with

The Vision of Tundale.' He held up the book. 'I understand that it was a favourite of your previous abbot, Ernald.'

Blank nods met his words.

'Now, it would appear,' continued Barling, 'that there is a marked similarity between the punishments of sinners described in the book and the murders that have taken place.'

As he'd expected, his words were met with a burst of appalled realisation, followed by questions and conjecture amongst the monks. He waited as brother turned to brother, some calling across to each other, each recalling parts of the book and the fates of those who had died.

'How dare you, sir!' This from Maurice. 'I will not countenance that Cuthbert was a murderer.' He waved an angry fist.

'It would be fair to say that the lady Juliana was proud,' said Reginald, surprisingly.

'I would say that Silvanus, God rest him, carried tales,' said Elias.

'Are you in possession of your wits, Elias?' Maurice shouted again, more riled than ever. 'And what has possessed you to come up with such utter nonsense?'

'Brothers!' Barling made his voice heard over the din. 'The body of Brother William was found only this morning. Yet here, in the book, we have a punishment that talks of a burden of corn. William was suffocated by a sack of grain. The book tells of spikes that pricked the feet of the sinner, a fate that befalls the man who steals those things that belong to the holy Church.'

'Fanciful rubbish!' called Maurice. 'Rubbish. And you should be ashamed of yourself, Elias.'

'It is not fanciful, Maurice,' snapped Elias. 'William had the missing chalice hidden in the infirmary. He'd stolen it!'

His reply led to a further wave of noise and questions.

'But.' The word uttered in the deep voice of Reginald cut through it all. 'I know the book inside out, for I copied every word. Barling: the fate you describe is the fifth. If William is the fifth, where is the fourth?'

A deep silence descended.

Barling looked around the room.

'What of Brother Osmund this morning?' Philip's voice sounded as taut as if somebody had placed a hand at his throat. He pointed at a couple of choir monks. 'Since he did not come to Compline, I ordered you to search at first light. Did you find him?'

'No, my lord,' they answered together.

'We started our search,' added one. 'But then came the news about Brother William.'

'But' – Reginald again – 'the fourth fate is for the covetous, is it not?' He looked directly at Philip.

'It is.' The abbot's voice tightened even more. 'And I have had cause to speak to Osmund in private about his unhealthy interest in the accumulation of extra wealth for the abbey. He is not at all skilled. But he is strangely obsessed.'

'Oh, may God protect us,' said Maurice.

'I would suggest that a search is undertaken for him as a matter of urgency,' said Barling.

'And I would suggest' – Reginald sneered the word – 'that what we need is to go into the church for Lauds. Prayer. That is what we need. Then we can search.'

A loud chorus of agreement met his words.

Reginald rose to his feet. 'My lord abbot?'

Philip nodded. 'I agree.'

Barling raised his voice. 'Before you do, I would draw your attention to the remaining punishments and the sins associated with them.'

Outrage now echoed through the room.

'Barling!' Philip looked and sounded livid. 'Are you accusing people here of sin? In my Chapter House?'

'I have had enough of this too.' Maurice stood up. 'We must pray and then we must find our brother Osmund. May our prayers lead us to him. Come, brothers.'

Maurice stormed out, the other monks following.

Barling opened the book as they did so. 'Sexual sins. Lustful clergy. Those who have added sin to sin. All of these are still to come.'

'Barling, have you lost your mind? Give it to me.' Philip grabbed it from him. 'You have completely overstepped the mark. Completely.' He slammed the book shut and stormed out after his monks without a backward glance, slowing only a little to help Reginald along.

Silence fell.

Barling pulled in a long breath. He hoped his plan to provoke the murderer had worked. He looked at Stanton. 'Well?'

'Well, I saw anger, fury, shock.'

'And?'

'And nothing.' Stanton's face fell. 'Barling, I couldn't see anything else. They were all equally roused. There was nothing at all that made one stand out from another. Nothing.'

Chapter Forty-One

The sound of Lauds being sung in the church floated through to the Chapter House. Stanton looked at the clerk, disappointment etched on Barling's face now as well as exhaustion.

Without saying a word, Barling went and sat down heavily on one of the seats.

Stanton's instincts told him to leave the clerk be, to wait until Barling was ready to speak.

As the monks sang on for several minutes, Barling seemed to be in a world of his own.

When he finally spoke, his voice as well as his gaze lacked their usual certainty. 'I tried, Stanton. Perhaps I tried too hard.'

While often Stanton despaired of the clerk's arrogance, he hated to see him as defeated-looking as he was now. 'Look, Barling, it was certainly worth a try. You've confronted them with what we know, which may yet flush someone out.'

Barling shook his head. 'God help me, I think I did nothing except make matters worse.'

'I think you should get some sleep, Barling.'

'But I thought that, by saying what I did, I would get a reaction, that someone would stand out.'

'Sleep, Barling. That's what you need now. You'll be able to think better once you have.'

Lauds finished and the sound of the monks hurrying to the cloister echoed in, voices low and anxious as they settled to their devotions.

'Come on, Barling.' Stanton put a hand under his arm and pulled him to his feet. 'You need to get to your bed.'

The clerk didn't resist but allowed himself to be led out.

They made their way back to the guesthouse along the path, the fog as bad as ever.

Ahead, Stanton could hear the sound of an argument by the gate.

'What is going on now?' asked Barling.

The sound of definite footsteps marched towards them and a couple of lay brothers emerged from the gloom.

'Excuse me, sirs,' said one. 'You don't happen to know why the front gate is locked, do you? We need to go out and there's no sign of Brother Lambert.'

'Afraid not,' said Stanton. 'We're only guests here.'

'Of course, sir. Sorry, sir.' The men hurried on their way.

'I hope brother Lambert hasn't had too much ale again,' said Stanton.

'No.'

The clerk's tone was odd. Stanton turned to look at him.

Barling had gone deathly pale.

'Are you all right, Barling?'

'Sexual sins,' he replied. 'Not just monks. The book mentioned men.' He swallowed hard. 'And women.'

And then Stanton knew what Barling meant.

Agatha.

He started to run, run up the path to the gatehouse, hammering on the door, kicking it.

Then his heart almost stopped. He looked closer at the door lock, at the wood surrounding it. A dark, brownish-red substance smeared

213

them. His nostrils prickled at the unmistakable tang of iron. The stains were of blood.

He rushed over to the cart used for collecting firewood that the lay brothers had left. His hands closed on the axe, and he ran back to the door. He heaved the long-handled tool at the stout planks, desperately trying to break them open as the fog muffled the dull thuds of the blade.

But otherwise, there was silence.

Chapter Forty-Two

Stanton doubted if the sights that met him would ever leave him. Agatha. The blood – so much blood. An abandoned scythe lay on the floor in a pool of it. Sleek rats feeding at the lower half of her body, the vile creatures scattering when he and Barling smashed through the door.

'God preserve us,' said Barling behind him.

'Where have the rats come from?' Stanton moved forward, peering in the dim light. 'And why would they—' And then he saw. Terrible wounds and something placed in them that the rats had found irresistible.

'There is an empty cage in the corner,' said Barling. 'The rats were part of this passage in the book. It speaks of vermin.' He swallowed hard. 'Gnawing.'

Stanton turned and fled for the fresh air.

This is your fault, your fault. His conscience pounded a fierce chorus in his head. He clenched his fists to hold back the roar of anger that surged in him, thumped at the doorpost with one hand, then the other, over and over.

Barling hurried out after him, his breaths deep. 'Stanton, what is it?'

'What is it?' Now he shouted, he couldn't help it. 'You've used your eyes, man, same as I have!' He'd never dared speak to Barling like this before and he didn't care. 'Seen what's in there.' He jabbed a finger at the horror inside. 'And you ask me what is it?' He gave the door jamb another punch, ready to land one on the clerk if he tried a lecture.

'No.' The clerk stayed calm. 'You have viewed many corpses in my company. While this one is indeed amongst the most horrific, you have never reacted like this. I ask again: what is it?'

'Agatha. I saved her life. Just yesterday. She was so frightened, when . . . when she thought she was going to die. I saved her for—' He broke off to punch the door again, the pain helping to hold back his grief. 'It's my fault she was here.'

'You can hardly berate yourself, Stanton,' said Barling. 'Would you be happier had you let her drown yesterday?'

'That's not what I mean.'

'Then what do you mean?'

'I tried to persuade her not to go back to Lambert. But she wouldn't be told. I could have tried harder, but I didn't. I was so cold. Tired. Bothered that I'd failed to get out of this place.' He hit the wood hard once more. 'I failed her, Barling.'

'I disagree. You did not fail Agatha. You saved her life. She was, I am sure, profoundly grateful. As for what happened next, she very much knew her own mind and she made a choice. A terrible choice, as it turns out, but her choice nevertheless.'

Stanton said nothing. To his surprise, Barling briefly patted his arm.

The clerk went on. 'None of this is your fault, Stanton. Evil stalked that poor girl. It is too late for her now, but we have to stop it before it takes any more lives. And I fear it has already taken another.'

Stanton locked his hands behind his neck, tipped his head up to get air and to calm the angry race of his heart. 'Lambert?'

'Though the thought fills me with dread, I believe so,' said Barling. 'The book talks of a frozen swamp. I suspect he will be outside here somewhere.'

———————

They quickly found him, despite the fog.

The huge gatekeeper lay face down and completely still in one of the half-frozen pools of stinking yellow-brown slush that surrounded the manure pile. Blood stained the entire lower half of his habit.

'God have mercy,' said Barling as they came near the corpse.

Then the befouled cloth abruptly moved and shifted.

'Barling, I think he's still alive!' Stanton went to rush to the monk's aid.

'Stop.' Barling grabbed his arm. 'I do not think so.'

'But he's—'

'Look.' Barling's voice dropped to a whisper as he pointed.

Stanton doubted his own eyes.

From under Lambert's habit came the flick of a dark, scaled tail, just for a second, before it disappeared again.

'Another fate in *Tundale*,' said Barling. 'And where we have discovered rats on that poor girl, this fate talks of a serpent.'

Stanton swore in disgust. 'Then Lambert is dead.'

'Most definitely,' replied Barling. 'We cannot go near his body until we have help to deal with the creature that lies with it. Summon that help, please. At once.'

Stanton ran for the gate bell, pulling down on it as hard as he could. A fat old monk. A young girl. What coward would slay them in such a depraved way? 'Make haste! Brothers!'

A frightened call from the fog. 'Lambert? Is that you?'

'It's Stanton, the King's man. Come quickly!' His hands clutched the rope as he kept ringing, ringing.

More voices came: cowled figures were running from the fog.

The younger men first. Elias, a couple of lay brothers. Then Philip, Maurice holding tight to his arm in the murk of the fog.

'What's happening, Stanton?'

217

Stanton tried, tried so hard, to find the right words. All that came out was a confused jumble that somehow managed to convey the horror of what he'd seen.

His words were taken up by others as men made for the guesthouse, called for more help, uttered new cries of terror at what they saw.

Stanton walked away, breathing deeply, trying to pull himself together. He had to calm himself. He had to go back to Barling and help the clerk deal with these latest appalling discoveries.

Then, in the fog, he heard another sound. Not loud. But definite.

The single clack and then a scraping of wood on stone. Hard to tell in the fog. But it sounded like it came from the nearby walls.

He turned, started moving towards it.

Then came a flurry of regular sounds. Like someone walking up wooden steps.

Not walking. Scrambling. And not steps. A ladder.

'Hey!' He broke into a run. 'Hey!' Now running faster.

Just in time to see a bearded figure reach the top of the wall and disappear over it.

Daniel.

Chapter Forty-Three

Stanton reached the ladder. His stomach rebelled afresh.

Blood smeared each of the rungs, the marks made by Daniel's wide hands horribly clear. But he wouldn't let his disgust slow him. He flung himself at the ladder and clawed his way up it, two rungs at a time.

He got to the top of the wall to see the lay brother clamber to his feet, having jumped from the wall into the deep snow.

'Daniel, stop, you devil!'

The lay brother looked back up at him, his eyes wild as he shook his head. Then he took off through the knee-deep snow as fast as he was able, swinging his legs high and wide.

Stanton judged the height as best he could. And jumped.

Like Daniel, he landed in the snow, jarred but unhurt. He scrambled to his feet and set off after him.

The snow cloyed at his legs and boots. But he was gaining on him. Stanton was smaller, lighter than the bulky lay brother, the deep snow holding the other man back more. His breath rasped in his chest with effort.

Then Daniel stopped, bent to grab something that was half-buried in the snow.

Stanton was nearly on him. He tensed his arms and legs, ready for the fight.

He hardly saw the stout, heavy branch that Daniel threw right at his knees. It came through the air hard and fast, hitting them dead on. Pain burst through his kneecaps and his legs folded beneath him, sending him pitching forward into the snow.

Swearing hard, Stanton clawed his way upright.

Daniel had set off again, still at no great speed, but he'd widened the gap between them.

Stanton forced his legs to move, step by hobbling step, though each one was agony. The picture of Agatha's ruined body flashed before him again. His anger gave him fresh speed – his pain was nothing compared to what she'd suffered. 'You won't get away, Daniel!'

The lay brother glanced back at his shout. And he went down.

Whether it was a tree root, clumsiness, Stanton didn't know. All he knew was he had a chance to stop this vicious killer.

He surged forward, putting every ounce of strength he had into his charge.

Stanton hit him full force, body to torso, grabbing for his clothing.

'Get off!' Daniel's hefty swipe knocked him to one side.

He rolled over and over in the snow as Daniel tried to run once more.

Stanton scrambled after him, almost bent double, and got hold of another handful of clothing. He yanked the brother to a stop. 'You're coming back with me.'

'I said, get off!' Daniel tried to kick out at him. 'I've done nowt!'

Missed.

'You're a liar, Daniel.'

Missed another kick.

'I saw your handprints on the ladder.'

'Then go to hell, Stanton.' The brother swung a vicious punch.

Stanton ducked.

Daniel went to go for another.

Then a voice came from the fog. 'You'll have to stop me too.'

Elias, the library monk, stood there. He wielded the axe Stanton had thrown aside at the gatehouse.

And he looked like he knew exactly how to use it.

⎯⎯⎯⌣⎯⎯⎯

Barling stood with Stanton at the door of the Chapter House, where the monks had assembled. Daniel lay prostrate on the ground in the middle of the floor. This, thought Barling, was the discipline of the order in action before his very eyes.

Abbot Philip sat in his chair of office. He repeated the same questions at the lay brother, over and over. His fellow monks joined him with their own, a relentless, accusatory chorus raining down on the head of the quivering lay brother.

'Tell me the truth, Daniel. You were right next to the gatehouse this morning, when the bodies were found.'

Daniel spoke but he didn't dare to lift his head. 'I didn't touch Agatha, my lord abbot, I swear! Or Brother Lambert.'

Philip put a hand up.

The other monks went silent.

'But, Daniel,' said Philip, 'there was blood on the gatehouse door. The outside of the door, and a locked door at that. The King's man found your bloody handprints on the ladder. When we searched your clothing, we found you had a set of keys, also with smears of blood on them.' His mouth turned down in distaste. 'I can see from here that it is caked under your fingernails. What kind of a sinner are you, that you would persist in such lies?'

What, indeed? thought Barling. He folded his arms and waited for the answer, as he knew every ear in here did.

Daniel gave a long, low moan in response.

'Daniel?'

'I'm not lying, my lord abbot. I . . . I had a set of keys. I know I shouldn't have, but Brother Lambert gave me a copy. He'd lose his own all the time, and he had to be sure he had a set.'

'A very convenient response,' said Philip, 'when we have no way of checking this with the late Brother Lambert.'

Barling exchanged a brief nod with Stanton in agreement.

'I didn't know Lambert was dead, my lord. What I'm saying is true, my lord, it's all true. The gatehouse was closed up this morning, so I used the key to get in.' He moaned again. 'And then I found her, found my Agatha. I went to help her, though I knew it was useless. I got her blood all over my hands.'

'Your Agatha?' Philip's eyebrows shot up as a scandalised murmur rippled through the room.

'Yes, my lord abbot. She was mine. We . . . We were lovers.'

As the murmur turned to open gasps, Barling gave a quick look at Stanton. The younger man's face had darkened in anger. Barling prepared to order him out if he acted upon it. Emotions were running very high in here: he would not permit Stanton to worsen the situation through rash actions.

'You are telling us now,' said Philip, his voice tightening in disgust, 'that you loved her. Yet you find her body slain in the most hideous manner and your response is to run away. Fight the King's man hard when he tries to stop you. And you might have succeeded in getting away had it not been for the intervention of—'

'I ran because I thought I was next!' Daniel's yell echoed in the room, bringing a shocked silence.

He went on, his words tripping over one another in his haste to get them out. 'I found Agatha and I knew, knew that whoever had killed her was the same devil that had killed all the others. The King's man talked about the punishment of lustful clergy being one of the fates. I feared I was dead if I stayed there. For all I knew, the killer still lurked in the gatehouse, watching me. So I locked the door to keep him in. And I ran. That is the truth, I swear it, I swear.'

Philip shook his head. 'Daniel, only a few moments ago, you swore you had never touched Agatha. When that didn't work, you admitted your sin of fornication, a sin that is very much touching her. You swear to that now. You also swear that you touched her dead body. Which is it, Daniel? How many more lies will Satan put on your wicked tongue?'

'I'm not lying. I'm telling the truth.'

Philip dropped his hand and the chorus started again.

'The truth, boy.'

'Brother Silvanus despaired of your rudeness to him. He said so. You silenced him with a pitchfork.'

'God sees the sin in your heart.'

'Repent, Daniel. Confess your sins.'

'And Brother William? Not only did you slay him, you took a sacred chalice!'

'The lady Juliana. A defenceless, noble woman. Yet you put your evil hands upon her. Confess it, Daniel.'

On and on, until Philip raised a hand again for silence. 'Daniel, your refusal to confess to the most serious sins saddens all our hearts. Yet there are many transgressions that we know of. Fornication. Running away. Lying. I order you to be taken to the cell beneath my hall, where you will be locked up until you confess and repent. You will receive a flogging tomorrow for the sins of the flesh. You will fast for six months for running away and for your lies. That is my judgement as father of this house. I will seek advice from our General Chapter about further punishments that they will wish to impose for these grave sins.' Philip beckoned to a couple of other lay brothers who waited outside.

They moved forward to approach Daniel.

'You may rise,' said Philip.

The broad lay brother stood up, his face flushed and angry. 'I never killed anybody.' He jabbed a finger at the abbot. 'Never.'

A deep gasp of outrage met his words.

He stepped forward again. 'Never. Do you hear me?' He wheeled round to shout at the whole room. 'Do you?'

Several of the monks shrank back with prayers for help.

His fellow brothers stepped in and grabbed him. 'That's enough, Daniel.'

He tried to shake them off. 'Let go of me.'

'Take him to the cell,' said the abbot. 'I shall accompany you there.' His gaze met Barling's. 'I would ask that you accompany us. You need to witness that the criminal is securely under lock and key.'

'Certainly, my lord.' As Barling stepped forward to follow the group that was dragging the shouting, protesting Daniel away, he saw Stanton's fists tighten again.

He gave his assistant a warning shake of his head. For Stanton to start a fight in the Chapter House would be of no help at all.

'I think you should stay back a little, Philip.' Barling kept his voice low as they walked out into the cloister, although he doubted if the yelling, struggling Daniel would hear him even if he spoke in normal tones.

'I am not afraid of him,' replied Philip, though an anxious sheen of sweat on his face betrayed his words. 'I am still his father.'

Barling eyed the fight that Daniel was putting up. 'Nevertheless, he may do you harm. He is quite beside himself in his anger.' The lay brother continued to shout about his innocence. Barling was unimpressed, much as he had been in the Chapter House when Daniel's stories had changed in such quick succession.

'It's not the first time I have dealt with anger,' said Philip, 'though it is the first time I have had to imprison someone in the cell. Ernald had it built below the abbot's hall. He used it quite frequently and to great effect. Perhaps I should have been doing the same.'

They came out of the cloister.

The hall was now a short distance away, much to Barling's quiet relief. He was not Daniel's father and would not welcome an assault from the burly lay brother.

'I would not worry about the past, Philip,' he said. 'What is of concern is the immediate present and you are doing everything that is needed.'

Philip nodded and raised his voice. 'Daniel.'

The lay brother looked around, breathing hard, as were the brothers who held him.

Philip went on. 'You need to stop your fighting and accept your fate. If you struggle with the brothers on the stairwell, you could break your neck, or theirs. If you continue, I will have you chained up. Do you hear me?' Philip's sharp words seemed not so much to calm Daniel as to induce a sense of defeat.

They entered a side door to the hall which Barling had not used before. It led to a short flight of stone stairs, and the brothers and their prisoner waited at the top, Barling to one side, while Philip took a lit lamp from the wall and used it to light his way down to unlock the door. The abbot held the lamp aloft so he could select the right key.

He unlocked the door and pushed it open, the lamp casting a glow on the complete darkness within.

Darkness, but not emptiness.

Philip staggered back with a cry as Barling recoiled in horror.

A mutilated, white-cowled body, lying on the floor. Skulls arranged around it, their mouths agape and something dark and gleaming between each jaw.

They had found Brother Osmund.

Chapter Forty-Four

Stanton sat with Barling in the clerk's room at the guesthouse. The clerk had just given him a description of the hellish tableau in which Osmund's body had been arranged in the cell below the abbot's hall.

'God alive.' Stanton shuddered. 'It's another from the book of Tundale, isn't it?'

'It is. The fourth murder in the telling of the book. The covetous, devoured by a beast. Now we have seven in total. Pray God this is the last, with Daniel now in captivity.'

Stanton snorted. 'The captivity of the monks, though. Not the King.'

'It is indeed highly unlikely that Daniel will ever face the King's justice,' said Barling. 'He will be in the abbot's prison once they have cleared away Brother Osmund's body. And that is where he will stay.' He sighed. 'What he has done in there should give him cause to repent. Yet he still says it wasn't him, despite everything.'

'He fought me like the devil to get away,' said Stanton. 'I wouldn't have got him back here, had it not been for the library monk and his axe.'

'There are still many, many questions that he has to answer aside from all that was asked of him in the Chapter House. We have confirmed that Osmund is dead too, and Daniel was very belligerent with him also. He has learned about books with Elias, which is a breaking of the Rule, yet that has not been mentioned. We need to get the whole story out of him, Philip and I.'

'You do.' Stanton shook his head. 'I can't believe that I quite liked him. More fool me. I suppose I should be glad that I didn't end up a victim of his handiwork as well.'

'Work that is done,' said Barling.

'Speaking of work that is done, it turned out to be hugely to our benefit that you'd read the book of Tundale, Barling. If you hadn't read it, you wouldn't have known about those punished for sexual sin. But because you did, we realised at once what must have happened at the gatehouse. If we hadn't got there so quickly, Daniel would have escaped.'

'Not deserved, Stanton, but thank you. Reading is never a chore. I think I will have a couple of hours' sleep until it is time for me to see the abbot. We need to write an account of what has happened here to share with his General Chapter and for me to bring back to de Glanville. We are doing it after Compline. The brethren need to pray their hours more than ever.'

'That they do,' said Stanton. 'I'll leave you in peace to get some rest.'

Barling sat in the abbot's hall with Philip, feeling much restored after his sleep.

'By the looks of you, Philip,' he said, 'you need to get some rest even more than I did.'

The man sat at his table, his pale face drawn. 'How can I ever sleep again, Barling?' He rubbed at his face and gave a low moan of despair. 'I have been no father to these men. No defender. Evil has walked amongst us and I could not stop it.'

'You have done everything you could, Philip.'

'But it was not enough, was it? So many lives have been lost in the most depraved way.'

'Philip, all you – all we – can do is write these letters. Let us turn our attention to that, shall we?'

'We shall.' Philip gave a miserable nod, then his face contorted in a painful grimace.

'Are you all right, Philip?'

'Yes, please do not be concerned, it's—' He bit his lip to suppress a gasp of pain and put a hand to his stomach.

'I believe I should be. You do not look well.'

Philip nodded, still clutching at his stomach. 'I have to confess that I am not entirely hale. My innards have been giving me the greatest discomfort recently. I have some herbs that poor William gave me. If you will excuse me, I need to go and fetch them.' He got to his feet.

'Take your time,' said Barling.

As Philip headed out in the direction of his personal quarters, Barling began to lay out his writing materials. Usually that gave him great comfort. But such was the turmoil here, it was not of great use. As he laid down an inkpot, Philip came back in looking grim-faced. 'I have none left. Now I fear I will have a sleepless night of pain ahead.'

'Surely there are more of the herbs in the infirmary?' asked Barling. 'I saw many jars when I was in there the other day.'

'I wouldn't know where to find anything in there. It's late and it's cold, Barling,' said Philip. 'I shall manage, and we need to get on with writing those letters.' He sat back down, grimacing again.

That decided it. 'Philip,' said Barling, 'we are not writing a list of how many pails of milk the kitchen requires. This needs to be done properly. Either we fetch your herbs or we wait until you are feeling better.'

'You're right, Barling. As always.'

Barling collected his cloak and they walked out into the night, heading for the infirmary, their shoes crunching quietly on the frozen snow.

Suddenly Philip stopped dead and grabbed for Barling's arm.

'What is—' began Barling.

'Shh.' Philip raised a hand, a hand that shook. 'I just saw something. Somebody tall. Dressed in a black cloak.'

Barling's heart tripped faster. 'Where?' he whispered back.

'There.' Philip pointed to the shadows at the side of the infirmary.

'But nobody wears a black cloak here,' said Barling. 'Except me.'

'I know.' Philip grasped for Barling's arm. 'But what if Daniel wasn't acting alone?' What little colour he had drained from his face. 'What if he had an accomplice, one who wishes to fulfil the rest of Tundale's fates?'

Barling's mouth dried. A second murderer. One who was still on the loose.

Chapter Forty-Five

Stanton lay on his back in his bed in the guesthouse, fully dressed, staring sightlessly at the ceiling. By the usual routines of the abbey he knew it was very late. For him, it was less so. He wasn't ready to settle down for the night just yet, though he'd been dozing on and off.

He couldn't wait to get out of this place. There was something about being helpless in the snow's grip. He'd always liked open spaces where he could ride fast and far, and knowing such space was beyond the walls would usually have given him a sense of freedom. Now he felt trapped. He'd also give a whole purse of money for a night in a decent alehouse. Never mind, that would come soon.

He yawned deep and long. Wait. What was that? He sat up and listened out.

Nothing. Nothing except the rumble of the river.

He lay back down. There it was again. A sort of hammering noise. Not close. At least not very.

Stanton threw on his cloak and shoved his feet into his boots. He went out of his room but all seemed quiet within the guesthouse. He frowned. There it was again, faint and definitely not from within these walls. He made his way to the main door and opened it. The freezing night wind rushed in.

He stepped outside. Heavy clouds raced across the moonlit sky.

The hammering came again, brought here on the wind and louder now that he was outside.

But there was something else on the wind too.

The smell of smoke. Stanton frowned to himself. The monastery fires would all have been damped down for the night hours ago.

He started off in the direction of the noise, which was coming from somewhere over to the right. He quickened his pace.

As he drew nearer to the group of buildings where the lay brothers worked, the smell grew even stronger and the noise of the hammering grew louder. And he could now make out a male voice along with the urgent hammering. 'Help me!'

Then he saw it, a flicker of orange light.

Fire.

Stanton ran down the path towards it. Now he could see where it was coming from. The abbey's forge.

Crackling flames leapt from a burning window shutter along with billowing smoke.

The hammering carried on and Stanton could see why. The door was shut. Locked.

'Hello!' He ran faster towards it, and heard the voice, that of a man, yell out in terror again.

'For the love of God, somebody help me!' A storm of coughing.

Hell's teeth. It was Philip in there. 'Hang on!'

Stanton flung himself at the door handle, wrenched it round. No good. He pounded on the door with his knuckles. 'My lord abbot!'

'Stanton? Is that you?'

'It is, my lord.'

'Help me.' More coughing. 'I beg you!'

'Stand back!' Stanton raised a boot and kicked at the door. It bounced on its hinges but stayed firm.

'Stanton! Hurry!'

He kicked again. The planks bent. A little. Another. More. He summoned all his strength, slammed into them as hard as he could, and two gave. It was enough.

Stanton tore the damaged wood out with his hands, uncaring of the skin on his palms, hauling a screaming Philip through the gap.

Philip dropped to his hands and knees on to the snow-covered ground, coughing and retching and still screaming. His white habit was filthy, as were his face and hands. And his screaming wasn't stopping. It was one word, over and over and over again.

Satan.

Stanton crouched down to him. 'My lord?'

Philip looked at him with eyes wild with terror. He stopped screaming, panted for breath, grasped hold of Stanton's arms. 'The church. I have to get to the church. Do you hear me, Stanton?' Philip shook him as much as he was able in his weakened state, coughing hard again.

'I don't think you should try to move, my lord. It's not wise.'

'The church.' It came out as a croak. 'That is my order.'

'Yes, my lord.' Stanton broke the abbot's hold and shoved his shoulder under one of Philip's arms, grabbing hold of him as he did so.

They set off, Stanton bearing most of Philip's weight. The man could hardly walk, stumbling every second step and half-sobbing in breathless fear.

Shouts of alarm sounded from the inner precinct, followed by the flicker of light from lamps and torches. The monks were rushing to the burning forge.

'Brothers!' Philip's hoarse shout sent him into a fresh spasm of coughing. 'The church. You must make for the church!'

His body sagged even heavier in Stanton's hold and Stanton feared the man's collapse. 'My lord—'

'The church. I beg you. For all our sakes.'

Chapter Forty-Six

Stanton bore Philip into the church, a church that now teemed with frightened monks and brothers.

'The altar, Stanton,' came Philip's hoarse order.

Stanton complied, willing hands stretching out from the brethren to help their abbot to his rightful place.

As they reached the altar, Maurice pushed through the crowd and put his arms around the abbot, taking him from Stanton's hold. 'Philip, my boy.'

The abbot managed to stay standing with Maurice's help, though he was not steady on his feet. The fire and smoke had come close to taking him: as well as his laboured breath and constant coughing, his face and hands and habit were stained and marked.

Stanton stepped back out of the way, nursing his palms. The skin was ripped and bleeding from his assault on the door. He'd not felt a thing as he'd fought to get Philip out of the burning forge. Now that his pulse had slowed, the stinging pain had begun to take hold. He scanned the crowded church for the one face that he couldn't see: Barling's. He frowned to himself. The clerk must be in here somewhere. Otherwise, where was he?

Philip was speaking from the altar now, weakened and coughing every few words. 'My brothers, I thought that when we caught Daniel at his wickedness, and had locked him up, that we had defeated the evil that had visited this place. But we have not. The devil still stalks us.'

The brethren called out in their fear.

'Tonight, that devil brought me right to the gates of hell. I was rendered senseless and locked into the forge, which was set on fire, so that I might suffer not just death, but a particular death.' He coughed long and hard again. 'Brothers, I was to suffer one of the fates of the sinners in *The Vision of Tundale*: to be cast into an infernal forge and burned to ash. The eighth fate.'

The chorus of fear swelled louder, along with prayers for salvation.

Philip raised a hand as much as he could to get silence.

Every monk and brother gave it, waiting for his next words.

They were not ones Stanton or the brethren expected.

'But hear my confession, I beseech you: it was a fate I deserved, for I am a sinner!'

The stunned faces before Stanton could be identical, along with the cries of shock and disbelief.

'My sins,' said Philip, struggling to be heard, 'are those as described in Tundale for the eighth fate. I have had such deep anger in my heart for brethren who have slighted me. I have lain abed and slept in my lodge. Consumed food and wine in sickening gluttony. I have added sin to sin to sin. That is why Satan found me and almost sent me to hell! I am a sinner – we are all sinners. We must repent, so no others will be taken in death. We must repent!' He fell prostrate to the floor, calls for God's mercy and protection rising up in a loud chorus as Philip wept aloud.

Maurice knelt down to tend to him.

Yet Stanton still could not see Barling.

His heart began to beat faster again. He stepped back on to the altar and crouched down to speak to Philip.

'My lord abbot,' he said.

'Go away,' said Maurice. 'Can you not see that our lord abbot is suffering?'

'Maurice, please,' said Philip, coughing once more. 'Without the intervention of Hugo Stanton here, I would surely have perished.'

Maurice muttered something that Stanton couldn't catch as the monks who stood closest broke into loud thanks.

'God be praised!'

'The blessings of eternity to you, sir!'

'May you have your eternal reward!'

Stanton gave an embarrassed nod. He didn't care about the thanks. He'd been relieved to have got Philip out alive, to save a life in this place of death. 'My lord abbot,' said Stanton, 'I only need to ask you if you know where Barling is.'

'Barling?' Philip looked in confusion at Stanton. 'He's with you, isn't he? He sent you in to save me.'

Now Stanton's heart was a thud in his chest that he couldn't ignore. 'No, Barling wasn't with me. Your noises from the forge summoned me. The last time I saw the clerk, he was going to help you with some letters in your hall.'

'He was with me,' said Philip. 'But we needed to go to the infirmary for some of my stomach herbs. Then I saw a figure, a black-hooded figure near the infirmary. Barling forbade me, but I set off in pursuit. Then I knew no more. When I woke, I was locked in the burning forge, where you—' Philip stopped, his eyes growing wide in horror. 'But if the devil got me, he must have got Barling too. And now we are all in mortal danger. Don't you see?'

The monks around him cried out in terror, in a bewilderment that Stanton shared, along with his own fear: not of the devil but that something terrible had happened to Barling.

'Maurice,' said Philip, 'help me to rise.'

'No, my lord.'

235

'Maurice.'

The novice master did as ordered with another mutter.

'My brothers, oh, my brothers.' Philip swayed as he stood. 'First I must ask and I pray I will get an answer: has anyone seen the King's man, Aelred Barling?'

Stanton waited for the call that someone had. That the clerk was at the back of the church. Out in the cloister. Sheltering in the warming room. Every moment that went past was another where his heart beat faster. But nothing came, nothing except a buzz of quiet questions.

Stanton's mouth dried as he met Philip's appalled gaze.

'Then, brothers,' said Philip, 'we are nearer the peril of damnation than I have ever known. If Barling has been taken, then his is the ninth fate. And once the ninth fate has taken place, then it is time for the Prince of Darkness to arrive. Oh, God help us.' His knees buckled and he sank to the floor of the altar, to screams and shouts of fear from the monks. 'Pray. I must pray – we must all pray! Satan, begone. Begone!'

The brethren took up his call, chanting it over and over.

Stanton grabbed hold of Maurice's shoulder.

'What is it, boy?' hissed Maurice.

'Brother, what's the ninth fate?'

'Not now. Can't you see we are in turmoil?'

'Please, brother.'

'The ninth fate is that the sinner will descend into the very depths of hell. Down to the deepest, darkest place of all. Where there is no light, only blackness. For all eternity.'

Stanton willed his words to change, but they did not.

They could only mean one place. One place where it would be dark forever. The thought threatened to fell him.

Barling, I've failed you too. Failed you utterly.

Chapter Forty-Seven

Stanton ran through the library, making for the door that led to the graveyard, terror clawing at his heart. He should never have left the small-framed clerk alone.

Never.

He hauled the door open and caught his breath. The scudding clouds had blocked out the moon.

And cutting through the black of the night was snow. More snow. A thick, swirling curtain of it.

Covering the stones, the ground, in a thick, fresh layer.

Any disturbed ground was being covered before his very eyes.

He ran, ran between the gravestones, kicking snow, dropping to his knees to shovel it aside with his hands, shouting Barling's name, over and over.

It was no good.

He could see nothing, find nothing. His grief roared through him.

Barling was lost.

His head. Dear God, his head. Barling forced his eyes open, braced for the stab of fresh pain that the light would bring.

Nothing.

He closed his eyes again, opened them.

Yet he could still see nothing. Nothing at all.

His fuddled mind fought to make sense of what was happening to him.

His eyes – he should rub them. Yes, that would help. He dared to move his right hand, cautious lest that was injured along with his head. He could scarce feel it.

But no. It was just cold. Cold. He was cold all over. Especially his back. Something hard and lumpy pressed into it too. He went to raise his right hand to rub his eyes.

His knuckles struck against wood before he raised them more than a few inches.

Barling swallowed hard.

Blinked harder.

There was nothing wrong with his eyes. He knew that now. He tried to bend his knees.

Again, they struck wood. Solid wood. He scrabbled hard with his fingers. An edge, there had to be an edge to it. An opening. He couldn't find one.

A sweat coated his entire body despite the deep chill that possessed him.

He swallowed hard again, filled his lungs.

'Help me!' His shout sounded muffled, hollow.

The dread that had been circling at the edge of his mind tore through it, sending his heart into spasms that he feared would shatter his chest.

There was nothing wrong with his eyes: the dust-tasting darkness was utter and complete.

Barling knew that now, knew it as screams that could be those of a terrified animal broke from him. Screams he could not stop, though each one robbed him of his precious air.

He lay in a coffin. And it was one that he shared with someone else.

Stanton knelt on the deep snow, shivering hard. He might have lost Barling.

And by all that was holy, he'd get the devil who'd killed him.

But he didn't know who that was and without Barling, maybe he never would.

Yet he had to try – he had to.

The book, *The Vision of Tundale*. The answer lay in there somewhere.

He stood up. He had to take it. Take it away from here and bring it to somebody who could read it all, make sense of it.

There were many pairs of eyes here that could. But any one of the monks could be the devil laughing at him behind the mask of a pious man.

Wait.

There was one man. One who could not have attacked the abbot or Barling, for he was under lock and key. One who might turn out to be in league with the devil. But one who might not.

Stanton hurried off in the direction of the abbot's hall.

And offered up a prayer that his instincts were right about the man locked up in the cell below it.

Chapter Forty-Eight

Stanton hammered on the door of the cell under the abbot's lodging. 'Daniel. It's Stanton. Move away from the door.' He raised the stout hatchet he held, taken from the kitchen, and brought it down once, twice, tearing his damaged palms further. The lock splintered away and with a hard kick he was in.

Daniel stood in one corner. His eyes went to the hatchet. To Stanton's face. And back. 'What is it?' Wary. 'What do you want?'

'I want the truth, Daniel,' said Stanton. 'And I haven't time for chapter meetings or whatever it is you're used to.' He pointed the axe at him. 'Did you kill Agatha?'

'No.' Daniel drew himself up to his full, considerable height. 'I never hurt a hair on her head. I'd chop one of my hands off with that blade if it would make you believe me.'

Stanton knew he would. He nodded. That was good enough. 'You asked me what was going on. There have been more attacks. Philip was the latest victim. Or he would have been if I hadn't saved him. When I should have been saving Barling.' Grief threatened to take him. He forced it down. 'I have to find the devil who's done this. To do that, I need the book, the book of Tundale. The monks have the copy that Reginald made but I think there should be an original copy, an old one, that belonged to Abbot Ernald. You know the layout of the library, don't you?'

'Yes.' Daniel was still wary.

'Then you can help me.' Stanton held up the hatchet again. 'And if you plan on attacking me, think again.'

'Stanton, I swear to you, I won't do you any harm. I've never done anybody any harm. You've got to believe me. I loved Agatha. I want to find the murdering bastard as much as you do.'

Stanton went to repeat his threat.

'I swear.'

He hadn't time. 'Then come on: the library.'

Daniel hurried over to him. 'What if somebody sees me? I'm supposed to be locked up.'

'They're all in the church,' said Stanton. 'And I've got a blade that'll stop any argument. Now, let's go. Quiet as we can.'

Stanton followed as Daniel led the way in through the sacristy to the back chamber.

His judgement had been right. The many voices raised in fearful prayer still came from the church, but they'd not seen a soul.

Daniel lit a taper and handed it to Stanton. 'Elias has a system for his books. He would keep Ernald's favourite books in that locked cupboard. Still does.' He rummaged under a chest in one corner and produced a key. 'Elias's spare. I swear the monks scatter keys like birds scatter grain.' He unlocked the cupboard and started to go through the books, squinting in the poor light that Stanton held up. 'Here it is.' He went to hand it to Stanton.

Stanton put the hatchet down and took the book. Tattered and old, it looked far less grand than the copy made by Reginald.

241

But in it were the words that had ended the life of the clerk Aelred Barling. Ended it in a way that was the worst of nightmares. Yes, he might find out who had done this. But he'd failed. Failed a good man. He choked back a furious sob. 'Damn it all to hell. I've failed. Completely.'

'Not completely, Stanton. If you hadn't been here, the abbot would have lost his life.'

Stanton froze. Stared at him. 'If I hadn't been here?'

'Yes, you've saved a life. Without you, Philip would have died.'

'No.' Stanton shook his head. 'No. That's not it.'

'You're not making sense—'

'I shouldn't have been here. Don't you see?'

Daniel looked at him, bewildered. 'No.'

'All of this evil has been planned.' Those had been Barling's words, the day they rode back from seeing the village priest: *. . . it was not the result of a chance encounter with evil . . . it was very much planned. And that, in my long experience in the law, is the worst kind of evil.* Stanton held out the book of Tundale. 'This, *The Vision of Tundale*, is the plan.'

'Yes, you said. But—'

'The murderer is following this plan, making each fate real. Barling was the last victim. He's part of the plan, like all the victims. But I never was, because I shouldn't be here. I never should have been.' Silvanus, the guestmaster, on the day Stanton had arrived in this place with Barling: *A second visitor from the court of the King? . . . Unfortunately, I have not yet had your room prepared as I was not informed that we were receiving you.* Stanton swore loud and long. 'I think I know who it is now. And that bastard sent Barling to hell. The last fate, the darkest place for all eternity. He has buried him.'

Daniel's face changed. 'Then there may well still be time.'

'Time? Of course there's no time. I ran to the graveyard. The snow is so heavy I can't even see which grave he's put him in.'

'But there are no fresh graves,' said Daniel.

'What do you mean?'

'The ground is frozen solid. The bodies are in the crypt. They stay frozen there in this weather.'

Stanton's mouth dried. 'And where is the crypt?'

'Under the south transept of the church.'

'Then it's also under a church full of monks and lay brothers. And only one devil. Daniel, we must unmask him. But I need your help. And we will only have one chance.'

Chapter Forty-Nine

Stanton opened the door of the church to a wave of light and the sound of the monks' voices raised in desperate pleas to banish Satan.

'Go,' he whispered to Daniel.

Daniel marched in, marched in the door that led to the monks' choir, the east end of the church, from which he was forbidden.

Marched in too as the man accused of grievous murder.

The first monk saw him. 'By the name of the Virgin!' He dropped his prayer book and fled.

'Oh, God save us!' called out another as he saw the burly lay brother striding freely across the church. Others now saw him and all began to shout and point, many more fleeing as they did so.

The chaos spread, Daniel still marching. He headed for the south transept.

But Stanton only watched for the one reaction that mattered.

And there it was. An angry, angry shout. 'Daniel, stay away from that crypt!'

A shout that came from Abbot Philip.

Though he felt cold no longer, Barling's consciousness was fading fast.

Perhaps not fading, no. Too many colours swirled around him for that. Red. Blue. Like my lady's robe.

Precise, Barling, you must always be precise.

How could he be standing in front of himself, lecturing, wagging a finger?

'Help me.' He struggled to form the words through lips that were dead with cold. He could not tell whether he uttered the words aloud or whether they were only in his head.

More colours, but now they were pale and cold and arched over him. His mind was slipping. One could not build arches from colour.

And colour did not whisper, either.

Whispers that turned to the hiss of snakes that he was sure coiled their way around his arms, his legs.

The serpent of evil. The devil.

And the devil was made flesh and dwelt amongst us.

The devil who'd buried him in here, who'd killed all those others.

Philip, whose words had flowed like a serpent's poison into Barling's ears as he'd gloated to him of his depravity, as Barling lay almost without sense and unable to move from the blow to his head.

Cuthbert, my very first. I went and summoned him in the hours after Compline. All of the monks were fast asleep in the dormitory, even Maurice had closed his eyes. If someone had stirred, what would they have seen in the dark of that room? A cowled figure. That's all.

I got Silvanus at a quiet time, when I knew everybody would be occupied. All so conscientious.

With the lady Juliana, it was so easy to slip from cloister in the early hours of prayer. Pitch dark and the monks either praying or sleeping in their carrels in the cloister. Both take the monks into a world where they notice nothing.

Osmund? Hopeless, of course. But he'd do anything I said. I was giving him a wise lesson in discipline, showing him the cell and telling him how best he could use it with the lay brothers. The sheep skulls were already waiting in a sack.

William was a mistake. It should have been an old, sick monk. But William arrived unexpectedly as he was worried about one of his patients. Never mind. He served my purpose just as well.

Old Lambert and his little whore, Agatha, were far too easy, in the gatehouse that's apart from the rest of the abbey.

I myself shall be the victim of the eighth fate, though I have of course ensured that I will be able to rescue myself in a convenient miracle if the fools here fail to notice my commotion. I am quite looking forward to the excitement.

As for you, you know what you've done, and I know it too. You're going to hell, Aelred Barling. So good of you to allow me to send you there.

The colours were gone again, all gone.

Now it was black, only black. He could see nothing.

The words of his fate from the book of Tundale beat in his head like a drum.

Forever in darkness you will be, light no more will ever see.

He was falling, falling, the air rushing past, yet he could not feel it.

He could not feel anything. Anything at all.

Now it was quiet, so quiet.

The thud of his heart sounded far, far away. So very, very slow.

And then came a tremendous crash, followed by a bang.

Shouts. Noise.

'Barling! Where are you?'

Another bang and his whole body jolted.

And then, dear God, there was a flood of light, so bright it hurt his eyes and there was air and Stanton had his arms around him, hauling him out, and there were more shouts, more voices. More air.

And he, just like Tundale, was moving back from the depths.

Chapter Fifty

'Barling!' Stanton knelt over the clerk on the frigid floor of the crypt, his own heart pounding. They'd found him, found him, crammed into a coffin with the dead Silvanus. But he was ice cold, his thin lips blue. Stanton shook him hard. 'Can you hear me?'

Barling's lips twitched.

Relief surged through Stanton.

'He's alive.' Elias, next to him. 'Let's get him into the warm. Quickly as possible.'

'Let me. I can pick him up.' Daniel went to do so.

'I need to have Philip locked up.' Stanton hurried back up the crypt steps and into the church, where monks and lay brothers milled in loud confusion.

His gaze lit on Reginald and he ran over to him. 'Where's Philip?'

'If you mean Abbot Philip—'

'I mean the devil we've been seeking, brother.'

A louder commotion broke out as Daniel emerged from the crypt carrying the senseless Barling.

Realisation flared in the prior's sharp eyes. 'May the saints preserve us. Philip told me he was going to his hall.' His glance went to where

Barling was now being tended to on the floor by Elias. 'But I doubt that is the case.'

'Damn it all. He's getting away.'

The prior unhooked his keys from his belt and thrust them at Stanton. 'Here. These will get you through any door.'

Stanton set off at a run for the exit of the church. 'Daniel, with me!'

They raced out into the cloister.

'Look, the main door's open,' said Daniel.

'Quick,' said Stanton. 'He can't have got far.'

As they ran out Daniel shouted. 'I have him.'

Stanton followed his point. The snow had stopped once more and the full moon lit the frozen snow clear as day.

Running for the main gate was Philip, his long strides giving him great speed.

'Come on.'

As they chased after him, Philip glanced around.

The abbot had seen them. He ran faster than ever and reached the gate. It took him two tries to get it open.

'The snow's making it stick,' said Daniel. 'We're nearly on him.'

Philip didn't bother closing the gate again as he fled.

Then Stanton and Daniel were through and out the other side.

The white road glowed in the moonlight. Deserted. But the light showed Philip's footsteps, leading off to the right.

'He's headed for the woods,' panted Daniel.

'I can see him.' Stanton pulled in an extra breath to raise his voice as he ran. 'Philip! Stop!'

'Doesn't matter,' said Daniel. 'We'll get him easy in there.'

Now they were climbing, and the rumble of the water was getting louder.

'The river will stop him. There's nowhere to go after that.'

As they broke cover into the clearing, Philip was nearing the water's edge.

Then Stanton knew. 'Damn it to hell, he's going to jump it. If he gets to the other side, we'll lose him.'

Daniel swore. 'He won't make it. He can't.'

As the words came out of his mouth, Philip put on a last burst of speed. He raced to the narrowest part of the torrent and leapt.

For the moment that he hung in the air, Stanton thought he'd gone too high.

But no.

Philip made it to the other side. The rocks that he landed on were slick with ice and wet moss. He slid down, down towards the water, with a last grab at a snow-covered shrub. He stopped. Pulled himself back up. Got cautiously to his feet, breathing hard but with a wide smile. He raised his voice over the roar of the water.

'Too slow, both of you. Slow minds as well. So easy. All of it.'

Fury pounded through Stanton along with the race of his heart. 'Make no mistake, I will hunt you down, Philip!'

'But why would you do that, Stanton? You saved me from peril in the forge, did so most impressively. Trouble is, you should've been looking out for your master.'

Stanton wouldn't respond to his mocking. 'You'll feel the hand of the justice of the King. You will hang. And I will be there to watch it.'

'No, I won't, Stanton.' Philip's smile got even wider. 'I shall seek refuge at another holy house. Confess all my sins. I may be flogged and imprisoned. But I will live. The Church believes in repentance. All I have to do is throw myself upon its mercy. The King's justice can't touch me. For I am a man of God and not subject to Henry for my crimes. I might have hated the life of a monk that I was forced into, but I have my reward for all those wasted years. My vows are what'll save me from the noose.'

'You're no man of God, Philip. You're a monster.'

'Oh, but I am a man of God. One who ruled over an ordered life, an order that I could demand, which meant I could move freely through the abbey. Nobody ever questioned it when I approached them, telling them I had something of importance to discuss with them, each and every one trusting the holy abbot.' He grinned. 'Except for your whore, Daniel. I didn't even bother saying anything to her.'

'Shut your mouth, you hear me?' yelled Daniel.

Philip ignored him. 'She and pissed old Lambert were almost too easy. I killed her first. Her neck broke and opened like a bird's as I swung my scythe. Lambert actually tried to fight me to save her.' He laughed. 'Can you imagine? He was crying for her when I killed him. All fools, even the keen-minded Aelred Barling. He followed me outside like a lamb, went down in the snow with one strike to the head. Too easy, really.'

'You'll go to hell, Philip,' shouted Stanton, rage hot in his chest. 'You're the worst sinner. Not any of them.'

He shrugged. 'It didn't actually matter if they were sinners or not. What mattered was what people thought. Believed. And people are fools. They never see what's in front of them.' He gave a nasty wink. 'But you might want to ask your friend Barling about Paris.'

Daniel yelled at him again. 'That I could get my hands on you. I'd throttle you in a heartbeat.'

'But you can't, can you, Daniel?' replied Philip. 'You're a big clumsy ox and twice as stupid. You'd never make the jump.'

Daniel muttered something and bent down to rummage through the snow. He stood up with a grunt of effort, a huge rock in his right fist.

Philip just laughed. 'Even you can't throw that thing this far. Try if you like. You'll see.'

Daniel hurled it at Philip with all his might. It bounced harmlessly off the rocks and fell into the torrent with a mighty splash, watched by a delighted Philip.

'See? Stupid. I told you.' He looked back up at Stanton and Daniel. And his face changed.

Changed at the moment Stanton saw another stone, smaller, faster, fly through the air and strike Philip hard on one temple.

The abbot screamed at its impact. Took a stagger to one side. On feet that stood on wet moss and ice.

After, Stanton would think of Philip's slipping, sliding feet as a long dance, one that tipped him towards the torrent as he fought, failed, fought to regain his footing.

In truth, it was a blink of an eye.

Philip fell in, his mouth open in a high cry that cut off as soon as he hit the roaring water. The torrent pummelled down on him, flung him from side to side against the brutal rocks for a few moments, then swallowed him down into its depths.

'Two of these.' Daniel held up both hands. 'Two rocks.' He spat hard into the water. 'Folk never see what's in front of them.'

Chapter Fifty-One

'And we pray, dear brothers, that God will help guide us in our deliberations this morn. Amen.' Brother Reginald finished the prayer.

Barling joined in with the loud response of 'Amen' that sounded in the Chapter House, as Stanton, sitting next to him, did too. All the monks were assembled, with the lay brothers standing in the doorways.

'My brothers,' said Reginald, 'with the authority that my office of prior gives me, and in recognition of the nature of this special chapter meeting, I have invited the King's men to sit amongst us.'

As the prior carried on with the formalities, Barling kept his expression composed. It did not matter that he was not the one leading the announcement of the findings of the enquiries at Fairmore Abbey. He was lucky to be alive. He should not feel the twinge of envy at Reginald that he did.

'To commence,' said Reginald, 'I will ask the King's men, Aelred Barling and Hugo Stanton, to give their accounts, which they have already shared with me. There has also of course been a great deal of discussion over the last couple of days between many individuals and me. We will draw all the information together. I will be formally notifying the General Chapter of our order. Barling will share his findings with Ranulf de Glanville, justice of the King.' Reginald looked at Stanton.

'You and Daniel, lay brother of this abbey, pursued Philip after he fled the abbey. He lost his life in the river during the pursuit. Can you revisit your account, please?'

Stanton did so, providing a clear and concise summary.

Barling listened with approval at how well Stanton acquitted himself. He had heard the full version from Stanton and Daniel in private with the prior. To Barling's relief, Reginald had decided not to punish Daniel in any way for his actions against Philip. Barling thought that Reginald would perhaps have done exactly the same thing, should the old monk's hands have been in full working order.

'That is my true account, brother,' finished Stanton.

More than a few quiet, stifled sobs came from the gathered audience.

'Thank you,' said Reginald. 'And not only for your account. Our sincere thanks also for being the man who found the truth. Yet while your account is of great value in establishing how the wicked Philip met his deserved end, we also need to have a full account of what he did, and we also need to examine why. I will ask Aelred Barling, the only victim of Philip to survive, to tell us what Philip spoke of to him when he imprisoned him in the crypt. I know that there are many of the brothers present who will add to it. Barling, would you like to begin?'

'I will, brother.' Again, it felt odd to be on the receiving end of the questions. But that was nothing compared to revisiting that terrifying time in the crypt. A time when he was sure that he was going to die. Yet he would push aside such feelings here. Emotion had no place in the law, he had said that enough times. 'Philip, as you have mentioned, was taking a depraved delight in what he was doing. Like many who are so driven, he wanted to boast of it. So he boasted of it to me, even as he was preparing my death.'

Barling repeated Philip's foul list as sensitively as he could, aware that he spoke of so many horrific deaths.

Reginald nodded when he had finished. 'Then that tells us all how Philip went about his crimes.' He shook his head. 'By using the sacred order and structure of our lives against us.' He passed a gnarled hand over his face. 'As to why, we have heard some of it from Stanton. But Philip also spoke of that to you, Barling, did he not?'

'He did,' replied Barling. 'Like so many who go down the path of wrongdoing, his actions were born from a place of deep, deep anger. He told me that he had never wanted to enter a monastery. That he had hated the idea. But that it was his father who had insisted, a man who, in Philip's eyes, was devoted to Philip's older brother but had little time for him. Philip was particularly aggrieved by this, as he believed his older brother to be of vastly inferior intellect to him.'

'His father's choice would not have been out of favouritism,' said Reginald, 'but by right of order of birth. As it should be.'

'I agree entirely,' said Barling. 'But Philip did not see it that way.'

'I concur with all that,' said Maurice. 'As a young novice, Philip arrived under my tutelage in a state of constant anger. So arrogant, so sure of his own great worth. He hated his father for sending him away. And he hated being here: away from the world and denied all its earthly pleasures. He found all sorts of ways in which he could cause trouble. I used every method of discipline and punishment that I could. He ended up in the cell many times.' Maurice shook his head. 'I should say that Philip was not unique in this. I have had many novices cause me heartache and headaches. But what was of note was just how creative he could be in his bad behaviour. I had to seek help from Abbot Ernald in the end. Something I very, very rarely had to do.'

'And that was the turning point, Philip told me,' said Barling. 'Ernald warned him that he would be locked up for good by the order if he carried on the way he was. But Ernald had recognised his outstanding cleverness. He told Philip that if he were to embrace life within these walls, he could do great things. It worked. Eventually Philip became cellarer at a very young age.'

'That was indeed a gift of Ernald's: finding exactly the right talent for an individual monk or brother,' said Reginald, his words bringing forth many nods and murmurs of agreement. 'Letting them serve their God through work in which they thrived.'

'I have seen that that is the case here in the abbey,' said Barling. 'But for Philip, there were darker forces at work. His words to me were: "I think Ernald always saw me as his greatest triumph. In his eyes, I was the sinner who not only repented but who embraced God fully and completely. If only he knew." Indeed.' Barling paused so that all could grasp how Philip's thoughts ran. 'Nonetheless, Philip told me he loved being cellarer and was good at it, especially as so much of it was to do with finance and commerce and nothing whatsoever to do with endless devotions. He always wanted to do more but Ernald kept a tight rein on him, reminding Philip that his earning of money should be to serve the glory of God within this secluded holy house, away from the world and not for wealth for its own sake.'

'But all that time, Philip was not working for God's glory, was he?' asked Reginald.

'No,' said Barling. 'He enjoyed amassing wealth. He particularly enjoyed his power as cellarer over the lay brothers. Here were men who had to obey his bidding, whether they liked it or not.'

'Here I must pause to address something which is shameful on my part, on the part of all the brothers,' said Reginald. 'Barling and I have spoken to the lay brothers, with Daniel's help. It would appear that Philip had instilled great fear in them over the years. Where Ernald disciplined for sin, it would appear that Philip did it for pleasure. Not as Abbot Ernald would have done, with the lash of the whip. But with humiliations dragged out and unjust punishments and false accusations. Those spread to here, as well. We heard over and over from Philip about how the lay brothers needed the strongest of guidance as they had little wit of their own. To our shame, we stopped questioning it as we had no reason to think otherwise. I offer my heartfelt sorrow, brothers, and a promise that things will not be like that again.'

The lay brothers responded with humble thanks of their own and a nod from Daniel.

'And then,' said Barling, 'Abbot Ernald died last summer. Setting these horrific events in motion.'

'A loss we all felt and still feel, Barling,' said Maurice. 'Even though it was expected. Ernald had known he was dying for some time. He will be in God's arms for all eternity.'

'Philip said he genuinely grieved too,' said Barling. 'He said that Ernald was more of a father to him than his had ever been.'

'Then came the elections for the new abbot.' Reginald's mouth set in a thin line. 'And we elected Philip.'

'Which caused Philip great elation,' said Barling. 'No longer an unwanted son, he had become the beloved father – father of the whole house. He believed his talents were finally being recognised by every monk here. But they were not, were they, brothers?' His gaze moved to Reginald, then Maurice.

'No,' said Reginald. 'Ernald had made all of us senior monks, his obedientiaries, swear to keep our duties after his death.'

'Indeed he did,' added Elias. 'Ernald told me, as I am sure he told everyone, that he had chosen us for our worth and experience and that Fairmore was a great house because of it.'

'As for Philip,' said Reginald, 'Ernald told Maurice and me, the only two monks who remained from the foundation of the house, that Philip should become the next abbot.'

'When we objected,' said Maurice, 'citing Philip's past sinful conduct, Ernald reminded us of the parable of the prodigal son. Philip was his redeemed son and that was that. Ernald told us that we were like the sons who worked steadily and dependably, and would receive our reward in heaven.'

'I wish to confess to all here,' said Reginald, his voice low, 'that I was bitterly disappointed in being passed over for the position of abbot. So, although I knew of Philip's past, as did Maurice, we did not say anything to the King's men. I knew I would never get to be abbot of this great house, but at least I was still its prior. I feared that, should we say anything, I might lose my post, for the Rule says a prior can be deposed. I was well aware of Philip's vindictive streak. I put the maintenance of my own position above the good of the house. For that I am deeply sorry.'

The old man looked utterly dejected. Diminished.

Barling carried on. 'Philip now decided he would grow the wealth of Fairmore exactly as he pleased. He didn't want any opposition so he appointed Osmund as cellarer. Osmund could easily be ordered to do anything he said. Philip was, in effect, still cellarer. You have found evidence of that, have you not, Elias?'

Elias nodded. 'I have been through the books that Osmund kept. Osmund had no idea of what he was doing. But I also found many examples of where a page was missing, or half-torn. I believe that this was done on purpose, as even with the most detailed examination it renders many of the records meaningless. Osmund would have had no way of deciphering what was going on.'

'Do you suspect the work of Philip's hand?' asked Reginald, a little more restored-looking now.

'Very much so.' Elias gave a sad smile. 'If only because our dear brother Osmund would not have had the wit to do that himself.'

'Philip formed falsehood after falsehood about those he killed,' said Reginald. 'He essentially concocted sin where there was none. He told Stanton and Daniel that at the river.'

Now the murmurs of the monks and brothers were of disgust, of anger.

Barling did not join in. He could not truthfully speak of his own spotless conscience.

'I would ask for your attention, brothers,' said Reginald. 'Please continue, Barling.'

Barling did so. 'Within a couple of weeks, Philip found out that he hadn't been appointed out of admiration by his peers. Silvanus let it – how shall I put this? – slip. But it didn't upset Philip at all. In fact, it made him very happy. It had taken him the best years of his life, but he had made a complete fool of a father, his father Ernald. Now Philip had what he had always been denied: he had control over his destiny.'

The monks and brothers had quietened, hanging on every word of Barling's.

'Philip had no wish to leave the monastery and go out into the world. The power of the abbacy was immense and now he had it. But, he said, his plan was to bring the world to him. And the way to do that was through the spectacle of sin. He'd seen the huge crowds at the ordeal in York. The wealth, the fame that would follow: Fairmore would become one of the greatest sites of pilgrimage in the world. And Philip would be at its centre, lauded and renowned. So he set about bringing *The Vision of Tundale* to life. The story of Fairmore would be that sinners fell to Satan, but that through prayers and repentance, Satan was defeated.' He clasped his hands. 'While all the time, the only devil here was Philip.' He was done.

A great silence followed.

It was Reginald who broke it. 'Philip carried out acts of great evil. It is tempting to believe that our house will never recover from this. But no matter how hard the work is ahead of us, we should remember that Tundale's vision is not just about darkness. Tundale comes back into the light. And we will too.' He raised a hand in blessing. 'Thanks to Aelred Barling and Hugo Stanton: the King's men.'

Chapter Fifty-Two

The rumble of the river torrent never seemed to change or lessen, whether in snow or rain or fog. Or, as on this morning, a frost-edged morning with a bright blue sky and a sun that dazzled. Maybe the force of the water died down in the summer.

Stanton didn't care. He wouldn't be here to see it. He and Barling would be leaving soon. As he walked up the steep slope along the river, he could see Barling sitting on a rock near the edge, watching its unceasing flow.

The clerk had been unusually subdued since his rescue from the crypt. Not surprising, given the horrors the man had been through and how close he had come to death. But his quietness hadn't been consistent. Barling had been as efficient as ever in dealing with the aftermath of the recent events. Remarkably so. He'd helped Reginald with speaking to the lay brothers. He'd written many notes. He'd spoken calmly at the chapter meeting, giving his account to the monks and lay brothers in a clear and thorough way. No, his quietness was only around Stanton.

He looked up at Stanton's approach.

'I wondered where you'd got to,' said Stanton. 'But Daniel told me he saw you heading off up here.'

'Ah,' replied Barling. 'Daniel. The man responsible for Philip meeting his end. A hero, in many eyes.'

'I'd give him that.' Stanton took a seat on the wide rock next to Barling. 'And this is where it happened.' He looked at Barling. 'But you knew that.'

'I wanted some time to think,' said Barling.

'Fair enough,' said Stanton. 'There's been quite a lot going on, hasn't there?'

As ever, the clerk didn't respond to his smile in kind.

'I needed time to think, Stanton, because I did not solve this enquiry.'

'You weren't brought here to solve it. You were brought here to die. It was all part of Philip's plan. Like I already told you, it was your words that gave me the answer: *planned evil. The very worst there is.* You were certainly right about that.'

'Not right enough.'

'You were an innocent victim, used by Philip. Can't you see that?'

'Not innocent. At all.' He turned to look at Stanton with the haunted look on his face that Stanton had seen before. He'd witnessed it a couple of times last summer, and again when they'd first arrived at the abbey, when Stanton had joked to Barling about the clerk's past life in Paris.

'Barling, I don't know what's troubling you. But just before Philip fell into the water he said I should ask you about Paris. Should I? Because if it's something that you don't want me to know about, then that's the end of it.'

'I would rather you did not. But because of me, because of my past sin, you were dragged into Philip's plan too. You could have died out in the storm. And he didn't care if you did. He simply wanted you out of the way.' He pulled in a long breath. 'You have always spoken of the need to get at the truth, Stanton. I need to tell you mine. It is the least I can do.'

The clerk's look hadn't improved but Stanton was intrigued to finally hear its cause. 'Then let me hear it.'

'You already know I went to Paris to study as a young man.'

Stanton nodded. 'Yes, you and Philip.'

'Along with many, many hundreds of others. Nothing, but nothing, could have prepared me for it. My feast of learning became one of gluttony, greedily consuming what I was being taught by my many masters. There were also luxuries beyond measure before my eyes, even as many of us students lived in squalor, albeit a type of squalor that had its own glory. So many taverns. So many young men, all learning, debating. Which is how I knew Philip, if only vaguely. He was only one among a huge number of acquaintances.'

'But he knew you.'

'I shall come to that,' said Barling. 'There is good reason why he did. The taverns were called the devil's monasteries, and rightly so. We drank pots and pots of wine, talking long into the night. Along with the drink, there was so much temptation. The call of so many young women from dark corners, offering their bodies with skill and cunning. I never paid them any heed, save just once when I won a wager. The other student paid the girl and staggered off into the night leaving her for me. It did not go well. She was willing, lively. Pretty.' He paused while he collected himself.

Lively. Pretty. Stanton thought of poor Agatha. He hoped a demon was pouring pitch into Philip's weak maw for all eternity.

Barling went on, but it was as if Stanton wasn't there now and he spoke only to the river. 'Yet I could not service the girl to begin with. I managed it in the end. But only because she helped me with her mouth first and I imagined it being that of another.' He paused.

Stanton waited, picked up a few snow-covered pebbles and threw them into the water.

'That of Richard,' said Barling. 'A young fellow student.'

Stanton said nothing, threw some more.

Barling wouldn't look at him. 'If I disgust you, please say so.'

'No, you don't.' The desire of men for men. Stanton knew of it well, though he could never understand it. The only flesh that ever called to his was soft and female. As for Barling being a man who held such desires, a lot of what happened last summer now made more sense. So did Barling's anger at Stanton jesting about the clerk's past life. 'You said you wanted to tell me the truth, Barling. Then carry on.'

Richard was tall, clean-shaven and had green eyes that reminded me of trees in first leaf. And his hands: broad, square-fingered, settling awkwardly around a quill, and his smooth forehead creasing in his battle for concentration as we sat in the scribes' room and I saw him for the first time. All the others had left and it was him and me alone.

He looked up unexpectedly and caught my eye. I flushed but he just gave me a wide, easy smile. 'Well you might stare,' he said. 'I have the talents of an ape at this.'

'I can assure you I am not staring.' I wished to the heavens that I did not speak like such an old woman. 'Not in the least.'

'You're Aelred Barling, aren't you?'

I nodded. He knew my name. It sounded warm in his mouth. His beautiful mouth.

'The other fellows told me about you.' He smiled again. 'They say you have the most brilliant mind of all. They all say that you will be the master one day.'

I shrugged, thrilled inside. 'Gossip.'

'I don't think so. I've seen your work.' His gaze met mine. 'Perhaps you could be my master for now.' The green eyes pleaded, went back to his poor work. 'Aelred.'

'Let me see.' I got down from my stool, slowly. Carefully. I was trembling at the idea of moving closer to this man. I came to his side, acutely aware of my meagre frame compared to his. Of the ink that stained my fingers, my hands, my face and no doubt my thin hair. Yet Richard cast me the warmest look.

'You save my life,' he said.

I took the quill from him, reset it in his warm, dry hand. 'Now, follow my movements,' I said. So close I could smell his body, his hair, his sweet, sweet breath. I wanted time to stop, to keep me here forever, my hand over his, guiding him. But of course it had to end. Once we had finished two lines, he sighed.

'That's done, praise the Almighty,' he said. 'Now. A tavern?'

'I had three months in Paris that were the happiest of my entire existence because Richard was in my life,' continued Barling. 'I was helping him with his work. I did it and I did not mind, though his progress continued to be slow. He was from a very wealthy family but had always been bored by study. If I could have, I would have learned everything for him. Yet I should have realised that I was well on the road to damnation. Our gluttony with wine and rich food, all paid for thanks to our arrangement. All were vices that were growing within me, taking hold of my soul.'

'What arrangement was that, Barling?'

'We'd been short of money. Well, Richard had, and then he discovered I could sing.'

'Sing? You?' Stanton couldn't help his rude question.

Barling nodded. 'It was purely by chance. One night, as we were making our unsteady way through the back streets, we came across a man singing a popular love song to an admiring crowd. The man's reaching of the notes was not always accurate. But I had had plenty of wine and so joined in, quietly at first. Heads turned. Towards me. People nudged each other. Whispered. I stopped, embarrassed. Richard put an arm over my shoulder and murmured to me to carry on.' The clerk's face lit up at the memory. 'So I did, louder and louder, my confidence growing not only from the wine but from Richard's strong arm embracing me. When the song finished, people clapped and whistled. For me. One man threw a coin. The street singer looked furious. I dragged Richard away, for I had no wish to rob this man of his livelihood.'

A drunk Barling, singing in the street: Stanton could only smile at such an unlikely picture.

'But Richard had a plan: I should sing in the taverns. People would reward us handsomely.'

'I thought you said Richard was wealthy?'

'He was. Just useless at minding his money. Anyway, I agreed. How could I not? Richard said he would teach me all the popular songs he knew. His voice was passable, but no more. So he taught me. Some were bawdy, filthy. I found it hard to sing those, and I could see the frustration grow in his green eyes. But I persisted with the tuition and it paid off. Richard used his contacts in the taverns, pushed for me to be allowed to perform. He watched me – watched over me. He collected the coins, dealt with drunks who wanted to quieten me. Philip's was a face familiar from many of those audiences.'

'I've been in lots of similar audiences,' said Stanton. 'Though I hope I've not met any other Philips.'

'Who knows?' Barling shook his head. 'You would perhaps not have thought that I was guilty of great wrong. And yet I am.' He drew in a long breath. 'For then it happened. My committing of the worst sin. Late one night, Richard and I were back in his rooms, having finished counting out a great night's takings. Richard was lying back on his bed drinking more wine. I rose to go. But he persuaded me not to. For the first time, I touched another body just like my own. Not only on that night, but on further nights when he asked me to stay. There were not many. I wished it was every night. And every day. But I accepted his offers like a dog snaps at meat scraps thrown from a table.'

Stanton could hear the utter desperation in Barling's voice, even after all these years. 'Lots of young men do all sorts of things,' was all he said, aware his words would give scant comfort. 'A lot of the time, we're not even sure why we're doing them.'

'Oh, I knew what I was doing. What we did, were doing, was utterly unnatural, though the devil had blinded my eyes with lust. There was much talk around Paris that many students were doing exactly as we were. Philip sneered that at me when he was locking me up. But that was how I explained it to myself. Here I was, independent in mind and taking my pleasure as others did. The devil must have been helping me. But I cared not. I loved Richard and Richard loved me. That was the difference between us and the other young men who would find each other in the dark taverns and streets. I knew it would only be a matter of time until we declared it to each other, though I was not sure how to go about it. But Richard hit upon a brilliant method of doing so.'

'And what was Richard's brilliant plan?' asked Stanton. The clerk might have loved this Richard fellow but Stanton thought the man sounded like the worst kind of leech.

Barling didn't seem to notice the hardness in his question. 'One morning, as we waited for the master, Richard asked me to compose my own love song, one that he would keep. I worked on it for weeks, barely noticing that Richard seemed especially busy. This was our declaration of our love. It had to be perfect. Once I had it, I waited. And waited. Then a message came. Could I come with him for a night in the taverns? We did so, and to my joy we did not stay long. I walked back to his lodgings, my knees hardly able to support me. It was tonight: tonight, I would give him the gift he sought and that I was desperate to give. When we entered his room, I should have noticed that something was different. It was far too orderly. But I was so wrapped up in my song . . .' He shook his head. 'I told him I had it, showed him the parchment and sang it quietly to him. I finished on the last note, waited for him to embrace me, to make me his again, once and for all.'

'He didn't, though, did he?' asked Stanton.

'No,' whispered Barling. 'He did not.'

'Wonderful – that song should have the desired effect.' Richard opened his palm for the parchment. *'Thank you, Aelred.'*

I gave it to him, with a hand that was less than steady. 'Then you liked it?' My voice was not much better.

'Of course.' He lifted the lid on one of his chests and threw it in. A chest that was stacked with neatly folded clothing. He stood up. 'I'm sure my betrothed will too.'

My mouth dried and I swear my heart stopped for a couple of beats. 'Your betrothed?'

Richard closed the lid of the chest. 'Alys de Wollmer. Last time I saw her she was a mouse of a thing, so I hope that's not changed. I can't abide a woman who doesn't do as she's told. But my father says she has become very comely, with breasts that could smother a man. Hope he's telling the truth.' He grinned, then yawned again. 'I suppose we should say our farewells now, Aelred. I leave for England at first light.'

'Leave?'

'Yes. I just said so.' He frowned. 'What's up with you, man? You're acting very strangely.'

'You cannot.'

'Cannot what?'

'Leave me.'

'Aelred, you're talking like a madman still. Go and see the physician in the morning if you're still the same. Goodbye, my friend.' He went to move to the door.

It was as if he broke a spell. I stepped after him, grabbed him by the arm. 'Your friend? Friend?' My voice rose, I could not help it. 'Richard, I am your love. As you are mine.' I went to embrace him, but he shoved me away. Hard.

'Get off me, man. What do you think you're doing?'

'Doing?' I grabbed his arm again, tried to pull him towards me. 'I was showing you the depths of my love, my—'

'Get off me!' This shove sent me to the floor, where I landed hard.

I scrambled to my knees, tried to grasp for his cloak. 'Richard. Richard.' I grasped the cloth, refused to let it go. 'You must stay. Stay here. With me.'

266

Another push had me down again. Sobs that I had not summoned broke from me as he looked at me in disgust. 'Do you think I would want it to be so?'

'Yes.' Now tears choked my sight, my voice. 'Yes. As do I.'

'For a clever man, you're a complete fool.'

'But you asked me for a love song. How could I think otherwise?'

'Oh, Aelred.' He laughed: loud, long and hard. 'You thought I wanted a song for us? Us?' Still laughed. 'That I would want to spend my life with a filthy little sodomite like you?' All merriment left his eyes. 'Then you thought wrongly. As wrongly as it is possible to think. You were a distraction here, that's all. One sin among so many others.'

I got to my feet as the bitter, heart-breaking truth rained down on me.

'Now, Aelred, the time has come for me to cleanse myself of Paris, of you, the others. To make my penance and return to England to make my new life.'

It could not be so. It could not. But it was. His face told me it was, his beautiful face that I knew better than my own. I scrubbed at my tears. 'Then give me back my song.'

He scowled. 'Don't be pathetic, Aelred.'

'Give me back my song!' My rage-filled scream echoed in the room.

He took a step back in surprise, opened up the chest and thrust the parchment at me. 'I have no need of it, anyway.' His haughty smile returned. 'After all, I didn't need to sing to you to get you into my bed. I'm sure my new wife will be just as willing. Now get out of my sight.'

For a moment, I feared I would kill him. But I could not, for I still loved him. I took hold of the parchment and walked to the door.

'Goodbye, Aelred.'

I could not look around, could not see him for what I knew would be the last time. For if I did, I knew I would die of grief.

'And I believe I almost did die,' said Barling. 'I returned to my lodgings and stayed there for a week, claiming a fever. I could not set foot outside for fear of seeing Richard and then for fear of not seeing him.

The world had stopped for me. A few times, I held my precious song to the candle flame. But I could not bring myself to destroy it. I simply could not. I lay without sleep for much of the time, Richard's words an unceasing pounding pulse in my head. *A distraction. A filthy little sodomite. I need to cleanse myself of you. To make my penance.* My head span from it. Richard was the one who had first touched me, I argued to myself. Richard had started all this. Richard. But I knew in my soul I was the greater sinner. Richard was doing penance, was taking a wife. As for me, I had no desire for a wife. None. I must still be in the devil's grip. So I did what I knew best. I emerged from my room, went back to my masters and went back to learning.'

Stanton had often wondered why Barling lost himself in his work. Now he knew the reason.

Barling went on. 'I made my way immediately to a priest and confessed everything, much to his horror for my eternal fate. Fifteen years' penance was a small price to pay for my soul. In the course of my learning, I came across the writings of Saint Peter Damian. The priest had been right: Saint Peter could not have been clearer about the absolute seriousness of my sin, that it would take me down into the deepest pit of hell.'

'And no doubt Philip had come across these writings too.'

'Of course. And you yourself have heard him say that he recognised me immediately at York, at the ordeal. Abbot Ernald was still alive then, so Philip had yet to set his deadly acts in motion. But when he did, he thought that I, the King's man, would make a wonderful prize. Little did the monks in the Chapter House know that I was an extra-rich prize for Philip, not only as a royal clerk. But because he knew of my sin.'

'Had he not aimed so high, he might have succeeded with what he was trying to do,' said Stanton. 'Serves him right.'

'Meanwhile, I worked and worked and worked at my studies in Paris. The times I woke in tears became fewer and fewer. I got used to the loneliness, the isolation from my fellow students, who gave up asking me to join them in the taverns. I was no longer Aelred, Richard's friend who could hold the world with a song. I became Barling, who could argue that black was white and evidence it from seventeen sources, humiliating his opponents in argument. When I went back to London, I easily secured a place in the King's writing office. I have been there ever since.' He met Stanton's eye for a moment, then dropped his gaze again. 'Now you know the truth, Stanton. You see who the man you call master really is.'

Stanton didn't say anything. Barling's story was one that answered many questions Stanton had had about the murders in the village of Claresham last year. That explained Barling's fury when Stanton had suggested poor Lady Kersley might have lusted after the clerk. That answered many about the man himself.

It was Barling who broke the silence. 'And do you have a response?'

Stanton shrugged. 'I think it's a sad secret that you have had to keep.'

'That is all?' His face and voice lifted. 'You mean, you are not repelled by me, by my past?'

Stanton shrugged again. His own past wasn't much better, but that wasn't for now. 'Not especially. In truth, it's not for me to sit in judgement on you, or anyone. And not to worry, I'll keep your secrets. I'm good at that.' Stanton got to his feet. 'I'm going to head off now. I need to get ready for the journey.'

'I think I shall sit here for a while, Stanton.'

'But don't be too long.'

A faint smile twitched at the corner of Barling's mouth. 'I will not. I still have much to go over in my mind. Whatever you say, I should have seen Philip's wickedness, Stanton.'

'I disagree. The bearward leads the bear to the fight, Barling. But Ursus doesn't look to battle him. His mind is on the dogs.' He allowed himself a satisfied nod and a grin at Barling. 'See? I'm a good pupil.'

Though the clerk gave a sharp sigh, Stanton could tell he kept in a smile. 'One that has much to learn, I can assure you.'

That was more like it. 'I'll leave you be. But don't take long here. We need to get back to Westminster and it's a very long ride.' Stanton grinned again and went to set off back to the abbey. 'And you're a terrible rider, remember?'

'Not terrible. Adequate.' The clerk gave him his best displeased frown.

And Hugo Stanton's heart filled with thanks. With silent, fervent thanks that his friend, Aelred Barling, was still here to deliver it.

Historical Note

Fairmore Abbey is a fictional Cistercian house but is a composite based on a number of real twelfth-century Yorkshire monasteries.

Cistercian abbeys tended to follow the same uniform layout. Remoteness and seclusion were also important in determining their location. I used elements of the following abbeys: Rievaulx, Byland, Roche and Bolton. Although all lie in ruins, they are well worth a visit, with each site visually stunning and atmospheric. Anybody who is familiar with Bolton Abbey will recognise my depiction of the Strid in the novel. For those who are not, the Strid is a spectacular torrent of water, where the river narrows to force the water through rock at great and lethal pressure. Many lives have tragically been lost there.

The Cistercian order was and is a real order and continues to thrive to this day. It was founded in the eleventh century by monks and nuns who wished to bring about reform of the Benedictines. They wanted a return to the fundamentals of the Rule of Saint Benedict, with a more austere lifestyle and a commitment to physical labour as well as to prayer. The structure and daily regime of monastic life that I portray is based on the arduous real life of the White Monks. They were so called because they wore habits of undyed wool.

It is possible that the order would have remained relatively small and without great influence. But it was the work of Saint Bernard of Clairvaux, who died in 1153 and was canonised in 1174, that ensured the major expansion of the Cistercian houses. The White Monks were expert at reclaiming land, at farming and at wool production, which ensured they acquired great wealth and power over time. The lay brothers who feature in the book played a key role in this: they were a large, reliable workforce that could be depended upon to perform the necessary hard physical labour without question. Dissatisfaction ultimately spread amongst this workforce and there were acts of violence and rebellion by some lay brothers against the monks.

The novel also features the book called *The Vision of Tundale*, which bears some resemblance to Dante's fourteenth-century *Inferno*. *Inferno* is one of the three major sections of his *Divine Comedy*. But *Tundale* was written in 1149 by an Irish monk named Marcus, who ended up at a monastery in Regensburg in Bavaria. The book was hugely popular throughout the Middle Ages and was translated into over a dozen languages. It was especially popular in the Cistercian order.

It was my discovery of *Tundale* that inspired my novel. I was already pleased to find a link to Ireland through its authorship by an Irish monk. But when I began to read it and discovered that the story related that Tundale was in the city of Cork, my home city, when he collapsed and met his fates, I knew that it was meant to be.

Acknowledgments

The thanks that I give here can never truly reflect the debt I owe to so many people for their help and support in making this book happen. My agent, Josh Getzler, is as big a cheerleader for the twelfth century as I could ever hope him to be. My publishers, Thomas & Mercer, have been as wonderful as always. Jack Butler has brought Stanton and Barling to so many readers, as well as providing the best editorial insight and guidance. He also gave me the great gift of Mike Jones as an editor, and the eagle-eyed Ian Critchley. Mike's wealth of experience helped me to bring this book to a different level and to make it really shine. Ian made sure that every dot was joined up, for which I am hugely grateful. Hatty Stiles was tireless as ever in making sure that the world gets to hear about my novels, helped by Nicole Wagner, who went the extra mile many times for me. There are many historians whose excellent work I have consulted and who are mentioned in the bibliography. I have the most stalwart readers and reviewers, who never let me down with their unwavering support. And, as always, my Jon and my Angela: to thank them feels utterly inadequate as they are my world.

List of Characters

The King's Men
Hugo Stanton, messenger to the law court and pupil of Aelred Barling
Aelred Barling, senior royal clerk
Ranulf de Glanville, justice of King Henry II

The Monks of Fairmore Abbey
Philip, abbot and father of the abbey
Reginald, the prior and deputy to the abbot
Maurice, the novice master
Osmund, the cellarer
William, the infirmarer
Elias, the librarian
Silvanus, the guestmaster
Lambert, the gatekeeper
Cuthbert, the late sacrist
Ernald, the late abbot
Daniel, a lay brother

Visitors to the Abbey
Juliana, a benefactor of the abbey
Agatha, a beggar
Nicholas, visiting abbot of Linwood Abbey

Others
Theobald, priest of the local parish of Gottburn

Bibliography

No historical novelist could do what they do without the sterling work of historians, and I am no exception. Any factual inaccuracies in my book are of course down to me and not to them. For anybody wishing to delve deeper into the real history behind this novel, I can highly recommend the following:

Barrow, Julia, *The Clergy in the Medieval World: Secular Clerics, Their Families and Careers in North-Western Europe, c. 800–c. 1200* (Cambridge: Cambridge University Press, 2015).

Birkedal-Brunn, Mette, ed., *The Cambridge Companion to the Cistercian Order* (Cambridge: Cambridge University Press, 2013).

Brundage, James A., *Medieval Canon Law* (London: Routledge, 2013).

Burton, Janet, *The Monastic Order in Yorkshire 1069–1215*, (Cambridge: Cambridge University Press, 1999).

Burton, Janet & Kerr, Julie, *The Cistercians in the Middle Ages* (Woodbridge: The Boydell Press, 2011).

Foster, Edward E., ed., *Three Purgatory Poems: The Gast of Gy, Sir Owain, The Vision of Tundale* (Kalamazoo: Western Michigan University, 2004).

France, James, *Separate but Equal: Cistercian Lay Brothers 1120–1350*, (Minnesota: Cistercian Publications, 2012).

Gardiner, Eileen, ed., *Visions of Heaven & Hell Before Dante* (New York: Italica Press, 1989).

Kerr, Julie, *Life in the Medieval Cloister* (London: Continuum Publishing, 2009).

About the Author

E.M. Powell's historical thriller Fifth Knight novels have been #1 Amazon and *Bild* bestsellers. *The Monastery Murders* is the second novel in her Stanton and Barling medieval murder mystery series. She is a contributing editor to International Thriller Writers' *The Big Thrill* magazine, blogs for English Historical Fiction Authors and is the social media manager for the Historical Novel Society.

Born and raised in the Republic of Ireland into the family of Michael Collins (the legendary revolutionary and founder of the Irish Free State), she now lives in North-West England with her husband, daughter and a Facebook-friendly dog. Find out more by visiting www.empowell.com.

Printed in Great Britain
by Amazon